I0746815

Praise for Panji's Quest

"The saga of Panji, as told in *Panji's Quest,* intertwines numerous fascinating adventures and intricate episodes of didacticism, and revives a cultural heritage of Javanese/Indonesian/Southeast Asian literature and performing arts that was recognized by UNESCO's 'Memory of the World Programme' in 2017.

"The wealth of the elegant Panji collection, recorded in various formats, languages, and scripts, should be further preserved and promoted in research, teaching, and learning as "Panjiology" by current and future generations of scholars in Southeast Asia and beyond. Panji aficionados will know that *Panji's Quest* originates from the *Angreni from Palembang* manuscript, the love story of Sekartaji, crown princess of the kingdom of Kadiri, and Panji, crown prince of the kingdom of Janggala — two 12th-century Javanese kingdoms that were ruled by rival siblings.

"Translator Oni Suryaman has carefully preserved Setiyono's eloquent writing style in this rendering of a 12th-century Javanese folktale written to capture the interest of 21st-century readers. I look forward to adding *Panji's Quest* and *Tembang dan Perang,* its original, to our collection."

—Virginia Shih, Southeast Asia Curator,
South/Southeast Asia Library,
University of California, Berkeley, USA

"Junaedi Setiyono presents a popular folktale in a detective story-like mode that makes the novel intriguing and compelling. For those knowledgeable about the Panji legend, the story's ending is already known, but Setiyono's elegant writing brings out suspense, unforeseen conflicts, and emotional turmoil, interweaving dark and moving moments with ecstatic thrills that bring tears of sadness and joy.

"While the novel's philosophical aspect portrays a universe where human life is governed by divine providence, human agency still plays defining roles. The most conscience-stirring part of the story is the tragic murder of Angreni, which remains of haunting relevance today. Capturing the atmosphere and mood of the original novel, translator Oni Suryaman transports his readers to the 12th-century Kadiri and Janggala kingdoms in *Panji's Quest.*"

—Eka Budianta,
Indonesian Poet and Literary Critic

Panji's Quest

**Junaedi Setiyono
Translated from the Indonesian by
Oni Suryaman**

Dalang Publishing

Dalang Publishing LLC

San Mateo, California

www.dalangpublishing.com

dalangpublishing@gmail.com

ISBN 978-1-7357210-1-9

Library of Congress Control Number: 2021942534

Publisher's Cataloging-In-Publication Data

Names: Setiyono, Junaedi, 1965- author. | Suryaman, Oni, translator.
Title: Panji's quest / Junaedi Setiyono ; translated from the Indonesian by Oni Suryaman.
Other Titles: Tembang dan Perang. English
Description: San Mateo, California : Dalang Publishing, [2021] | Translation of: Tembang dan Perang. Yogyakarta, Indonesia : Penerbit Kanisius, 2020.
Identifiers: ISBN 9781735721019 (paperback)
Subjects: LCSH: Princes--Indonesia--History--To 1500--Fiction. | Man-woman relationships--Indonesia--History--To 1500--Fiction. | Warlordism--Indonesia--History--To 1500--Fiction. | Arranged marriage--Indonesia--History--To 1500--Fiction. | LCGFT: Historical fiction. | Romance fiction.
Classification: LCC PL5089.S4453 T4613 2021 | DDC 899/.22133--dc23

Panji's Quest

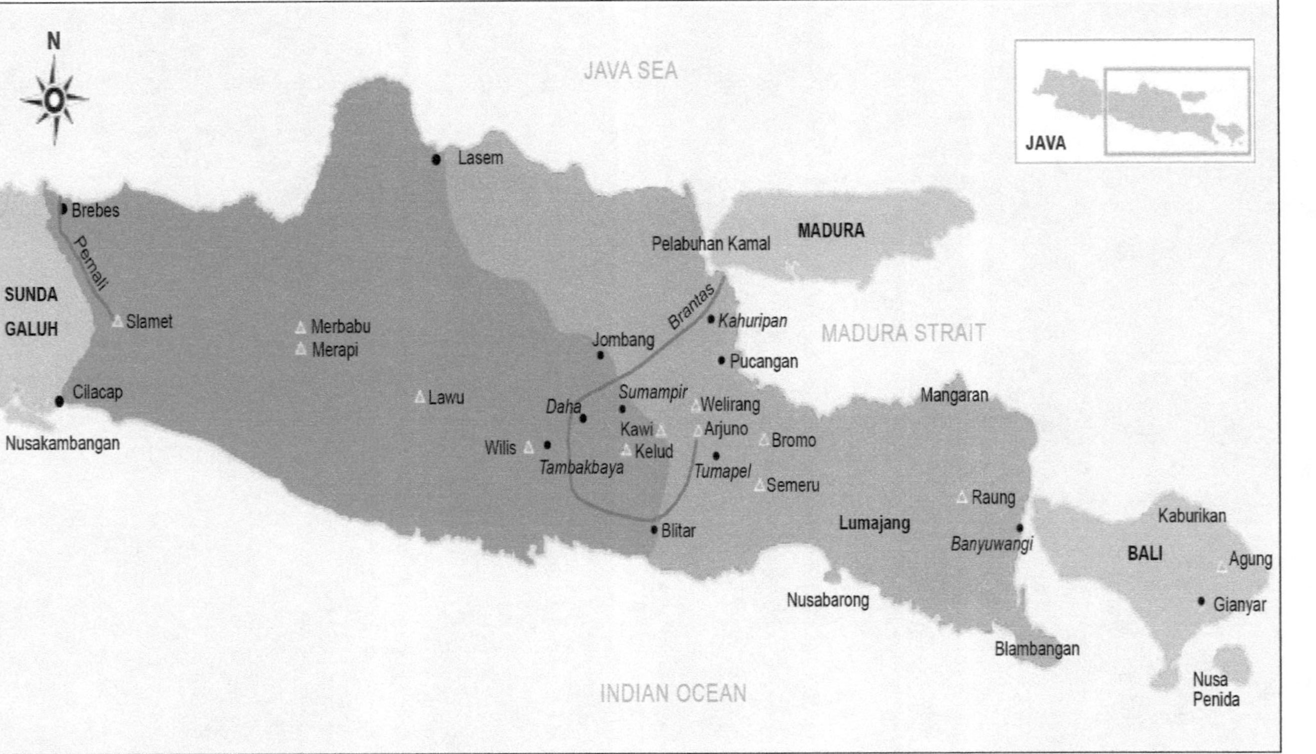

N
JAVA
JAVA SEA
Lasem
Brebes
Pemali
SUNDA
GALUH
Slamet
Merbabu
Merapi
Cilacap
Nusakambangan
Lawu
MADURA
Pelabuhan Kamal
Brantas
Kahuripan
Jombang
Pucangan
MADURA STRAIT
Sumampir
Daha
Welirang
Kawi
Arjuno
Bromo
Mangaran
Wilis
Kelud
Tambakbaya
Tumapel
Semeru
Blitar
Lumajang
Raung
Banyuwangi
Kaburikan
BALI
Agung
Nusabarong
Gianyar
Blambangan
Nusa
Penida
INDIAN OCEAN

GENEALOGY OF THE KINGS FROM ERLANGGA TO PANJI

Medhang Kingdom – Erlangga, reigned 1009–1042

Descendants of Erlangga's Queen Mahajiwatma:

Sanggramawijaya, daughter, refused the crown
Samarawijaya, son
    Samarotsaha, son
        Bameswara, son
            Jayabaya (Bameswara's son):
                Pramesthi (Rara Suci),
                daughter,
            refused the crown
            Amerdadu, son
            Amiluhur, son

Descendants of Erlangga's concubine Mandanu:

    Garasakan, son
    Lanjung Heyes, son
        Jayawarsa, son

TIMELINE

1042 - Erlangga divided Medhang Kingdom into two kingdoms:

Kadiri Kingdom
Samarawijaya, reigned 1042-1044

Janggala Kingdom
Garasakan, reigned 1042-1052
In 1044 Garasakan conquered Samarawijaya – both kingdoms became Janggala.
Lanjung Heyes, reigned 1052-1059
In 1052 Lanjung Heyes overthrew his brother and reigned over Janggala till 1059.

Samarotsaha, reigned 1059-1089
In 1059 Samarotsaha conquered Lanjung Heyes – the kingdom was known as Kadiri until 1089.

Jayawarsa, reigned 1089-1117
In 1089 Jayawarsa conquered Samarotsaha and changed the kingdom's name back to Janggala till 1117.

Bameswara, reigned 1117-1131
In 1117 Bameswara conquered Jayawarsa and changed the kingdom's name back to Kadiri again till 1131

1131 – Bameswara abdicated the throne for his son Jayabaya.
Jayabaya, reigned over Kadiri 1131-1135.

1135 – Jayabaya divided the kingdom between his 2 sons: Amerdadu and Amiluhur

Kadiri Kingdom
Amerdadu, reigned 1135-1185
Sekartaji, crown princess, born 1140
Gunungsari, son, born 1142
Mindaka, daughter, born 1146

Janggala Kingdom
Amiluhur, reigned 1135-1185
Panji, crown prince, born 1139
Carangwaspa, son, born 1146
Onengan, daughter, born 1149

In 1185, Panji, the son of Amiluhur and crown prince of Janggala, married Sekartaji, the daughter of Amerdadu and crown princess of Kadiri. Panji was later known as Kameswara, and the two kingdoms were united into the Kadiri Kingdom.

TRANSLATOR'S NOTE

The *Panji Tales* are quite well known among Indonesians, especially the Javanese. It is not an overstatement that these stories are among the most famous original myths in Indonesia, after the Mahabharata and Ramayana, which originate from India. The *Panji Tales* are mostly known from plays in various traditional theater, for example, the play of *Panji Semirang*. What is not well known is the fact that there are many versions of the *Panji Tales*. This novel is an effort to bring one of those versions to modern readers.

Panji's Quest is based on *Panji Angreni Palembang*, a manuscript written in Javanese, which was discovered in Palembang, a city in Southern Sumatra. This document is not the original work, but rather a copy of it that was ordered by a Palembang princess. For general readers, the translation of this story in Indonesian can be found in Prof. Dr. Poerbatjaraka's book *Tjeritera Pandji dalam Perbandingan* (Gunung Agung, 1968), which is unfortunately out of print but still available from university and government libraries. Therefore, this novel — despite its romanticized version — can serve as a gateway to the world of the *Panji Tales*.

Set in the Javanese medieval era, the narrative is culturally and linguistically bound to that era. As the translator of this work, I was faced with the choice of whether to keep certain Javanese phrases, for the sake of retaining a "foreignness," or to translate the phrases for the sake of a more understandable read. I chose to translate the many Javanese phrases that were retained in the Indonesian publication into English to lessen the burden on the readers. The small number of Javanese words and phrases that were kept as-is in the English translation, are immediately followed by a short, clarifying explanation. I am well aware that my choice might have resulted in losing some nuances of the original work.

The original Panji manuscript mentioned a lot of tree and flower specimens endemic to the island of Java. Many of those species do not have an English name. Therefore, only some species are retained in this translation, such as the angsana (*Pterocarpus indicus*), which plays a major role in the story development, while others might have simply been translated as "tree."

Similar to the Native American custom, several character names have a symbolic meaning. It was custom in ancient Java to bestow animal names upon someone to personify the power of that animal's nature. These names were kept in their original form without being translated; for example, in the name Kebotendas, *kebo* means "water buffalo," and in the name Lembu Amiluhur, *lembu* means "ox."

The names of the cities and places in this novel are those known during the time of the story. Some never changed and are currently still in use, but some are transformed or have become less known. For example, the name of a major city in ancient times may now be the name of a remote village, known only by the local inhabitants. For the sake of originality, all the geographical names use the ancient name; their locations can be found on the map at the front of this book.

As the translator of this ancient Javanese tale, I hope that *Panji's Quest* can be a bridge to the rich world of the *Panji Tales* for English-speaking readers. I would like to express my personal gratitude to the author, Junaedi Setiyono, for his tireless efforts in transforming an ancient text into a modern novel, and to Lian Gouw and Dalang Publishing for giving me a chance to work with them as a translator. I am honored to be a part of this wonderful team.

Oni Suryaman
Sleman, 1 April 2021

Panji's Quest

Chapter 1

THE SONG OF A VILLAGE ARTIST

As far back as King Lembu Amiluhur's rule over the Janggala Kingdom in 1135 CE, most parents managed to instill a feeling of homeland pride in their children, but this was not the case with Tendas's father. Even Tendas himself was not sure if his father wanted him to feel proud. The older Tendas grew, the more his self-esteem diminished.

Tendas was sixteen years old when King Lembu Amiluhur started ruling Janggala. He loved to play the *gambang*, a wooden, xylophone-like instrument, only because his father smiled when he played. Tendas's happiness derived from making his father happy.

Even though the gambang was very popular in Janggala, not many people could make the instrument. Tendas's father — people called him *Ki* Siwur — was among the few who had mastered the craft.

King Jayabaya, father of the Kadiri Kingdom's present king, had massacred all the descendants and followers of King Garasakan, the first king of Janggala. Siwur, who served as a guest artist for the court, was among those who should have been killed.

It was commonly accepted that those defeated in battle deserved a horrible fate. If they were not killed or imprisoned, they were banished.

1

Siwur received the lightest sentence and was banished. His skill as a gambang craftsman saved his life.

"Where is Ki Siwur?" Brajanata asked Tendas, who was playing the gambang on the veranda of his village home. Prince Brajanata, the eldest son of Janggala King Amiluhur's concubine, stood tall and smiled. His spirited but disciplined horse grazed not far from him.

"He's gathering wood in the forest." Tendas's visitor was an aristocrat. Nobility from the Janggala Kingdom were easily recognized by their appearance. They wore knee-length trousers covered with a batik cloth, held together by a cummerbund. They wore a gold ring on both middle fingers, bracelets on their wrists and upper arms, and big anklets. A crescent-shaped pendant adorned their chest. Their hair, tied in a bun on the crown of their head, was secured with a headband. And, of course, they carried a *kris*, a short, double-edged dagger, tucked into their cummerbund, right in front of their stomach.

Brajanata's horse, befitting Janggala nobility, was as gallant as his lord. The horse came from the Bima region on the island of Sumbawa. Fifteen years old, it still looked impressive with strong muscles visible beneath its well-groomed, white coat. Sumba horses stood about twelve hands tall and were favored by nobility because of their good temperament. The breed could withstand hot weather and was often used in the cavalry because of the animal's strength and agility. Tethered to a shade tree, Brajanata's horse grazed calmly, only swishing its tail to ward off flies.

"All right, I will come back tomorrow." Brajanata turned and walked to his horse. Before mounting, he said, "Tell Ki Siwur that Brajanata would like to meet him here tomorrow morning."

⊢——•◦•——⊣

Siwur had been moving gambangs from his workshop to the veranda since sunrise, and the sun's brightness took over the light from the cooking fires. He did not want to inconvenience his guests by making them walk to his workshop, located at the back of his house.

Brajanata and his two escorts arrived early in the morning, before the sun exhibited its full might and scorched the day.

"Forgive me, *Raden*, your honor," Siwur said nervously, after his guests were seated on the pandanus mats he had unrolled on the porch — a courtesy every commoner would extend to nobility. "I didn't expect your visit yesterday."

"There's no need to apologize. I'm at fault for not informing you." Brajanata looked at the gambangs Siwur had neatly lined up.

A moment later, the craftsman and Brajanata approached the row of gambangs. Brajanata casually reached for one and tried to play it.

"That is the best gambang I have made so far," said Siwur approvingly. "Its bars are made of ironwood, whereas the box is made of teak."

"Do you plan to make a larger version?" Brajanata asked.

"I could make a larger version of this one from the wood I gathered yesterday," said Siwur, pointing to a tree trunk still lying on a cart. "But the earliest I can start working on it is next month, because the dryness of the wood greatly affects the gambang's tune and strength."

The conversation between seller and buyer didn't last long. The large gambang was soon loaded onto Brajanata's horse cart.

Tendas learned a valuable lesson from his father's meeting with Brajanata, a lesson his father had never taught him: how honorable it was to be a royal servant. By *honorable*, he meant the respect a person in that position was given. He thought about this, trying to figure out what he based his thinking on, and concluded: First, royal servants were dressed in elegant clothes that made their appearance even more attractive; second, they spoke in a particular manner, soft but firm; and third, they were rich. Money seemed readily available to them, without them having to worry about earning it.

Those three reasons were enough to make Tendas dream of becoming a nobleman.

"You are welcome to take Tendas with you to repair the gambangs and teach the gentry how to play," Siwur said, after Brajanata told him there were many broken gambangs in his court, in addition to gentry who didn't know how to play the instrument.

"All right. I will take your son with me." Smiling at Tendas, the prince continued, "I'm sure you'd like to stay with me, right, Tendas?"

Tendas nodded firmly. He did want to see the homes of the people he admired so much.

For almost a full month, Tendas lived as an artisan at Brajanata's mansion. His tasks were less taxing than those of the other servants. His main duty was to repair broken gambangs and teach the gentry to play the instrument.

One morning, while repairing Brajanata's favorite gambang on the porch in the shade of a cananga tree, Tendas heard hurried footsteps.

"Welcome, *kakang*, my brother, Kusni." Brajanata welcomed his friend using the common Javanese address. "Come in, please." Although most guests were received briefly at the *pendapa*, the large open pavilion in front of the mansion, Brajanata accompanied this guest to chat not far from the cananga tree where Tendas was busy working.

Standing in the doorway, the two immediately engaged in an intimate conversation. From time to time, Tendas saw Brajanata pat Kusni on his shoulder.

"How is your younger brother, Panji, doing, Raden?" Kusni asked.

"My younger brother is doing well," Brajanata said. "As a matter of fact, too well."

"Too well?" Kusni asked, puzzled. "What do you mean?"

The prince didn't answer immediately. He cleared his throat and looked at the wongai plum tree's whitish leaves blowing in the wind. The tree, usually planted in gardens of the royalty, symbolized well-being. Finally, he said, "His Majesty's wish to make Panji a greater king than himself has robbed the crown prince of his childhood and young adulthood." Brajanata looked into the distance with dreamy eyes.

"Robbed?" Kusni raised his eyebrows slightly. "Isn't it normal for a king to treat the crown prince that way?"

"Whatever is done excessively will not be good in the end, even if it is done with good intentions." Brajanata sighed. "Spiritual exercise, in the form of religious study, and physical exercise, such as martial arts, are both essentially good disciplines, but if they are executed excessively, neither would bring any good."

"Yes. Yes, indeed." Kusni began to understand what Brajanata meant.

The silence that ensued was broken only by bird song and the restless rustle of leaves as wind moved through the treetops.

"If you believe that what is happening to your brother is not good, are you planning to help him?" Kusni's voice rose slightly.

"Help him?" It was Brajanata's turn to raise his eyebrows. "He doesn't need any help. He has all the help he needs. What he needs are distractions — I mean, *we* need to distract him."

Kusni frowned before bursting into laughter. As far as Tendas knew, only this guest dared to laugh so freely in front of Brajanata.

Tendas's duties — repairing the gambangs and teaching the gentry to play them — did not allow him to carefully observe all the events that took place in the mansion. He focused more on the gambang's bars than on the bustle around him.

Later, Tendas asked Kertala, the gardener, about this special guest. Kertala was some five years older than Tendas, and Tendas had befriended him.

"What makes you think that this guest is special?" Kertala asked.

"He is the only person I've ever heard laugh out loud in front of our master, Raden Brajanata," Tendas promptly answered.

"Do you know what they were laughing about?"

"As far as I could hear, Raden Brajanata was talking about how His Majesty the King spoils Brajanata's younger brother, the crown prince," Tendas said.

"You're correct," Kertala grumbled, like a cranky old man who had lost his cane. "The king is truly over-indulging him."

Kertala's expression and gestures made Tendas curious. Kertala talked about this guest as if he was really someone special. "You seem to know a lot about this guest," Tendas said politely. "Can you tell me more, kang?"

"Take a guess where the guest came from," Kertala said.

"I am sure that he didn't come from either the Janggala or Kadiri kingdoms," Tendas answered promptly. "Our master's guest is not like the people we usually see around here; he is dressed like a Brahmin in the temple. But unlike those holy men, who move slowly and gently, this man's movements are as fast and agile as a knight's. Also, he doesn't wear the finery that priests usually wear."

"You're correct. He comes from the Perlak Kingdom, at the northern end of the island of Sumatra. It takes several weeks of traveling by ship to reach the port at the eastern part of Janggala."

"Perlak?" It was the first time Tendas had heard about this strange place.

"I'm sure you've never heard about this kingdom. The guest's name also sounds strange to our ears: Kusni. I believe his full name is Kaji Kusni Ngali."

"Yes, both Perlak and Kusni sound strange to me."

Tendas and Kertala fell silent for a while, contemplating this guest's background.

"Why does Ki Kusni seem to be so close to Raden Brajanata?" Tendas asked.

"Aha, that is an important question. But unfortunately, I don't know the answer. You'd have to ask Raden Brajanata directly." Kertala turned to leave but suddenly stopped. "But don't ask him now. I'm worried that you still don't know the proper way to compose questions to nobility. Remember, he's a prince, not a commoner like me." Kertala pointed to his skinny chest.

Kertala was right to warn Tendas to first learn the proper words for speaking to nobility. Tendas was taught to carve gambang bars, not to compose a sentence. He was better trained to arrange the tools in the workshop than to arrange words for a conversation with a prince.

Tendas's father, brother, and mother were quiet people. They worked more than they talked. "Silence is golden" was his family's motto. Tendas was certain that this philosophy came from their circumstances: They were a family of defeated people.

Although Siwur had served Janggala's King Garasakan — who opposed King Jayabaya, now living in Kadiri as king emeritus — Siwur and his family were still alive because Brajanata had not only taken pity on them, but they were needed to make high-quality gambangs to accompany the princesses' singing in the palace.

Tendas learned new words from song lyrics. Words attracted him because of their sound and meaning. He had to admit that he did not always know the exact meaning of most of the words, but, oddly enough, their sound alone impressed him. He improved his vocabulary by asking his mother about their meaning. While the gambang brought him closer to his father, the songs brought him closer to his mother. But nothing brought him closer to Tandang, his brother, the only sibling he had. Tandang, a quiet young man, was closer to his horse than to his brother.

Tendas didn't dare ask Brajanata about his close friendship with Kusni. Even after Tendas had lived and worked at Brajanata's residence for almost two years, he still didn't dare to ask the question. By that time, he was almost eighteen years old, and many events had changed his outlook on life.

The biggest event that changed his life was Siwur's accident while he was felling a tree in the forest. The tree toppled before he could get out of the way and left him paralyzed. The incident prompted Tendas to return home.

The instrument shop was at the back of their house, and Tendas continued the work that Siwur used to do. Less than twenty years old, Tendas had to supervise more than twenty workers. Only one-third of his employees worked in the shop; another third gathered wood in the forest; and another third peddled the gambangs in the estates of aristocrats. This peddling had never been done before. To have roaming salesmen for their gambangs was entirely Tendas's idea.

From Tendas's interactions with the gentry and royal servants when he lived and worked at Brajanata's residence, he concluded that the nobles needed the gambang to balance their difficult — sometimes violent — lives. The more someone was affected by violence, the more they needed tenderness. The gambang provided that tenderness; the sound was soothing and not as loud as the gamelan, a Javanese musical ensemble, with its metal blades.

Tendas's idea was fruitful. Now his workers were as close as Tendas was to the nobles, the class of people who owned the Janggala kingdom. Some of the aristocratic customers were princes — sons of the king and his concubines, like Brajanata. Some were even willing to come to Tendas's instrument shop. During his interactions with these royal customers, in addition to what he heard from his workers, Tendas learned a few things about Brajanata's younger brother.

Panji Inu Kertapati, better known as Panji, was the crown prince of Janggala. In contrast to Brajanata, whose mother was a concubine of the king, Panji was conceived by the queen. From Brajanata's stories, Tendas knew that Panji and he, Tendas, were the same age. From Brajanata, too, Tendas knew that Panji's life was the life every man in Janggala dreamed of.

Panji's obligation to diligently study books on religion and state affairs was immediately rewarded by the king, who gave Panji the liberty to enjoy every pleasure he desired. At the age of nineteen, Panji's favorite pastime, apart from hunting wild animals, was the pursuit of beautiful women.

Beautiful girls readily lined up waiting for Panji to summon them. A girl considered it a great honor if the crown prince desired her. She would happily bestow her virginity to the handsome Panji, whose appearance was god-like.

———•••———

The heat of the day on the outskirts of the Janggala capital, where Siwur and his family lived, was made slightly more tolerable by Tendas's soft, melodious singing. Tendas did not hear the approaching hoofbeats. Suddenly, Brajanata appeared in the doorway of the workshop, as if welcomed by a light breeze and the songs of lingering morning birds through the shop's wide-open doors and windows.

"I don't see Ki Siwur, your father." Brajanata glanced quickly around the shop.

"He is still in his room." Tendas signaled the prince with his thumb.

"In his room?" Brajanata rubbed his chin.

"He has recovered from his accident, Raden, but he still feels weak," Tendas quickly explained. Tendas, wearing only a loincloth, as was the custom of most people in the countryside, lowered his eyes and took in the prince's knee-length trousers embroidered with glittering gold thread. He said, "I will tell him that you are here."

A few moments later, Siwur hurriedly entered the shop on wobbly legs. Bowing respectfully, Siwur, gripping his cane, welcomed the prince. "Your visit is an honor for my family, Raden."

Behind him, Siwur's wife also bowed deeply, folding her hands in front of her chest. Then, while still bowing, she backed out of the room. She soon returned with a tray of beverages and snacks, and the group moved outside to the veranda.

"After hunting from early morning until noon without catching a single tiger, the only consolation for our disappointment is to stop by your shop, Ki Siwur," Brajanata said.

Among the soldiers who accompanied Brajanata was a man dressed as a Brahmin — it was Kusni, the traveler from Perlak.

"Please, enjoy our very simple food." With a shaky hand, Siwur invited Brajanata to partake in the drinks and snacks his wife had prepared. They all sat on the veranda eating while talking about the scarcity of game that day.

"Ki Siwur, will you play the gambang and ask Tendas to sing?" Brajanata asked.

"We are no performers, Raden. We are just manual laborers. Forgive us if our performance does not entertain you." Siwur motioned to Tendas.

Tendas quickly brought their best gambang out to the veranda, then sat cross-legged next to his father and sang as best as he could.

The visit ended after Tendas finished his third song.

Siwur, his wife, and both of their sons, Tendas and Tandang, accompanied Brajanata and his small party to the roadside where their horses were tethered to the cottonwood trees. After the soldiers and Brajanata mounted their horses and rode away, one horse still remained under the trees. Its rider, Kusni, looked as if he had deliberately delayed his departure.

"I am interested in your songs, Tendas," Kusni said, as Siwur, his wife, and Tandang walked back to the house. "I would like to know more about the meaning of the lyrics you sang."

Tendas thought, *In Java, people do not so easily inquire about the knowledge of a person they just met.* Kusni's words made him uncomfortable. Was Kusni testing him? How embarrassed he would be if Kusni found out that he did not know the meaning of the songs he had just sung with all his heart!

"As far as I know..." Tendas paused, feeling stuck. He needed a moment to sort out his answer. Then he said, "This song gives advice about how to live a simple life. Simplicity can be shown by eating just enough to sustain life and sleeping just enough to be rested. Thus, it is sinful to eat until you are so full that you're still asleep when the sun has already lighted the eastern horizon."

"You are right, Tendas," Kusni said slowly. "It is important to avoid living excessively, especially nowadays."

"That is what we have been taught," Tendas agreed.

"Who taught you that?" asked Kusni.

"The songs we inherit from our ancestors."

Kusni nodded. "Your family is very fortunate."

"Fortunate?" Tendas couldn't believe his ears. "We rarely encounter the things enjoyed by most people, let alone the pleasures granted to the people living in the palace!"

"The people living in the palace are mostly unfortunate." Kusni's voice was low but firm. "And the most unfortunate person living in the palace is Raden Panji, the future king, and he is not even twenty years old."

"Raden Panji?" Tendas's eyes widened as he stared at Kusni in disbelief. "Am I hearing you correctly, Ki?"

"It's true. Raden Panji is indeed the most unfortunate person."

Tendas did not understand what Kusni meant, so he chose to stay quiet. Siwur had warned him that meddling in palace affairs was dangerous and had advised Tendas to distance himself from royalty as much as possible.

"His self-indulgent lifestyle will poison him." Kusni continued solemnly, "I want to tell you a story to help you understand what being fortunate means."

Then, Kusni told Tendas the life story of the crown prince Panji, who was being trained to become a perfect monarch.

"His Majesty's strong desire for Panji to become a king who is admired by friends and foes alike has caused the king to neglect one of the most natural needs of a child, which is parental affection." Despite his limited knowledge of Javanese, Kusni — a person from Perlak who had not even lived in Janggala for five years — told the story quite well. But by the time the story ended, Tendas still thought that Panji was the most fortunate man in the entire Janggala kingdom.

⊷•⊶

Running his father's business gave Tendas the opportunity to meet powerful people like Brajanata and Kusni, but he saw now that power came in different forms. The extent of Brajanata's power was obvious. He only needed to lift a finger to mobilize hundreds of mounted soldiers willing to risk their lives to follow his command.

Kusni's power was different. His ability to make Tendas see that he should not regret the simple life he had lived so far, but instead consider himself fortunate and be grateful for it, marked his greatness. Kusni taught Tendas that to be fortunate meant to be thankful. "To be a gambang-maker is something to be grateful for," Kusni explained.

"The most important thing in life is to make other people thankful for our presence."

Kusni stressed that he was grateful for Tendas and Siwur's beautiful musical performance. "Listening to your singing and finding out the meaning of the lyrics has given me an idea," Kusni said suddenly. "I never thought of this before. I will use your songs to teach Panji about the simplicity of life. I'm certain that your melodious voice will intrigue Panji, and he will ask about the meaning of the songs."

Kusni rode away, and the atmosphere in Tendas's house returned to normal. Siwur's wife, who told time by the shadows of an areca nut palm in front of the house, saw that it was time for the shop workers' lunch.

When Siwur's wife carried a tray laden with food into the workshop, the workers knew it was time to take a break. The workers in charge of making the gambang bars started to stretch and groan. It was time to straighten their backs and relax.

Tendas sat cross-legged on the woven mat in the workshop, contemplating the nuances of his conversation with Kusni. Meanwhile, his mother walked back and forth, carrying trays of food from the kitchen. Because the number of workers had increased after Tendas replaced his father as the workshop master, his mother had to employ a helper in the kitchen.

When Siwur managed the instrument shop, he focused more on repairing gambangs than making new ones. But after Tendas took over, it was the other way around; they were now producing more new gambangs than repairing old ones. Tendas rarely involved himself with carving gambang bars out of logs; he mostly worked on tuning the gambangs.

Tendas did not expect Kusni's return to his shop two days later. Apparently, Kusni was determined to quickly execute his carefully arranged plan to teach Panji about the simplicity of life, and he had returned to Tendas's shop for this purpose.

"Don't you want to see my father?" Tendas asked Kusni.

"Don't disturb your father. I can make my arrangements with you." Kusni pulled up a bamboo chair for himself and kept Tendas from calling his father.

Kusni outlined his plan again. To Tendas, Kusni's plan didn't make sense at all. But he nodded politely as if he understood and agreed.

When Kusni asked him for help with carrying out his plans, Tendas remained silent for a long time. He wanted to tell Kusni that he thought his plan would fail. But, afraid to disappoint Kusni, he decided not to say anything.

"You may doubt my plan." Kusni looked Tendas straight in the eye. "But to me, the most important thing is that we have tried. That alone can ease my guilt." When Kusni used the word "we" so proudly, Tendas was unable to deny his request.

"Can you ask Raden Panji to invite me to his residence?" Tendas was sure that not just anyone could ask Panji to do something — or would dare to.

"Of course, but I won't do it myself. I will discuss it with Raden Brajanata. Hopefully, as Panji's older brother, Raden Brajanata will ask Raden Panji to invite you and your father."

"And all I have to do is sing for Raden Panji at his residence?"

"Yes, and my task will be to explain the meaning of your songs."

Tendas felt that he had been assigned to carry a heavy burden, much heavier than carrying logs from the middle of the forest to his shop. It was very hard to go along with Kusni's idea because he was certain of its failure.

Kusni glanced at Tendas, who looked far from happy. "You don't seem confident that we will be successful."

Tendas not only doubted Kusni's plan, he also worried that Panji would be offended by the meaning of his songs. He knew very well that the king's son would not easily listen to advice, especially when being told he was wrong.

Kusni pushed on. "After you finish the first song, you will immediately continue with the song I have prepared. Of course, you will use the same melody. You may add and delete words as needed for the song's rhythm, as long as you show me the changes first. I just don't want the changes to affect the song's meaning."

Kusni handed Tendas a lontar leaf with verses written on it. He quoted some of the lines: "You undoubtedly will see hell; you will definitely see it. Then one day, you will be questioned about the worldly pleasures you boast about." He stopped and asked Tendas to sing the song:

> *Living luxuriously in the world has made you negligent,*
> *Oh man.*
> *You continue to be negligent, until the time you enter your*
> *grave.*
> *Don't be negligent as such.*
> *Later you will know the consequences of your negligence.*
> *If you knew those with certainty,*
> *You would not live like this.*

It was not difficult for Tendas to carry out Kusni's order and sing the song. He not only saw the satisfaction on Kusni's face, but he also saw the middle-aged man's eyes fill with tears as he smiled happily.

Kusni's plan began.

Tendas was invited to sing at Panji's residence. He was given only one day to prepare everything. The most troublesome part would be transporting his father. The idea of taking Siwur, whose frail body carried a broken spirit and was supported by a cane, felt like pulling a cart without a horse; it would be agonizing.

As soon as the sun rose in the eastern horizon, Tendas and his father left their house. Tendas drove their horse-drawn carriage to Panji's estate, in the capital of Janggala. Only the two of them went. The distance between their house and Panji's estate was not far for the average person, but for Siwur, it was a troublesome journey.

When the sun was directly above their heads, they slowly entered the large courtyard of Panji's estate. Tendas had not dared to drive his carriage faster, because the slightest jolt made Siwur moan and hold his chest.

Approaching Panji's residential area, Tendas noticed the signs of its owner's stature. The bushes looked neater; even the rocks looked cleaner. Amid the bright blooming flowers and clean red bricks, Tendas felt that their carriage was like a dirty black toad, swimming in a blossoming lotus pond.

As soon as their carriage rattled closer to the mansion, several servants ran to meet them. Tendas knew that their arrival was expected. The servants escorted them up to the pendapa, where Panji sat surrounded by young, kneeling women. Judging by the smiles on their faces, they were talking about something pleasant. The servants bowed respectfully before leaving Tendas and his father with an *emban*, a handmaid, who showed them the rest of the way. Supporting his father, Tendas slowly followed.

And so, on that clear, breezy afternoon, Tendas finally met the person who filled the minds of — and was the subject of conversation of — all the young women in the country: Panji, the crown prince of Janggala.

Tendas and his father prostrated in front of the handsome crown prince sitting in his chair. Then they seated themselves cross-legged on the floor and awaited orders from their host. A gambang had already been placed near them, so Tendas did not need to use the gambang he had brought; a servant placed it beside the pendapa steps.

"Welcome, Ki Siwur, and you also, Tendas," Panji said, leaning back in his chair.

Tendas glanced up at Panji, then looked down again. Although Tendas knew that he and Panji were about the same age, Panji appeared much younger. His relaxed manner of sitting lightened the atmosphere. Even though his voice was friendly, Tendas thought Panji's facial expression lacked warmth. His gestures too, lacked enthusiasm.

"My dear brother Brajanata asked me to invite you, famous craftsman and artist, to perform at my residence," Panji said softly.

Panji's saying that he was "asked" by his brother to invite them was enough to tell Tendas why Panji's expression was not as friendly as his voice, why his gestures were not as convincing as the gold jewelry on his strong body.

"We are not really a craftsman and artist," said Siwur, bowing his head. "We are only gambang-makers who don't deserve this kind of honor. If our performance does not please you, you can send us home immediately."

The exchange of pleasantries did not last long. Soon, Tendas and his father started the performance Kusni had arranged. Tendas did not see Kusni at the pendapa until the performance had already begun.

When Siwur started playing the gambang, all became quiet. Then Tendas began to sing.

The first song was an ordinary one often sung at weddings or childbirth ceremonies. Tendas glanced at the growing number of people watching the performance. People filled the middle, right, and left sides of the pendapa. The people in the middle section, of course, seated themselves behind Panji.

Tendas tried to read Panji's expression as he started the second song.

Panji's expression did not change, even when the song was almost finished. He had only clasped his hands and looked up intently, as if a cat-sized gecko were crawling on the ceiling beams. He remained seated that way until Tendas finished the song.

As Kusni had arranged, Tendas stopped singing after the second song. He and his father asked for permission to pause for a moment and wait for a response from the host. Of course, the decision whether to just pause the performance or end it, was left up to Panji.

"What a great performance," Panji said kindly, but indifferently.

Hearing Panji's comment, the audience smiled and nodded.

"Please forgive us; that's all we can do." Siwur bowed.

"I have often listened to the mellow sound of a gambang, as well as to a princess singing," Panji said. "But I have never heard such a melodious accompaniment."

Tendas tried again to read the look on Panji's face, but the crown prince still had the same expression: indifferent, even cold. His expression had not changed since they arrived.

"Ki Siwur, Tendas, please continue the performance. I'm sorry I won't be able to enjoy the remainder because I have other affairs to attend to." Panji rose, then slowly walked away.

Tendas and his father continued their performance. As Tendas expected, the atmosphere changed after Panji departed. Some people were now whispering and others moved around. By the time the craftsman and the artist started their fifth song, the audience was reduced by half. Tendas and his father exchanged glances and silently agreed to end the performance.

On their way home, Tendas and his father were escorted by two unarmed soldiers. Being given escorts meant that the crown prince had not been disappointed by their performance.

Tendas did not have high hopes that Kusni's plan to end Panji's destructive behavior would succeed. But the outcome did not matter to him.

⊢—•—⊣

A week later, a messenger arrived at Tendas's shop. The middle-aged man was bare-chested and only wore a loincloth, the way a servant dressed. He reminded Tendas of Kertala.

"Raden Panji sends you this." The messenger handed Tendas a basket — the kind often carried by village women — full of vegetables. "Although he did not give you gold or silver, this proves that he truly cares for you." It sounded like the messenger was just reciting the words Panji had told to him to say.

"Thank you, Ki…" Tendas did not know the messenger's name.

"My name is Prasanta. I'm sorry I forgot to introduce myself."

Tendas recognized the name. Kertala had once whispered to Tendas that the relationship between Panji and Prasanta was similar to the close relationship between Brajanata and Kusni. Thus, Tendas dared to conclude that Prasanta had great influence on Panji.

"Thank you, Ki Prasanta. We are honored that Prince Panji cares for us." Tendas bowed.

Prasanta pressed his folded hands against his chest. He spoke to Tendas as a confidant. "You need to know that Raden Panji changed a lot after your visit last week."

"Whatever the changes are, I hope they are for the better," Tendas said softly.

Prasanta went on, excited with his news. "After your performance, Raden Panji asked me to call his older brother. Because Raden Brajanata had a guest, he asked permission to bring Ki Kusni with him. Then they both went to see Raden Panji."

"Perhaps," Tendas said smiling, "Raden Panji changed because of the meeting with Raden Brajanata and his guest, not because of our performance."

Prasanta shook his head. "No, I am sure they met because of your performance."

"If you would be so kind, would you please tell me what Raden Panji thought of our performance?" Tendas's heart was beating so fast, it felt about to jump out of his chest.

Prasanta said Panji's change was not entirely caused by the performance. "I overheard the discussion among Raden Panji, Raden Brajanata, and Ki Kusni about the meaning of the lyrics." According to Prasanta, it was the song that Kusni had composed that really affected the crown prince.

Panji's change of behavior did not really matter to Tendas. His introduction to Prasanta, Panji's closest companion, however, was of the utmost importance. If Prasanta said that Panji was affected by his singing, it meant that their visit had been meaningful — the lyrics of his song had sent Panji a message.

"You visited at the right time," Prasanta said, looking at Tendas. "Panji is going through a big change right now. Your song served as fertilizer for a seed about to sprout."

Listening to Prasanta's words, Tendas concluded that Panji was starting to get bored of his opulent lifestyle. Of the thousands of people in Janggala, Panji was the only one who enjoyed such luxuries. Many people said that a man derived his highest pleasure from a woman. It would be very difficult to name the kind of woman Panji had not enjoyed.

But according to Prasanta, Panji would now rather be alone to think about his unordinary lifestyle. Unlike before the performance, Panji would now rather spend time reading the lontar leaves at the palace library than socializing with the other princes and princesses. When he wasn't spending his time reading, he left the palace compound dressed like a commoner. Only Prasanta knew where he went.

After their first meeting, Prasanta often took Tendas to Panji's mansion to repair broken gambangs and teach young nobility to sing. Prasanta himself also frequently visited Tendas in his shop to look for a new gambang.

Siwur, however, did not seem to like their growing friendship. Not once did Siwur meet Prasanta — let alone greet him — when Prasanta visited the instrument shop. His father's attitude made Tendas wonder. He knew that his father respected powerful people, such as royalty, as well as the people associated with them. "Don't you want to meet our customer, Ki Prasanta?" Tendas once asked his father when he saw that Siwur did not get out of bed when Prasanta arrived.

"You can take care of him by yourself," his father answered, uninterested.

"He has bought many of our gambangs." Tendas was curious about his father's indifferent attitude.

"The one who bought our gambangs is his master, Raden Panji," Siwur retorted coldly.

Tendas didn't reply. It was useless to continue this conversation. In their family, they handled disagreements with silence. His mother would busy herself in the kitchen; his brother, Tandang, would go for a walk to the side of the house and stroke his horse.

Tendas assumed that his father disliked Prasanta because Prasanta was just a servant, but then he heard his father reprimand his mother's kitchen helper for getting too close to Prasanta. His father's last words to the woman were: "Beware, he worships Semar, a god who came to earth disguised as a royal servant."

Siwur and his family were not religious. They did not worship Shiva, Vishnu, or even Buddha. For them, religion was too complicated and expensive. For example, to ask for a god's providence, they had to use the exact words as written in the holy book for their prayers. They had to build a beautiful place to worship the gods — a place even better than the house they lived in — not to mention the various offerings they had to prepare. Only privileged people, such as the aristocrats, could afford the intricacies of being religious.

Tendas paid attention to everything Prasanta told him. One time, Prasanta said, "You need to know that before Raden Brajanata's frequent visits, Raden Panji didn't think that there was anything wrong with his way of living. I truly suspect that his brother has made him re-evaluate his lifestyle."

Tendas was very interested in all the stories about Panji, Prasanta's master. The most interesting story was about Panji's meeting with Angreni, the daughter of Janggala's *patih*, the prime minister Kudanawarsa.

Chapter 2

THE ENCHANTING FLOWER OF THE PRIME MINISTER'S GARDEN

Accompanied by his aide, Prasanta, Panji walked wherever his feet took him.

The previous day, Panji's father, King Lembu Amiluhur of Janggala, had reminded him about his engagement to the daughter of King Lembu Amerdadu of Kadiri, the Janggala king's brother and Panji's uncle. The engagement between Panji, the crown prince of Janggala, and Sekartaji, the crown princess of Kadiri, had been arranged almost fifteen years ago.

Panji's father had told Panji to prepare for his marriage to Sekartaji, which was scheduled to take place the following month. Panji was certain that his marriage to Sekartaji would clip his wings.

Panji wandered aimlessly, as did his mind. He imagined looking down on the two kingdoms — the kingdom of Janggala and the kingdom of Kadiri — side by side. He recalled his father telling him that the marriage between himself and Kadiri's crown princess would unite the two kingdoms peacefully. There would be no more suspicion, no more mistrust between Janggala and Kadiri.

Panji's aimless walking took him to a blooming lotus pond in the middle of a garden area on Patih Kudanawarsa's estate. The lotus flowers competed in showing off their brightness, and the branches of a blossoming orange jasmine tree partially covered the pond. Panji stopped in its shade.

"This place is lovely," he murmured. "Let's rest here, Prasanta."

Prasanta nodded. "This is a good place to rest your legs and relax, Raden." He hurried to a nearby banana tree grove and gathered some dry leaves for his master to sit on while he kept a watchful eye on the surrounding bushes and tall grasses.

Seated in the shade of the tree covered with blooming, fragrant flowers, Panji leaned against the trunk and soon fell asleep.

Whenever his master closed his eyes, Prasanta remained especially watchful to guard him against all potential dangers. The king had not assigned Prasanta as Panji's aide without good reason. Prasanta was the only person the court trusted to protect the crown prince, in addition to being a companion who entertained and comforted him.

Prasanta walked around, observing the surroundings. After he was certain that there were no signs of snakes or other venomous creatures, Prasanta seated himself cross-legged next to his master. Afraid of falling asleep like his master, he refrained from leaning back against the tree.

The garden was not far from the main residence of Patih Kudanawarsa, Janggala's prime minister, who was taking a leisurely walk to enjoy the beautiful garden. The patih quickened his steps when he noticed strangers in his garden.

Panji was still fast asleep against the tree when the patih reached the two. "Prasanta," whispered Kudanawarsa, who knew Prasanta very well, "why didn't you inform me of Raden Panji's visit?"

"I was just about to do that, but you arrived here before I had a chance to." Prasanta didn't want the patih to feel disrespected.

"Has Raden Panji been asleep there for a long time?"

"No, not long, Your Excellency."

Their whispered conversation awakened Panji. He slowly opened his eyes, then rose, smiling at his host.

"Forgive me, Raden," Kudanawarsa said nervously. "I have disturbed your rest."

"No, Patih," Panji quickly responded. "You didn't disturb me at all. It is I who owes you an apology for sleeping in your garden without your permission."

"It is an honor for me and my family that Your Royal Highness is willing to pay us a visit," Kudanawarsa replied, feeling calmer. "Let me take you to my residence. At dusk, the mosquitoes usually become a nuisance in the garden." The golden disc in the western sky was indeed rapidly sinking, and it was growing darker.

"I'd be really pleased to meet your entire family, Patih." Panji glanced at Prasanta and his eyes said: *We have to accept the patih's offer. I haven't visited him for a long time.*

The three of them walked toward the prime minister's mansion. Panji and the patih walked next to each other, while Prasanta followed from a short distance.

When they arrived at the mansion, their host escorted them into the front hall and invited them to be seated. Panji took a chair, while Prasanta seated himself cross-legged on the floor, not far from his master. Meanwhile, Kudanawarsa asked one of his family members to honor his guest with a tray of betel leaf chews and flowers.

Panji straightened in his chair and rested his palms on his knees. When a girl carried a silver tray with betel leaf chews and flowers into the room, Panji looked at her, enchanted. The girl's appearance was very simple yet very charming.

"Thank you." Panji's hand quivered slightly when he received the betel leaves and flowers. "It appears this is the first time we've met. What is your name?"

"I am Angreni, Your Highness," replied the girl, lowering her eyes.

Even with all of his experience with countless women, Panji knew right away that despite her simplicity, Angreni was the most beautiful girl he had ever met. He fell in love at first sight — and he vowed to have her. "You can call me by my name, Panji."

"That would not be proper, Your Highness," Angreni said. "You are my master."

As Angreni turned to leave, Panji grabbed her hand.

Prasanta, sitting behind them, clenched his fist. He was surprised to see Panji's old behavior return. He could clearly see how hard Angreni fought to free her hand from Panji's grip. When Angreni's eyes filled with tears and she looked about to cry, Panji released her hand, but the girl had definitely won his heart.

Panji was not only smitten by her beautiful face and shapely body, but was also enticed by Angreni's earnest effort to pull her hand out of his grip. Among commoners, it was nothing special for a girl to pull her hand away from a boy she'd just met. But for the handsome crown prince of Janggala, what had just happened was very unusual. Until now, all the beautiful girls vied for his attention — just a glance from Panji made them proud enough to boast about the experience with family and neighbors.

Panji could not remember how many girls had eagerly surrendered their virginity to him or how many women had hungrily slept with him. From the wives of high officials to those of lowly village officials, no woman was immune to his charm — any woman would happily submit her body to Panji.

Panji once told Prasanta that even the parents of the girls he slept with were proud of the fact. And if the girl became pregnant, the parents would not hesitate to brag about their grandchild having royal blood. The husbands of the wives he slept with were also very pleased. The fact that the prince was attracted to a man's wife proved that his wife was indeed special. Prasanta often wondered to himself: *Why didn't the parents or husbands resent Panji for his callous treatment of their beloved daughter or wife?*

Panji's surprise when Angreni clearly rejected his advances was real. The girl was like a fragrant flower protected by thorns. The difficulty in picking the beautiful, fragrant flower challenged him.

Kudanawarsa had seen the interchange and nervously approached Panji. "Please accept my profuse apologies, Raden. My daughter Angreni does have a mind of her own."

But Panji did not hear what the patih said. His eyes remained on the doorway that separated him from the girl who had unsettled his mind.

Panji's lack of response made the patih even more nervous. He fussed with the batik cloth wrapped around his lower body. His chest rose and fell rapidly with apprehension. "I will punish my insolent daughter, Raden," Kudanawarsa said as he, too, looked at the door. "She deserves a flogging."

"Who deserves the punishment, Patih?" Panji suddenly realized the wrong turn things before him were taking — a father worried over his daughter's behavior.

"Angreni, Raden," Kudanawarsa answered quickly. "Her behavior has displeased Your Highness."

"On the contrary, Patih. I am very pleased with the way she served the betel leaves and flowers." Panji's words astonished the patih. He breathed deeply and lowered his gaze. A slight smile crossed his lips.

"May I see her now, Patih?" Panji pressed. He surprised himself by speaking those words — this was the first time he had ever asked a parent for permission to see their daughter.

"I am very pleased to hear that you want to see my daughter now," Kudanawarsa stammered. "But notwithstanding Your Highness's position, it would be best to postpone the meeting till at least tomorrow morning." He then added, "It is already late now."

For a moment, neither Panji nor the patih spoke. The sound of the jackfruit tree leaves rustling in the wind was suddenly so loud. The whistling wind and buzzing night insects competed with each other to fill the evening's silence.

Prasanta, closely watching the events unfolding in front of him, coughed uncomfortably.

"Very well, Patih. Tomorrow morning will be even better." Panji rose and turned to Prasanta, who stood and moved closer to his master.

Then they both said goodbye to the prime minister, who escorted his guests to the estate's gate.

—•—

After returning from the prime minister's estate, Panji went to his personal library that he had ordered built a week ago to replicate the palace library. But when midnight came, he had not read a single page. Filled with anxiety, he left the library and slowly walked toward his room. He crossed the garden and, with trembling fingers, picked a rose. Even after he lay down in his room, he was unable to close his eyes. It was not until morning that he fell asleep, still holding the rose.

The servants' morning activities awakened Panji. He immediately thought of Angreni. Fingering the rose petals, he whispered, "Angreni, Angreni." He rushed to find Prasanta. "Prasanta!" he said when he found his aide. "I want to visit Angreni as soon as possible."

"Apparently Raden is very impressed with the beauty of the prime minister's daughter," Prasanta said, making small talk as they walked to the stables.

"It's not only her beauty that impresses me ..." Panji seemed about to continue, but didn't.

Prasanta already guessed that it was not only her beauty that impressed Panji, but also her rejection of him. As far as Prasanta knew, Angreni was the only girl in Janggala who had ever pushed Panji's hand away. "She's indeed very special, Raden," Prasanta said.

Prasanta beckoned the stableman. Soon, Panji and Prasanta were on horseback headed for the patih's estate.

It was still early in the morning when Panji and his loyal aide arrived at the estate of the second-most influential person in Janggala. Patih Kudanawarsa was second only to the Janggala king, King Lembu Amiluhur.

Expecting the arrival of an important guest, the patih's household bustled with activities. Everywhere in the compound — the main house along with the smaller houses to the left, right, and behind it

— servants were busily engaged. The hosts, Patih Kudanawarsa and his wife, were dressed as if attending a great event at the palace.

Unlike on the previous visit, when he had worn plain clothes, Panji had dressed up for his second visit to the patih. For this visit, Panji rode a spirited, dapple-gray horse and was dressed like a prince on his way to the palace to pay his respects to the king. Prasanta rode a smaller black horse.

As soon as Kudanawarsa saw his guests approaching, he sent two servants to welcome Panji and Prasanta. The servants immediately tethered the horses under a shade tree and walked behind the guests to the mansion.

"Patih, I want to marry Angreni and ask for your blessing," Panji said to Kudanawarsa as soon as they were seated.

The presence of servants still serving snacks and beverages prevented the patih from answering.

"So, what is your answer, Patih?" Panji asked impatiently, leaning forward.

Noticing Panji's eagerness, the prime minister smiled slightly, as if to say: *Ah, a typical young man.* Kudanawarsa invited Panji to drink the steaming hot tea, then said slowly, "We, as Angreni's parents, are indeed delighted to know that Raden cares for our daughter."

"In that case, I ask for your permission to take her with me today." Panji held his teacup without drinking from it.

"Of course, I will allow it, Raden," Kudanawarsa said softly. "However, there is nothing wrong with meeting her before you move her to your residence."

"Yes, of course, Patih," said Panji. "May I meet her now in the garden?"

"Oh, I just remembered." The prime minister straightened himself before continuing, "She has gone to the market. She enjoys going there to watch women do business, buying and selling spices and pottery."

"Is that so? All right, I will go there."

"She went to the small market in the south," Kudanawarsa added quickly, "not to the big market in the capital."

When Panji and Prasanta arrived at the small market and dismounted, Panji halted abruptly. He suddenly realized that finding someone in a market was not the same as finding someone in a garden. Panji had never been to a market before.

Prasanta, seeing Panji's confusion, stepped closer and said, "This is where most people in Janggala fulfill their needs, Raden. More than half of Janggala's population depends on the market for their livelihood."

Panji could not comprehend Prasanta's words. He only knew that one could live well if one had power. Power could be gained by strength. Strength consisted of physical fitness and intelligence. He currently pursued both of strength's components with body and soul. He honed his physical fitness and intelligence daily because afterward, there were rewards. His rewards were the ability to fulfill his desires — the same desires all young men of his age had. It was the ability to indulge in all kinds of delicious food and beverages, as well as the ability to make love with palace courtesans and village virgins.

Panji looked around, overwhelmed. "How can I find Angreni in this place?"

"We have to mingle with the crowd and look for her, Raden. But in order not to be conspicuous, we need to change into a commoner's garb."

Panji only nodded.

Prasanta now realized that the woman his master pined for was not an ordinary woman, but rather someone so unusual that she could easily reject the advances of a crown prince. She could have very well sneaked off when she found out that Panji was looking for her. To avoid any unpleasant surprises, Prasanta asked Panji to wait outside the market while he went shopping for clothes that would disguise them.

After they changed into the clothes Prasanta had bought, the two entered the market. Their disguise was successful. No one noticed the presence of the crown prince of Janggala and his loyal aide. Dressed like a commoner, Panji didn't look any different from the people milling around him. He observed the people closely, especially the girls who were either buying or selling.

The marketplace offered much more freedom than the world Panji knew behind the palace walls. This was something he had learned from a Brahmin who taught him about social matters. Here, the free atmosphere was created spontaneously. Everyone at the market was there by choice to meet a necessity. The world of the marketplace was indeed the opposite of the world of the palace. Everything that happened in the palace was dictated by rules and rituals which often did not make sense and were seldom based on a necessity.

Panji looked desperate. He was giving up hope of being able to find the woman of his dreams. "I will order some soldiers to find Angreni in this market."

"It would not be wise to use soldiers to find someone in this market, Raden," Prasanta counseled. "We better wait here."

"Wait here? Until when?" Frowning, Panji glanced at Prasanta.

"I am sure Angreni knows that we are here," Prasanta said.

"And we have to wait here for her?" Panji still did not understand his aide's reasoning.

"That's right, Raden. If she comes, it means you can proceed with your plans to marry her."

"If she doesn't come, I will still marry her, so what's the problem?" Panji grumbled. In the distance, Mount Arjuna towered in the blue sky.

"The problem is that you would only possess her physically, her body," Prasanta explained. "In a marriage, one not only has physical needs, but also spiritual ones."

Panji looked at the gravel between his feet. He didn't just lust for Angreni's body; he had enjoyed many girls' bodies. This time, he wanted something else.

Panji and Prasanta stood for a long time under the burning morning sun. Unable to bear the heat any longer, Panji turned to leave the market, only to find the girl who had disturbed his sleep the night before standing before him.

"Angreni! I've been looking for you for a long time!" Panji couldn't hide his joy. Before he could continue, Angreni offered him water from a coconut shell half with a carved wooden handle.

"Forgive me, Your Highness. I only have a coconut shell to serve your water in," Angreni said softly.

Panji grabbed the ladle and drank from it with big gulps. Some of the water spilled and wet his bare chest.

Prasanta, noticing the way Angreni was dressed, nodded happily. He was satisfied with the way things had unfolded. Angreni was dressed like the other women vendors at the market; no wonder they had a hard time finding her.

"Now I'm convinced that you are the girl who is destined to share my life," Panji said, returning the ladle.

Angreni simply looked down.

Panji couldn't take his eyes off the girl. "Let me take you home."

"Forgive me, Your Highness, I went to the market with Sumbita, my handmaid. Please allow me to walk home with her." Before Panji had a chance to reply, Angreni beckoned to someone standing near her. Angreni and Sumbita bowed, then both of them hurried away from the thinning market crowd.

Panji could only watch them go.

He and Prasanta rode back to the prime minister's residence, where Panji restated his intention to marry Angreni and asked Kudanawarsa for permission to take Angreni with him as soon as possible.

"Am I to understand that what you mean by 'as soon as possible' is not more than the time between two full moons, correct?" Kudanawarsa asked.

"What I mean is not more than one week, Patih," Panji said sheepishly.

"Oh, I see. All right then. Next week you may take Angreni to your residence. I believe you have already talked to her." The patih turned towards Angreni, who had slipped into the room and now sat behind him.

Angreni bowed deeply.

Kudanawarsa turned back to Panji. "You must tell your father, His Majesty the King, about your intention to marry Angreni."

Panji remembered his engagement to the crown princess of Kadiri. "Would you please inform His Majesty that I intend to marry Angreni next week?"

"All right, Raden. Tomorrow, I will tell His Majesty."

"Thank you, Patih." Panji turned to Prasanta sitting behind him and said, "Please go on home and tell my sister Onengan to clean and decorate the house."

"Yes, Your Highness. I will go now and tell your sister." Prasanta bowed before leaving the prime minister's mansion and riding directly to Onengan's quarters at the *keputren*, the compound where the female royalty lived.

Panji turned to Kudanawarsa. "I will return here in a week to move Angreni to the palace, Patih."

"We will prepare for her leave," Patih Kudanawarsa responded and bowed.

It was the first time ever that Panji had to wait a week before he could take the object of his desire with him. Usually — it had happened dozens of times in his early teens — the girl's father would allow Panji to immediately take his daughter with him.

It also was the first time Panji had met a girl with such peculiar behavior as finding enjoyment in spending time at a crowded marketplace. Usually, the daughters of gentry loved to play in a beautiful flower garden or near a pond stocked with a variety of fish. But Angreni preferred to be among people who were drenched in sweat, bartered loudly, and were even rude at times. She enjoyed being at a place where she could buy the goods she needed as cheaply as possible, as well as sell her wares for the highest price possible. Panji realized that Angreni was a constant surprise. She had made him wait impatiently because she would allow no one to force her. Still, he could not stop thinking about her and how alive she made him feel.

A week later, which to Panji felt like a year, he arrived at the patih's estate with his entourage. He was accompanied by his older brother

Brajanata, his younger sister Onengan, and, of course, Prasanta; all were part of the procession of a dozen horse carriages.

They were obviously expected. The pendapa and veranda of the patih's mansion were decorated with colorful flowers. Trays filled with refreshments were neatly served on beautifully carved wooden tables and lacy pandanus woven mats.

The conversation between the host and his guests followed the socially prescribed formula of phrases that conveyed respect and goodwill.

By the time the sun had sunk into the western horizon, the guests had finished their refreshments, and it was time to go. Panji bid farewell to Patih Kudanawarsa and his wife, then slowly led his bride to the waiting horse carriage. The rest of his party followed in their own carriages.

Standing in front of the pendapa, Patih Kudanawarsa and his extended family saw their guests off. They remained standing there until Panji and his party disappeared behind the trees in the distance.

———•◦•———

The sun had set and the tree leaves were bowed to pay respect to the master of the day when Panji and his entourage arrived at his estate.

They immediately headed for the veranda, which was decorated with floral arrangements. Food and drinks were already served on short tables and mats. Everyone who had accompanied Panji from the patih's residence — some close relatives and their servants — was invited to enjoy the prepared refreshments. Every so often, someone suppressed a burp.

The elder guests were the first to excuse themselves. Laden with parcels containing party food — a gift from the host — they all said goodbye. The last person to leave was Brajanata.

Now there were only Panji, Angreni, and Onengan left on the veranda. The servants, including Prasanta, had gone to the backyard, while others clustered near the gate.

"I hope you'll enjoy living here, Angreni," Onengan said to Angreni, who was still admiring the decorations.

"Who wouldn't be happy living in such a beautiful house, my dear sister." Angreni's faint smile by far expressed exalted happiness.

"Thank God." Onengan looked relieved. "In that case, I ask for permission to return to the keputren."

"I wouldn't dare keep you from leaving," Angreni said. "It's already late. Please be careful on your way home."

Onengan returned to the keputren, accompanied by a handmaid and escorted by two soldiers.

Now it was quiet on the veranda. Only a turtledove calling from behind the mansion, broke the silence of the night.

"Angreni, won't it be better if we go inside?" Panji's question sounded more like a request than a suggestion.

"I am still admiring the decorations, Raden." Angreni's answer sounded more like a refusal than a statement.

"You don't have to call me Raden; just call me by my name." Panji paused, then continued, trying to persuade Angreni. "Everything was decorated by my sister, Onengan, not by a hired hand."

"I like it this way," she said. "Anything more would have been too much. I don't like anything that is excessive, Raden — I apologize, I mean, Panji." Angreni smiled.

Panji took a deep breath. It appeared he would have to be patient — or, to be exact, restrain himself — and simply sit on the veranda. "If that's what you wish." Panji tried to remain calm.

They were quiet for a while, facing each other. From a distance, anyone who saw them would think that they were having a nice conversation.

Panji broke the silence. "Aren't you tired of sitting here? The night air is starting to get cold."

"I'm neither tired nor cold, Panji."

"Listen to the owl hoot. Aren't you sleepy?"

"I am not sleepy, and the birds keep me even more awake."

They fell into silence again. It was close to midnight when Angreni softly said, "Panji, I need to thank you for your patience. I realize that while I've irritated you since our first meeting, at least from what I can see, you're not angry with me."

"How could I be angry with you? Being angry with you is like throwing away a blooming rose, and the one who would cry over the loss would be me."

"Please take me to your room, my husband."

"Let us go, my wife."

They walked hand in hand towards the bridal room that Onengan and the handmaids had prepared. The fragrance of jasmine welcomed them as they entered the room. Jasmine flowers, a symbol of purity, were scattered on the white sheets and carpeted the floor.

Angreni stopped just inside the door.

Panji slowly closed the door behind them and led his bride to the prepared bridal bed. The bed creaked slightly as the two of them took a seat on the edge.

The wind settled between the tree branches. A cloud hid the moon. The buzzing night insects were the only sign of life.

That night, Panji and Angreni made love for the first time. Panji's admiration for the girl who had shown indifference towards the advances of a nobleman who was not an ordinary prince, ignited the fire of their union. The flames were fanned by Angreni's respect of a crown prince, willing to patiently wait for an ordinary girl.

The slow twisting and rapid turning of their bodies was something only they were fit to witness. In the length of time it would take to cook a pot of rice, the fiery flames were extinguished, and the virgin blood transformed admiration into a reverence that bordered on worship.

Panji and Angreni held each other in a blissful embrace until the rooster crowed and the light of dawn broke through the eastern horizon.

Angreni slowly rose.

The creaking bed awakened Panji. When he saw Angreni reach for her clothes, he quickly rose, too, and took his wife to a bathing pond with a waterspout next to their room. They both went in together. Panji finished first and helped his wife dress.

Angreni reached for a silver powder box and applied powder evenly on her feet, hands, and body. A batik cloth wrapped her body from stomach to ankles, secured by a cummerbund and fastened with a gold belt studded with diamonds. A gold necklace, earrings, and bracelets, enhanced with diamonds, illuminated her firm body. Angreni felt shy while Panji helped her put them on.

From a smaller container, Angreni took some fragrant powder and applied it on her neck and face. The intricate, jeweled hairpins used to put up her hair were difficult to handle. Several times, the glittery pins loosened and fell on the rug.

Angreni's skin powders served several functions: they warded off mosquitoes and other disturbing insects and made her skin and face shine. Last but not least, the fragrance was refreshing, not only for her but also for the people around her.

Outside the door, a handmaid sat on her knees waiting to help Angreni dress if necessary, but this morning, she had not been needed. After completing her toilette, Angreni walked out of the room towards the veranda.

While the grass was still wet with dew, the servants had already started to prepare everything their masters needed. As soon as Angreni seated herself on a chair overlooking the garden, a handmaid placed a cup of steaming hot tea on the round wooden table beside her.

Unlike the batik cloth Angreni wore, Panji wore looser clothes. The cloth of his trousers was woven with shimmering golden thread. He wore simpler jewelry on his head and body.

At noon, Onengan arrived with some of Panji's close relatives. The new husband happily presented his wife to them. Later, after Angreni had met all the close family and friends, Panji told her to rest in the garden and bask in the afternoon sun.

After most of the guests had left and Angreni had excused herself, Onengan said to Panji, "There was no one among the guests who did not admire Angreni's beauty and elegance."

Panji did not hide his pride. "Thank you, my dear sister. I am very lucky indeed to have Angreni."

Onengan had actually wanted to say that Angreni was *now* a perfect woman. The girl who was *almost* perfect was *now* perfect because she had married a crown prince. But Onengan worried about perfection. She worried that Angreni would cause envy, not only among the court princesses, but also among the angels in paradise. Envy could manifest into danger for a perfect woman. Not wanting to ruin her brother's happiness, Onengan kept her thoughts to herself.

The next day, Panji took his wife to the prime minister's mansion. Angreni's parents were expecting their visit and rushed to meet them in front of the pendapa. All the servants, including Sumbita, were present.

Nyai Patih, Angreni's mother, said that she wished their marriage would bring happiness to both of them. Panji promised that his meeting Angreni, followed by the marriage, would lead both of them to a happy life.

After a light meal, Nyai Patih turned to Panji and asked, "May I now say something, Raden?"

Panji was somewhat surprised by his mother-in-law's question. "You're welcome to speak at any time."

"I mean, now that you've enjoyed our simple food, there's something I want to tell you," Nyai Patih continued awkwardly. "I just want to remind you that as far as we know, the court — or, more precisely, the king — has not yet been informed about your marriage to Angreni."

"That's right, I haven't told His Majesty yet," Panji said flatly. He had a feeling that his father would object to this marriage. But knowing that his father and other princes had taken many women as concubines before marrying the formal queen, Panji didn't see any urgency to inform his father of his marriage. Panji said to Nyai Patih, "But remember, I asked the prime minister to inform the king."

"I think you'd better tell the king yourself," Nyai Patih said.

"And when do you think I should tell my father?" Panji asked.

The patih's wife glanced at her husband, who was in the front yard, talking with someone who looked like a messenger from the court. "We think it's best to go now."

"Now?"

"Yes, now." Nyai Patih knew it was important to tell the king about the marriage as soon as possible. Panji's marriage to Angreni was complicated. It was widely known that Panji was already engaged to Sekartaji, the crown princess of Kadiri. The prime minister's household was worried that Panji's marriage to Angreni would displease the king, which was why they hadn't thrown a big party or invited many guests, as was customary for high-society weddings.

"All right, we will immediately get ready and see the king." Panji turned to his wife.

"Of course, our entire family will accompany you to the palace," Nyai Patih said.

"It will be an honor to meet the king in the company of my wife's family."

After apologizing to Panji for not being able to accompany him because of a sudden assignment from the king, the patih departed.

Kudanawarsa's family had already prepared for a visit to the Janggala palace, so they were soon on their way. Panji and Angreni sat side by side on the palanquin, while Nyai Patih traveled in a horse-drawn carriage.

At the palace gate, Panji and Angreni quickly stepped out of the palanquin and continued the rest of the way to the palace on foot, followed by their entourage.

When they noticed the guests, the guards rushed to greet Panji, then led him, Angreni, and Nyai Patih to the *paseban*, a large, open audience hall where the king received guests.

The rest of their party, which numbered at least fifty, was taken to rest in the shade of a banyan tree, where bamboo mats had been placed around the trunk.

The news of Panji's visit spread quickly. All the women in the palace were eager to see the new bride.

The court priest and Her Holiness Rara Suci, the king's sister, welcomed the bride and the groom. Onengan was also among those welcoming the visitors.

"Please be seated," the court priest said to Panji, his wife, and Panji's mother-in-law. Then the court priest turned to Rara Suci, sitting next to him, and asked, "Where's His Majesty?"

"His Majesty is still sleeping," Rara Suci said. She turned to Onengan, sitting next to Angreni. "My daughter Onengan, please, wake up His Majesty." Rara Suci always addressed her niece as if she were her own daughter.

Onengan bowed and left the paseban. Only Onengan and Her Majesty, the queen of Janggala, dared to awaken the king.

The king's bedroom was located in the center of the palace. Onengan knocked softly on the door. Her mother, the queen, immediately opened it.

"What is it, Onengan?" the queen asked.

"Pardon me, Mother," Onengan replied respectfully. "I've been asked to waken the king. My brother Panji has married."

"He married?" The queen sounded indifferent to the news her youngest daughter brought her. "Can't Panji marry anyone he wants on any day?" The queen was unwilling to wake up the king for such trivial news.

Onengan folded her hands. "This time he married someone special, Mother. Panji married Patih Kudanawarsa's daughter." When her mother didn't respond, she continued, "Her name is Angreni."

"The prime minister has many daughters. What's so special about this one?"

"I have never seen Panji this happy." Onengan paused to find the right words. "Panji and Angreni are both waiting in the paseban."

"Oh. I see." Still looking uninterested, the queen sighed. "Very well, I will wake up His Majesty. Ask them to wait." The queen closed the door.

Not long afterward, the king walked out of his room. The servants kneeling on both sides of the door immediately moved back then rose.

Bowing with their hands folded and pressed against their stomachs, they waited for the king's orders.

Followed by dozens of his servants, the king walked to the *balairung,* the royal audience hall. His Majesty King Lembu Amiluhur took a seat on the throne, while the queen seated herself on a lower chair next to him. After they were seated, he ordered a soldier to bring in the guests waiting in the paseban.

Panji, Angreni, and Nyai Patih entered and knelt before the king.

The king raised his hand to signal two handmaids, kneeling slightly behind him on his left. One of the handmaids immediately prepared a chewing wad of betel leaves, betel nuts, and slaked lime for the king. The king put the wad into his mouth and chewed slowly.

The other handmaid inched towards the king with a brass spittoon. She placed the vessel near the king to prevent his red betel juice spit from staining the rug.

The audience hall was filled with a dead silence. No one whispered, let alone talk. With their lips pressed together and their heads bowed, everyone waited for the king to speak. The king continued to slowly chew his wad. His silent mastication was barely noticeable. Then he finally spat the whole chew into the spittoon, followed by another spurt of red spit.

"I am glad to see you all gathered here." King Amiluhur looked at his guests one by one before continuing. "I am pleased to meet Nyai Patih and her beautiful daughter."

Nyai Patih and Angreni rose for a moment and, bowing, raised their clasped hands with thumbs touching the mouth.

"Panji, my son." The king now looked at the crown prince. "I know the purpose of your visit. Patih Kudanawarsa has told me about your marriage to his daughter. I, of course, bless the wife of your choice."

Now it was Panji's turn to show his respect to the king by raising his clasped hands with the thumbs touching his mouth. But unlike Nyai Patih and Angreni, Panji tried to read the expression on the king's face. And even though he only caught a fleeting glance, Panji concluded that his visit with his new wife did not seem to spark the king's attention. His father's expression was blank. Panji saw his father stifle a yawn.

As if reminded by a mysterious whisperer, the king slowly straightened and said, "Of course we need to celebrate Panji's marriage to the prime minister's daughter." After issuing this order, King Amiluhur rose from his throne and slowly walked towards Panji and Angreni, who sat side by side. He stroked the heads of the newlyweds and then walked toward the inner section of the palace, followed by his servants.

The queen ordered the household staff to immediately prepare a banquet. Everyone — the people who came with Panji and anyone who just happened to be in the palace — was welcome to enjoy the royal banquet.

Outside, Prasanta had fallen asleep under the banyan tree. In the gentle breeze, he dreamed he was Semar, the servant of virtuous knights in Javanese mythology, who was actually an incarnation of a god. Because Semar was a man with the appearance of a servant but who possessed divine power, the king allowed him to marry royalty. In his dream, Prasanta, as Semar, could choose any princess, either from those in the palace or from the prime minister's household.

"Who would accept a servant as their husband?" Prasanta asked the king in his dream. "I am ugly and also old — I'm more than fifty years old. Besides that, I have many children. No one would want to take me as their son-in-law."

"Even if you ask for Onengan to be your wife, I will allow it," replied the king.

Prasanta then chose one of Patih Kudanawarsa's daughters, Angreni's younger sister, who was a part of Panji's convoy. In his dream, Prasanta and his chosen bride were paraded to the prime minister's residence to be wed.

The local people at the wedding in his dream pitied the beautiful girl who had to marry Prasanta. It was just like feeding delicious white rice to a mangy dog.

In the sky, a host of heavenly creatures hovered over the prime minister's residence. They flew in formation; some played the flute, others danced. They were the gods and dwellers of heaven. But, of course, only Prasanta could see them in his dream.

The girl did not want to marry an ugly old man. She repeatedly ripped off her wedding dress and was ready to stab herself with a dagger. Angels descended from heaven to calm the girl. They told her she was about to marry a god who resided in the palace of Mahadewa, the king of the gods. At the request of the angels, the girl looked up, and she saw Prasanta in his true handsome, godlike form.

The girl was captivated, and the marriage ceremony continued without any further trouble. After the ceremony, the king and his party returned to the palace. The gods who were present as witnesses to their marriage returned to heaven. Prasanta's dream wedding to the patih's daughter ended joyfully.

As his wife, this beautiful woman behaved very well. True to the custom of that era, she never ate with her husband but always later. She never went to bed earlier than her husband, and never rose later than he did. There were many other good things about her. Prasanta's dream wife was set as an example for other women in the Janggala kingdom.

Just as Prasanta was about to introduce his wife to his relatives, the chirping of a warbler perched on the branch above him woke him up. The thought of having a beautiful wife of high society made Prasanta smile. He took out a thumb-sized statuette of Semar from his pocket and gazed at it with reverence.

Chapter 3

A HERMIT HEART'S DESIRE

Many kings and princes from the surrounding areas of the Kadiri Kingdom came to propose to Sekartaji, the crown princess of Kadiri. But their proposals were always rejected because the king of Kadiri intended to marry his daughter to Panji, the crown prince of the Janggala kingdom.

The rejected suitors, according to information gathered by Kadiri spies, organized an alliance to attack Kadiri. The rumor said they were led by Metaun, a king presumably from Suwarnabhumi, an island northwest of Java. But the alliance vacillated on when to attack Kadiri. They were reportedly afraid of the mighty army of Janggala, because the king of Janggala was the younger brother of Kadiri's king.

·—•◦•—·

Sekartaji, surrounded by her handmaids, was enjoying the fragrance of the champaca flowers blooming in the garden.

Bayan, one of the handmaids, cleared her throat.

"It seems you have something to say, Bayan." Sekartaji was familiar with the behaviors of all her handmaids.

"You're correct, Your Highness," Bayan said nervously. "But I changed my mind."

"You make me curious. Quick, tell me what you wanted to say," Sekartaji ordered.

"Ah, no, Your Highness, I don't want to."

"You, watch your manners! Tell me what you have on your mind. This is an order!"

"All right, Your Highness." Still nervous, Bayan said, "But I need to apologize first if what I say is disrespectful."

"I will definitely forgive you, Bayan," the Kadiri crown princess said softly. The beautiful princess liked to joke and give presents, but she became dangerous when she was angry. Her handmaids knew that.

Bayan spoke with great difficulty. "I heard that your fiancé, Raden —"

"Yes, I've also heard the news." Sekartaji sighed, almost inaudibly. She had guessed what Bayan was about to say. "Tell me what you've heard so far."

"Raden Panji, your fiancé," Bayan dropped her head even lower, "has married the daughter of Janggala's prime minister, Kudanawarsa."

Sekartaji shifted her gaze from the bowed head of her favorite handmaid to the champaca flowers nearby, but she no longer saw their beauty. When she looked back at Bayan, she could only see her handmaid's hair bun. Bayan's forehead almost touched the ground.

Silence filled the air. A dozen of the handmaids who overheard the conversation bowed their heads. No one dared to speak. The circulating rumor said that the husband and wife, Panji and the prime minister's daughter, were madly in love. Further, many people believed that the long-planned marriage between Panji and the Kadiri crown princess would no longer take place.

Sekartaji rose and walked to her room. If she were the only one who had heard the news of Panji and Angreni's marriage, she would not have been so upset. But now, even her handmaids talked about it. Sekartaji was not sure whether her hurt was caused by sadness or embarrassment. She slammed her bedroom door and flung herself on her bed. With her face buried deep into the pillow, she burst into tears. Between sobs, she sighed, "Panji, it turns out that you are not a man of your word."

In the audience hall of the Kadiri palace, Amerdadu, the king of Kadiri, sat surrounded by his wives, children, and Kadiri's prime minister, Patih Gunabadra. Two of the king's sons and two of his daughters sat behind the prime minister. The king had also summoned his oldest daughter, Sekartaji, but she had not yet answered the summons.

After discussing the kingdom's welfare and security, the king said to the prime minister, "Patih Gunabadra, I heard that Panji has married a woman from Janggala. Is that true?"

"I also heard that rumor, Your Majesty," the prime minister said, looking down.

"It doesn't matter to me that Panji has married a woman in Janggala." The king looked at the bowed heads around him, then rested his eyes on the patih and said, "What matters to me are the rumors that Panji no longer wants to keep his promise to marry Sekartaji."

"I also heard that, Your Majesty."

"What do you think we should do, Patih?"

"In my opinion, Your Majesty, we must ask the court of Janggala for a formal explanation."

Silence filled the hall. Judging by their uneven breathing, both the king and the prime minister were uncertain what to do. The prime minister looked down as if consulting the cold hall floor. The king looked up as if studying the intricate wooden carvings on the ceiling. The queen looked right and left as if to observe her children's faces as they anxiously looked at one another.

The king's deep voice broke the silence. "Very well, then. I entrust this matter to you, Patih."

"Leave it to me, Your Majesty. I will send an envoy to Janggala to meet with King Amiluhur directly, or at least with Patih Kudanawarsa."

From the meeting in the palace's audience hall, Amerdadu, king of Kadiri, walked to the keputren and took a seat in the cool garden. He asked Bayan, Sekartaji's favorite handmaid, the whereabouts of his daughter.

"The princess is asleep, Your Majesty," replied Bayan respectfully.

"Ask the queen to wake her up," the king ordered.

"Yes, Your Majesty." Bayan bowed, then went to the queen to convey the king's order.

The queen immediately went to her oldest daughter's room. She gently knocked on the closed door and said, "Sekartaji, your father wants to see you."

"Now, mother?" Sekartaji asked, her face still buried in the pillow.

"Of course, my dear," answered the queen gently. "He is waiting for you in the keputren's garden."

When Sekartaji joined her father, the king said, "Your eyes are swollen, my dear. Have you been crying?"

Sekartaji only bowed her head.

"Please tell me, what is making you sad?" the king asked quietly.

Sekartaji remained silent.

"You can tell your father the truth," the queen urged Sekartaji. "Tell us what makes you cry."

But Sekartaji still remained silent.

"Bayan," the king looked at Sekartaji's loyal handmaid, "what were you talking about with the princess?"

"Forgive me, Your Majesty," Bayan bowed low, unable to say more.

"Were you talking about the marriage of Janggala's crown prince?" asked the king.

"Yes, Your Majesty." Bayan then told him about the conversation she had with Sekartaji the day before.

The king tried to console his daughter. "Don't be sad about your fiancé's marriage. I have sent an envoy to Janggala to ask for an explanation." Amerdadu sighed. "It is possible for a common man to unilaterally break off an engagement, but the engagement between a crown prince and a crown princess is not a common engagement. It is different. Very different, indeed."

The queen picked up where the king left off. "Don't worry, my dear. Have some fun. Perhaps you should go on a journey." The queen paused. "Besides, what can you expect from a man who doesn't keep his promise?" Locking her eyes with Sekartaji's, she added, "Wait patiently, maybe another prince will propose to you."

Surrounded by handmaids, Panji and Angreni were enjoying themselves when Rara Suci, Panji's hermitic aunt, came to see him. King Lembu Amiluhur of Janggala had asked his sister to remind Panji of the promise he'd made to wed Sekartaji, the daughter of his brother, His Majesty King Lembu Amerdadu of Kadiri. The wedding was supposed to take place in one month.

Rara Suci had deliberately taken Panji for a walk in the garden to distance him for a moment from Angreni, who was still chatting with her handmaids. "I hope you haven't forgotten your father's promise to your uncle, the king of Kadiri," Rara Suci said gently.

"I remember, Auntie." Panji picked a hibiscus flower and squeezed it between his fingers.

"Then when can your father fulfill his promise? Remember, Panji," Rara Suci reminded him carefully, "it is you who has to decide the right time for the marriage."

"Auntie, I have not forgotten my promise to marry Kadiri's crown princess, Sekartaji. But now, after becoming Angreni's husband, I no longer want to marry another woman. Angreni will be my only wife until I die. Sekartaji is free to marry another prince if she wants to." Panji's voice was soft but firm. He stared for a moment at the crushed hibiscus petals in his hand before throwing them into a ditch along the path.

Rara Suci, who had her share of life experiences, felt no need to further persuade Panji to keep his promise. She patted Panji's shoulder and said goodbye.

Panji accompanied his aunt to the gate of his estate, then returned to his wife, who was still chatting with her handmaids. Panji quickly seated himself next to his wife and joined in on their merriment.

In the palace hall, King Amiluhur of Janggala, and his sister, Rara Suci, discussed the marriage of crown prince Panji to Angreni, the daughter of Patih Kudanawarsa — a marriage that was creating serious problems for the court.

"Is it true that Panji doesn't want to take another wife after marrying Angreni?" King Amiluhur asked, skeptically.

"You are correct, my dear brother," said Rara Suci. "That is what Panji told me himself."

The king shook his head in disbelief. "Didn't Panji marry Angreni to be his concubine?"

Rara Suci did not answer her brother's question. Instead, she turned to the turtledove's cage swaying in the wind.

"Isn't Angreni only Panji's concubine?" King Amiluhur repeated his question.

"No, she's not just a concubine." Rara Suci avoided the king's eyes. "She is more than that to him."

"No, Angreni is Panji's concubine, nothing more than that," King Amiluhur grumbled as if speaking to convince himself. "I hope that my brother in Kadiri doesn't think that Angreni is Panji's official wife, let alone his queen."

That afternoon, the palace hall was quiet indeed. The king's words were commandments that could not be refuted.

The usually refreshing scent of incense now suffocated Rara Suci. She silently compared the warm atmosphere of Panji's residence with the chilly atmosphere of the palace hall now surrounding her.

"I was unable to weaken Panji's resolve." Rara Suci's voice faltered. "He still doesn't want to marry Sekartaji." Rara Suci was gravely concerned about the disaster this might cause.

"You're not saying that he refuses to marry Sekartaji, are you?"

"That's exactly what I'm saying."

Amiluhur's face turned red, and his body stiffened. He straightened his back. With a voice trembling with rage he said, "I ask you to summon Panji to your residence in Pucangan. Alone."

"When?"

"Next week."

"Next week? How about in a month? I just talked to him. The next full moon would be a perfect time to send for him. It would make sense, then, when I tell him that I miss him."

"Next week!" Amiluhur shouted. "Next week I will summon him and say that his aunt is waiting for him in Pucangan."

"As you wish. I will expect Panji to visit me at Pucangan in a week." Rara Suci trembled as she tried to hold back the pain her younger brother's tone of voice had caused. She didn't hide her resentment for being expected to summon Panji to her residence. Nor did she ask why she needed to — her guess of the reason made the hermitess cringe. She left without saying goodbye.

Amiluhur, still furious, paid no attention to Rara Suci's leaving.

Chapter 4

CRIMSON COASTAL GRASSES

Tendas became well known among the gentry. He'd become close to both common royal servants and nobles, among them two high-ranking royals, Brajanata and Panji. Because of his connections to them, Tendas, who was just a *shudra*, the working class, had climbed the social hierarchy to become a *vaishya*, the merchant and artisan class, and could get closer to the king.

One morning, Kertala, the gardener, arrived, panting, at Tendas's workshop.

"You are summoned by the king," Kertala gasped.

"His Majesty the King? Why did he send you and not a soldier?" Tendas asked casually to hide his nervousness and calm his racing heart.

"This is not a typical matter. It is not official. I will wait for you while you dress."

"But I should say something to my father before I leave. What should I say to him?"

"Just say that you are asked to accompany Raden Brajanata to the palace."

"Does Raden Brajanata know about this?"

"He sent me to you."

Soon, the two were riding on horseback to the palace.

Tendas had to wait a long time in the paseban to meet the king. It took so long that he started to think his meeting with the king might have been canceled or at least postponed.

When Tendas was finally summoned into the inner room of the palace, he only saw the king and Brajanata. As soon as Tendas entered, Brajanata hurried out of the room. Tendas was now left alone, face-to-face with the king.

"Have you waited long at the paseban, Tendas?" The king asked matter-of-factly.

This was the first time in his life that Tendas had heard the voice of a king.

"It wasn't very long, Your Majesty," Tendas answered politely with a nervous voice. He wondered if his untruthful answer would be considered polite. "Furthermore, I am supposed to wait."

"I hear that you want to be a soldier, am I correct?" The king's voice was still flat.

"That is my wish, Your Majesty. Of course, I am not worthy of having such high aspirations."

"Your wish will come true, Tendas. You will be trained as a soldier and specifically assigned to guard my son, Brajanata."

"It is too difficult to comprehend that such an honor should be bestowed upon me, Your Majesty."

"Well, it is a fact. Starting tomorrow, you will go to the wongai plum tree out there." Amiluhur gestured to a tree with dark bark that stood separate from the other trees. "Be there before sunrise to meet your drill sergeants, Tunggulwulung and his brother, Banyakwulung."

For exactly one week, Tendas underwent the tough training needed to become a bodyguard. During that short time, Tunggulwulung and Banyakwulung — exclusively appointed to train Tendas — taught him the skills to dodge an attack and use small arms. Every night when

Tendas came home after training, his body was so sore, it was as if he had been beaten with the bar of a gambang.

———•—•———

After the last day of his training, Tunggulwulung and Banyakwulung asked Tendas to wait in the audience hall of the palace until the king summoned him. When the sun had completely disappeared beneath the western horizon, a soldier came by and escorted him to the king.

"Tunggulwulung and Banyakwulung have reported the results of your training," Amiluhur said after observing Tendas closely. "Congratulations, you have graduated with honors. Therefore, I grant you the addition of *Kebo* to your name. From this day forward, your name will be Kebotendas."

Tendas, now a trained bodyguard, granted a new, longer name, prostrated before the king.

"Your first duty is to guard Brajanata when he goes to Panji's residence," ordered the king.

Kebotendas prostrated again. "I am honored to accept this assignment from Your Majesty."

Amiluhur lowered his voice and looked into the distance. "I will tell you a story that is meant for your ears only, Kebotendas. You are forbidden to tell what you are about to hear from me, even to your own parents."

Kebotendas prostrated for the third time.

"You need to know that the kingdom of Janggala and the kingdom of Kadiri were once one mighty kingdom. It was the kingdom of Medhang, which was governed by His Royal Highness King Erlangga. To maintain peace in his kingdom, King Erlangga divided the kingdom between his two sons before abdicating. He had to do this because his first child, a princess, had refused the throne. Instead, she chose to become a monk and live in a secluded place in the mountains. So the kingdom of Medhang became two kingdoms: Janggala and Kadiri.

"But it turned out that after the kingdom of Medhang was divided into two, and each half was being led by a son of King Erlangga, peace did not follow. There were many conflicts between the two brother kings. As always, a conflict between two nobles made the commoners suffer. Many soldiers and peasants were killed during the conflicts between those two sibling kings.

"I don't want my people to suffer the fate of my ancestors — the killing among relatives. I have an idea how to reconcile Janggala and Kadiri, and I am sure that this is the perfect time to execute my plan. I am father to a crown prince, Panji, a brave young man. My brother, King Amerdadu of Kadiri, is father to a crown princess, Sekartaji, a beautiful young girl. By marrying the two — who will make an excellent couple — I believe that not only will peace reign again, but also the glory of the previous mighty kingdom during the reign of His Royal Highness King Erlangga will return."

King Amiluhur paused for a moment before continuing. "I hope you have the patience to hear the rest of my story, Kebotendas."

Kebotendas prostrated for the fourth time.

"I have planned this carefully, and I have even put a part of it into action long ago by arranging for Sekartaji to marry my son. But now, my entire plan could be ruined because of a young girl named Angreni. Panji is so much in love with her that he decided he wants only one wife, Angreni. Panji wants to break the promise to marry Sekartaji, even though their wedding is supposed to be consummated next month.

"Panji and Angreni's marriage does not only disrupt my plan to reconcile the two kingdoms, but it could also incite a war. The spies I planted in Kadiri have already told me that the nobles in Kadiri know that Panji will retract his promise to marry Sekartaji. This is an insult to them. War is the only way for them to save face. And, of course, I don't want this to happen."

Amiluhur stopped his story. Both of his hands clasped the arms of his chair before he looked up, sighing heavily. A cuckoo sang its lonesome, sad song from afar.

"Kebotendas, what you hear must not leave this room, especially what I am going to tell you next." Amiluhur took a deep breath. "I have ordered Brajanata to separate Panji and Angreni, by taking Angreni away."

Hearing Amiluhur's calm, flat statement, Tendas tensed and straightened. His muscles hardened as if they had turned into firewood. He shook his head, not believing what he had just heard.

"You should not be shocked," said the king. "It is more important to save the lives of thousands than it is to save the life of one, Angreni. Ensuring peace between both kingdoms and reconciling them is more important than saving the union between Panji and Angreni. Unfortunately, only death can separate them. So be it.

"And you, Kebotendas, your task is to escort Brajanata to take Angreni away. Initially, I didn't want to involve another person; only Brajanata would know about this. But based on his reaction to my plan, I fear Brajanata can't carry out this task properly on his own. That's why I order you to accompany him. Angreni's life must end tomorrow."

Kebotendas bowed deeply, his face almost touching the floor. When he finally looked up, the king was no longer on his throne. Kebotendas slowly retreated, then left the room. The brightly lit room felt like a muddy, dark cave. When he walked out, he clicked his heels.

———•—•———

Panji and his wife were making love when Prasanta suddenly appeared outside the house. He called out, "Raden, a court messenger is here with a request from the king for you to see him."

Panji looked at his wife, who was quickly straightening her disheveled garments. Panji went to the door and met Prasanta and the messenger, who told him that the king expected him later that day in the reception hall. Panji agreed to meet the king and gave the messenger permission to return to the palace. Panji was baffled. It was unusual for His Majesty to summon him at such short notice.

"I will answer my father's summons," Panji said to Prasanta and turned to his wife, who had joined him in the doorway. "My love," he said, "I have to go to the court today. His Majesty has called for me."

"Right now, darling?"

"I guess it doesn't have to be right now. Let's go inside. The wind is getting quite cold." Panji turned to Prasanta, who still stood bowed with his hands clasped. "Prasanta," he called, "please, come in."

"I still have a lot to do, Raden. Please allow me to carry on with my duties."

Panji and Angreni had been enjoying each other's company all morning — if not in their room, then in the garden. Sometimes Angreni sang, accompanied by Panji who played the gambang. Sometimes they chased each other like a pair of teenagers who were madly in love.

By the afternoon, Angreni looked tired. Panji accompanied her to the bedroom facing the garden. After she fell asleep, Panji left her and rode to the palace. Angreni had a dream in which she was crying because someone she loved had left her.

At the palace, King Amiluhur and Brajanata were sitting together in the inner room. It was unusual that there were only two people in that room. It seemed that all the palace events for that afternoon had been suddenly canceled.

"Panji has still not arrived yet," Amiluhur said impatiently. "We have already waited a long time."

"I apologize, Your Majesty," Brajanata said. "I forgot to tell the messenger what time Panji should arrive at the palace. He was only told that Your Majesty expected him to arrive today."

Amiluhur nodded gently. Very gently. He stood and craned his neck out the window, trying to see down the road, some ten yards out.

"You do understand what I ordered you yesterday to do, don't you?" Amiluhur asked abruptly. He wanted to recheck Brajanata's understanding of the plan. They had been talking all morning about the marriage of Panji and Angreni, the marriage that could ruin the royal wedding between the crown prince of Janggala and the crown princess of Kadiri.

"I understand. But…" Brajanata closed his eyes tightly before continuing. "Isn't there anything else we could do, besides what you have told me to do?"

"Do you think that I issued the order without contemplating the matter thoroughly? No, my son. I have pondered the matter for a week. After leaving no stone unturned, I had to conclude that this is the best way." Amiluhur's expression changed from anger to sadness.

"Is this truly your own idea, dear Father?"

"I have, of course, consulted the court priest to find a way to save the royal wedding between Panji and Sekartaji." Amiluhur raised his voice slightly. His son's question didn't please him.

"I am sorry, dear Father. Brajanata wanted to ask why he was the one chosen to perform this task, and not another prince. But the question stuck in his throat and never made it to his lips. He was suddenly certain that his question would only make the king angrier.

"You want to ask why you are the one who must execute this deed?" Amiluhur finished his son's sentence. "You must understand, my son, that if I don't do this, neither my goals nor my brother's goals will be realized. My brother — your uncle, the king of Kadiri — and I already agreed to reunify the kingdom of Kadiri and the kingdom of Janggala, to be one great unified kingdom, mightier and more glorious than either of the small kingdoms now. The wedding between Panji, the crown prince of Janggala, and Sekartaji, the crown princess of Kadiri, will be the first step toward that unification.

"It may seem to you that you are carrying out my order. But you're actually not, my son. You're carrying out the order from the descendants of His Royal Highness King Erlangga, descendants born from the womb of his queen. These scions want to revive the glorious kingdom the way it was during the reign of His Royal Highness King Erlangga. They realize that the division of the kingdom into two parts was a mistake that should not be maintained."

As the sun set in the western horizon, they heard the neigh of Panji's horse. Brajanata bowed and retreated from his father's court.

Outside, the soldiers hurried to welcome Panji and escorted him to the king.

"Panji, my son, I have been waiting for you," King Amiluhur said after Panji seated himself cross-legged in front of his father.

"I am sorry, dear Father. I didn't know that I kept you waiting so long." Panji bowed his head deeply and continued, "The messenger only asked me to come to the court today; he didn't mention the exact time."

"I want you to know, my son, that your aunt, Rara Suci, wants to see you." Amiluhur's voice was firm. "She is already waiting for you at her dwelling in Pucangan. You must go and see her immediately."

"Leave now, dear Father?" Panji usually never questioned his father's orders, but dusk had begun to fall, and Panji felt it was too late in the day to start the journey through the thick forest to Pucangan.

"Yes, leave right now!" King Amiluhur issued the order so loudly, it sounded like a bark.

While Panji remained stunned in his seated position, the king strode away.

With the help of two court lackeys, Panji packed up for his journey to Pucangan. As it grew darker, Panji asked for a coach with a lantern. When a soldier offered to be the coachman, Panji refused. He felt that even though he was carrying out the king's order, seeing his aunt in Pucangan was his personal duty.

He was certain that the conversation with his aunt, like the cause of this summons, would be about his betrothal to the crown princess of Kadiri.

The coach clattered away at moderate speed. A pair of lanterns, the size of coconuts, did not do much to illuminate the graveled path. The long dry season had made the path quite wide, as it was now free from thick undergrowth and tall grass. During the journey, Panji kept thinking of Angreni, his wife he had left behind. He thought about her peaceful face when she was sleeping, and the uneventful journey did not feel too grueling.

The morning song from a bulbul bird flying low over Angreni's room awakened the new bride, who had spent the night alone because her husband had gone to the palace. She sat up impatiently, longing for Panji to return soon. Finally, she stepped down from her bed and walked to the front porch, wishing her husband had already arrived on the lawn. But even when the sun had almost reached its highest position in the sky, Panji had yet to return.

When Angreni heard the sound of galloping horses approach her house, she scurried to the front door. At the doorstep, she saw Brajanata dismount his horse and hurry to her. His escorts, five uniformed soldiers, remained mounted. There was also a coachman with an open horse carriage that carried a palanquin.

"My Lady Angreni, I apologize for my unannounced arrival." Brajanata folded his hands in front of his chest.

"Please come in, Brajanata. I thought it was Panji coming home."

"I am sorry, but we have to hurry." Brajanata turned to his escorts, who were now dismounting. After the coachman and the escorts offloaded the palanquin, the coachman turned the horse carriage around and left in the direction it had come from.

"We must quickly take you to meet Panji at Kamal Harbor."

"Kamal Harbor?" Angreni asked in disbelief. "My dear Panji is at Kamal Harbor?" Angreni couldn't believe that her husband was so far from home and not at the palace where she thought he was.

"His Majesty sent him to Kamal Harbor," Brajanata said. "I don't know what he is supposed to do there."

Angreni stood in the doorway as four of the soldier escorts carried the palanquin to her doorstep.

"Please get ready, My Lady. We are ready to escort you to your destination."

Panji's house servants saw the arrival of guests from the palace and gathered around the porch, waiting for orders. Meanwhile, the soldier escorts lined up behind Brajanata, who waited for Angreni getting ready to leave.

The new bride, not suspecting any foul play, quickly readied herself to meet her husband.

Brajanata helped Angreni into the palanquin, and four uniformed escorts carried her by foot away from her house.

That's how Brajanata deceived Angreni.

The fifth escort was Kebotendas, in soldier uniform. He tied the four soldiers' horses together so he could handle them as one. As soon as he saw the soldiers carrying the palanquin pass through the gate of Panji's estate, Kebotendas dismounted and hurried to close the double-leaf swing gate. Both parts of the gate were strong and sturdy — they were made of teak twice his height and twice the thickness of his own hand.

The house servants wanted to accompany their master's wife and were startled by Kebotendas's action. If he fully closed the gate, they would be locked inside. "My Lady!" the house servants called out to their mistress in unison.

Angreni looked back and saw the gates being forcefully closed so none of the house servants could accompany her. She began to realize that something was not right. She sensed danger and became restless. The fact that the four soldiers who carried the palanquin remained totally silent, added to her worry.

With a trembling hand, she motioned to her servants being locked inside the gate. "Emban!" Angreni called out. But her voice was too faint to be heard by her servant. Angreni could hardly hear herself. She tensed and gripped the sides of the palanquin.

Soon the servants' voices, like Angreni's, faded into whispers. The servants held each other's hands tightly, looking like a haphazard bamboo fence. Several younger servants paced anxiously at the entry to Panji's estate.

But although Panji's household was shocked by what had happened and sensed danger, they could not fathom what was really going on. Fear grew among the handmaids and servants.

Sumbita, Angreni's favorite handmaid, was the most agitated. She looked frantically for something she could use as a weapon to protect her mistress. She spotted a knife that the gardener had left near a whetstone on the grass, and she tucked it in her cummerbund while running towards the closing gate. She slipped through the final foot-wide opening before the gate fully closed.

Kebotendas tried to grab Sumbita to push her back inside. But Sumbita quickly dropped her body and rolled toward her disappearing mistress. Kebotendas started to pursue Sumbita, but Brajanata held him back and growled, "Secure the gate!"

While Kebotendas barred and nailed the gate shut, Sumbita ran after her mistress. Stumbling and crying, she caught up to the palanquin and held on with one hand. She didn't care when her bun came undone and her long hair spilled across her shoulders; she didn't care when her sarong ripped up to her knee.

A mile outside Panji's estate, the small group came upon the coachman and his open horse carriage. They stopped to place the palanquin onto the carriage. Placing the palanquin on the open carriage was an omen. A noble lady was never transported in a palanquin that was placed on a carriage. Hoofbeats heralded the arrival of Brajanata and Kebotendas, leading the four horses. After the soldier escorts remounted their steeds, the caravan headed out.

Wailing, Sumbita staggered alongside the carriage. Brajanata issued an order to the coachman, and the carriage increased speed, leaving Sumbita behind, screaming her mistress's name. Angreni, deeply moved by the sight of her handmaid trying to keep up with the carriage, could only wail. Stumbling, Sumbita tried to catch up with the carriage, but she fell farther and farther behind. Despite running as fast as she could, Sumbita watched the carriage grow smaller and smaller until it looked like a grain of rice — and finally vanished.

After the caravan had traveled for about twenty miles, Brajanata's group of five horsemen, a coachman, and a carriage carrying the palanquin with Angreni inside, arrived at the coast on the way to Kamal Harbor. Brajanata and Kebotendas headed for a grove of trees not far from the secluded beach. The four horsemen dismounted, then lifted the palanquin off the carriage and carried it on their shoulders to the grove of trees.

"We have arrived, My Lady," Brajanata said to Angreni, who sat, stunned, inside the palanquin. "Please step out."

"We have not reached Kamal Harbor yet, and I don't see my dear Panji here," Angreni said softly while slowly stepping out. It seemed she spoke to herself.

Brajanata didn't respond. Instead, he turned toward the four soldier escorts who had just carried the palanquin. He ordered them to place the empty palanquin back on the carriage and return to the palace. "Follow these four guards," he said to the coachman. "Once at the stables, call the drill sergeant Banyakwulung and hurry back here together. We will wait for you over there, under that tamarind tree."

Wiranata, the coachman, was a Janggala prince in disguise. Because of Wiranata's loyalty to the king, Brajanata had chosen him to help transport Angreni. But Brajanata did not want Wiranata to see what he was soon going to do.

Near midday, only Brajanata, Angreni, and Kebotendas were at the secluded beach, still quite a distance away from Kamal Harbor. Angreni stood under an angsana tree, which was in full bloom and covered with yellow flowers.

"Aren't we here to meet Panji? Angreni asked. "Where is my husband?"

"We are not here to meet your husband, My Lady." Brajanata tried to speak calmly but could not keep a tremor out of his voice.

"So, my suspicion is true after all. You lied. Now, tell me what you want. I am ready to face anything."

"I am ordered to separate you from your husband." Brajanata's voice faltered.

"I already expected this would happen, but I didn't think it would be this soon, and I wouldn't have guessed that *you* would be the perpetrator." Angreni tried to look Brajanata in the eyes, but he kept his gaze lowered. "As soon as Panji declared his love to me, I expected this to happen. Let it be, then, that this is the day our love ends."

The look Angreni gave Brajanata was neither filled with hatred nor threatening; nor did it invite pity. Still, it struck Brajanata deeply in his heart. His strong body recoiled.

Brajanata was relieved when Angreni looked away and stared at the vacant beach. "Please tell me why you have to end my life now, dear Brajanata."

"His Majesty thinks that as long as you are alive, Panji will never marry the crown princess of Kadiri. That's why he wants you to be eliminated." Brajanata bowed his head.

"I see." Angreni nodded calmly. When she started to speak again, it was as if she were talking to herself instead of to Brajanata. "You should know that I always pray to God that the royal wedding between my husband and the crown princess of Kadiri will be realized. With my body and soul, on this earth and in the hereafter, I don't mind the marriage at all." And then as if something startled her, Angreni looked closely at Brajanata and said, "But now, it looks like my own life has become the obstacle to that marriage."

Neither of them said anything. Brajanata's uneven breathing was the only sound heard.

"If that is the case, my dear Brajanata, prince of Janggala, whom I honor, then please take my life with your kris right now."

"If it is possible," Brajanata said brokenly, "I want to hide you until the royal wedding between Panji and the Kadiri crown princess has taken place." He paused, sending Angreni a fierce look. "Then, later on, I'd tell Panji what happened so he can introduce you to the Kadiri princess, and thus you and Panji could still live together."

Angreni's eyes misted over, and she turned pale. She did not fear her imminent death, but clung to her love for her husband, who had made her so happy. It would end soon. Tears ran down her cheeks and dripped onto her breasts. She wiped her eyes with her shawl. Finally, she said, "Please tell me where my husband is right now, Brajanata."

Brajanata remained silent. His face hardened. His neck felt stiff, and his eyes were burning hot.

Angreni sighed and murmured, "Where are you Panji, my dear husband?" The faint squawk of a seagull filled the air.

Brajanata, eyes brimming with tears, haltingly answered Angreni's question. "Your husband is on his way to Pucangan. He was summoned by his aunt, Her Holiness Rara Suci. That's all I know. At the time of his departure, I received His Majesty's orders to end your life."

The leaves of the angsana tree rustled in the wind. Some of its flowers drifted down. Using his thumb, Brajanata wiped his tears and continued, "If I don't follow the king's orders, the godly king, I will be cursed. And I am afraid of the curse."

"The curse" Brajanata would have to endure if he ran from the king's order to end Angreni's life was that he would have to face himself. If he wouldn't be ashamed to live a life of betrayal against his king, who had provided for him all this time, he could have easily run away to a place where no one knew him. But for Brajanata, who had been instructed since early childhood to follow the king's orders — because the king was the vicar of God in the realm of mankind — it would be easier to sacrifice his life for the king than to disobey him.

"Brajanata, please tell me honestly, what did I do to trespass against the king?" Angreni asked. She wanted to hear the answer to her question once more. The answer would give her the courage to leave this world willingly.

"My dear Angreni, you are guilty because you live as husband and wife with Panji," Brajanata said simply.

Angreni fell quiet for a moment, then nodded slowly. "Now I know my wrong-doing. Please give me a moment to remember and praise my beloved Panji's kindness." Angreni was silent again before continuing, "Please tell my beloved husband that I am sorry for all of the mistakes I have made. I am also sorry for any wrong that I have done to you, Brajanata. And I ask you to convey my apologies to the king for having troubled His Majesty.

"I would like to ask His Majesty the favor of treating my parents the same as before I married Panji. I beg His Majesty not to harm either of them, physically or mentally." Angreni took off a pair of diamond rings and handed them to Brajanata. "Please give these rings to Panji to be delivered to my parents as something to remember me by."

In her mind, Angreni saw her husband standing next to Brajanata. She said, "Now I surrender my soul so that the royal wedding between Janggala's crown prince and Kadiri's crown princess can take place."

Brajanata listened to Angreni's parting words to her husband. Then she said to him, "Now, Brajanata, take my life. I am afraid that my husband is already on his way home."

With a deathly pale face and teary eyes, Brajanata looked at the tamarind tree standing alone in the distance. The tree looked as if it were a black funeral umbrella. He turned to look at Kebotendas, who had been sitting quietly, cross-legged, some ten yards away.

Kebotendas took Brajanata's look as an order. He stood, drew his kris, and approached Angreni.

"Brajanata," Angreni called when she saw Kebotendas walking towards her. "Only *your* kris has the right to take my life. Yours is the kris that holds the king's orders."

Brajanata could only bow, speechless. His lips trembled, but no words came out of his mouth.

When Kebotendas came within striking distance, Angreni suddenly rose.

Kebotendas thrust his kris at her heart, but Angreni tilted her body and slipped away. Still, the kris had wounded her chest and arms. Blood dripped on the ground.

"Brajanata, this is the court's order!" Angreni called again, holding her bleeding chest. "I give you my life because you have received the order from His Majesty, my father-in-law. I will not give my life to this unknown person."

Once again, Kebotendas struck, thrusting his kris at Angreni's neck.

Angreni blocked the strike with her bare hands. Her palm was slashed and another gush of blood splashed on the ground below. Kebotendas, a trained bodyguard but an inexperienced soldier, had not expected Angreni's fierce resistance. He saw stars, as perspiration drenched his trembling body.

Kebotendas did not have time to dodge when Sumbita, Angreni's beloved handmaid, suddenly appeared and stabbed him between the ribs with the gardener's knife. The dull knife only wounded him slightly, but he could not believe that the handmaid they had left behind was now at her mistress's side and had just attacked him with an intended deadly strike. Regardless, he was a soldier and under direct orders from the king to help Brajanata end Angreni's life because the king had had enough life experience to foresee the possibility that his son would not have the heart to carry out his orders.

Sumbita's attack had distracted Kebotendas from Angreni, who had fallen. Angreni pressed her shaking left hand on her chest wound, while pressing her slashed right hand on her bleeding thigh. Through blurred vision, she looked around for something she could use as a weapon. Some four yards in front of her, Kebotendas and Sumbita were fighting a deadly battle.

Angreni saw Kebotendas thrust his kris into Sumbita's stomach. The loyal handmaid tried to dodge the strike, but she was not fast enough — Kebotendas's kris wounded her. She fell facedown, screaming.

Grabbing a thorny branch, Angreni waited as Kebotendas approached her, step by step.

Kebotendas was more careful now. He would not again underestimate the woman he initially thought to be nothing but a meek lady. With half of her body covered with blood, the woman still had the determination to fight him. Kebotendas thrust his weapon. But once again, Angreni dodged his attack while striking his face with the thorny branch.

Kebotendas howled in pain. A thorn had blinded his eye. Growling, he pounced on Angreni, who dodged him again. Kebotendas was now having a hard time seeing. He slipped and fell, hitting his head on a rock that knocked him unconscious.

Bleeding profusely from her gaping wounds, Angreni crawled towards her handmaid, lying facedown in silence. But before she could reach Sumbita, Angreni collapsed.

Sumbita, who was still alive, moved. With great effort, she dragged herself next to her mistress, who lay on her side, panting. When Angreni saw Sumbita near her, she whispered, "Sumbita, go home. Take my good wishes to my dear husband and my parents…"

Sumbita pulled herself up to sit cross-legged. Sobbing and hugging herself, she suddenly realized that there was no life left in her mistress's still-warm body. Sumbita wailed, "I prefer to die with you, My Lady, rather than take your good wishes to your husband and parents!"

Still bleeding from her stomach wound, Sumbita turned her pale face to Brajanata. "Kill me," she gasped. "I want to follow my lady." Then, Sumbita collapsed again, unconscious.

Brajanata was sitting in a dejected trance, when Kebotendas regained consciousness. Brajanata looked up as Kebotendas bowed before him.

"Kebotendas, collect as many angsana flowers as possible," Brajanata said huskily. "We need to cover Lady Angreni with fresh, fragrant flowers."

Kebotendas could not understand Brajanata's command. "Doesn't she deserve to be eliminated, Raden?" The resistance the two women had given him had riled him.

"We are supposed to respect her by covering her body." Brajanata said, raising his voice. He remembered that he had never ordered Kebotendas to kill Angreni.

"Is she not the enemy of the kingdom, Raden?" Kebotendas pressed.

Brajanata's anger suddenly flared. "Are you defying me, Tendas?"

"Forgive me, Raden," Kebotendas muttered. "It is my opinion that an enemy of the kingdom doesn't deserve to be honored."

Brajanata's wrath exploded. "There!" The kris he had originally carried to end Angreni's life was now pointed at Kebotendas's chest.

Kebotendas jumped back and ran. Without looking back, he ran frantically as far as possible from the beach. He needed to treat the wounds caused by Sumbita's knife and Angreni's thorny branch, but still he continued to run.

Brajanata watched Kebotendas run away. Then he turned his gaze to the figure lying a few yards in front of him. Angreni's corpse looked as if someone had already prepared it. Her body lay straight, with both arms crossed. Her face was calm, and she appeared to be smiling slightly.

Stunned, Brajanata backed away from the lifeless body, then hurriedly began collecting angsana flowers. Soon, a large heap of angsana flowers was piled next to Angreni's dead body. Brajanata was amazed at the number of flowers he had gathered. It was as if all the trees on the beach had turned into angsana trees, and all their leaves had turned into flowers. Brajanata completely covered Angreni's body with the flowers.

Brajanata turned when he heard the faint sound of carriage wheels rattling across the rocky road. Wiranata halted his carriage under the nearby tamarind tree. Wiranata and Banyakwulung jumped out and ran toward Brajanata.

"Wiranata, hurry!" Brajanata panted, pointing to Sumbita. "Take this handmaid to the court's physician. Her life depends on how quickly you can reach the Usada Hall."

Seeing the young handmaid covered with blood shocked Wiranata, but he didn't feel the need to ask what had happened. He ordered Banyakwulung to bring the carriage closer to where the handmaid was lying.

Silently, Brajanata and Wiranata lifted Sumbita into the carriage. Then Wiranata and Banyakwulung swung the carriage around and rushed towards Janggala's royal hospital. For a moment, Brajanata gazed at the mound of yellow angsana flowers, shifting gently under a soft breeze that seemed to shush a farewell. Then he mounted his horse and galloped off in the same direction the carriage had taken.

After arriving at the palace, Brajanata tethered his horse and staggered toward the inner room to meet King Amiluhur. He had to stop several times. The ordeal he had just experienced made breathing difficult and filled his feet with lead.

A soldier resting in the shade of a banyan tree next to the guard post jumped up when he saw Brajanata's erratic approach. He ran to Brajanata and bowed nervously. "His Majesty is in the palace hall, Raden."

"Has my brother Panji returned from Pucangan?" Brajanata was most interested in the answer.

"Yes, he has, Raden," the soldier said. "He returned a few moments ago, before the sun became so hot."

Suddenly, Brajanata turned around. Ignoring the soldier's confused stare, he hurried back to his tethered horse. He would not be able to speak to the king. He deeply regretted Angreni's death. The unpretentious woman had won the heart of a crown prince and was coveted by many girls in the palace, as well as among the commoners.

—————•◆•—————

"Thank you for taking the time to visit me, my son, Panji," Rara Suci greeted Panji when he arrived at her dwelling in Pucangan in the darkness before dawn.

"It is my duty to respond to your summons, Auntie," Panji replied dutifully.

"Did your father tell you why I summoned you?"

"His Majesty only asked me to see you, Auntie. It seems that you have something important to tell me."

"It's not me who has something important to tell you; it's you who has something important to tell me, something I need to know."

"Very well, Auntie. I believe this visit is closely related to my upcoming marriage with Sekartaji of Kadiri. All right, I hope you won't tire of listening to what I've to say, because I've said it more than once.

"You know, Auntie, that His Majesty educated me very well. He brought in the best teachers from all over the country, to train me in martial arts so I can defend myself and to teach me spiritualism, so I can control myself and thus be worthy of being the king of Janggala. His Majesty said that only his most competent son had the right to lead the kingdom. Yes, he had me trained to be the best possible human being.

"Not only has my physical appearance become the center of admiration for all Janggala people, but also my intelligence, which is evidenced by my vocabulary, was cultivated to impress all Janggala people. When I turned seventeen, the king's efforts already showed results, and this pleased him. He rewarded me for my obedience to his commands and instructions with compliments and gifts to enjoy. Is there any delicious food that I have never tasted? Are there any tasty beverages that I haven't sipped? Is there any beautiful virgin in the palace I have not slept with?

"*Perfect!* That's how the closest people to me describe my life. But as you once said, Auntie, perfection doesn't always mean happiness. My life is dedicated to the kingdom. I only live to make the king proud. At the age of nineteen, I began to tire of being forced to live by the rules of others. Even though I can defeat ten warriors in hand-to-hand combat and ten priests in word-for-word religious debates, I'm unable to overcome my overwhelming boredom. It strangles me. It feels as if a snake as thick as my calf is coiled around my body, crushing my bones. I often gasp and feel short of breath for no reason.

"When I tried to overcome my boredom by living the life of ordinary people, His Majesty immediately blocked my way. I really do not want to die of boredom. I already told you that Angreni is the first girl I ever had to conquer. She is not like the girls in the palace who easily surrendered their virginity to me. She's really different, Auntie. At her side, I feel like a real human being."

Panji took a deep breath. Then he sat, looking at the floor.

Rara Suci had deliberately let him talk until he had no more words left. She wanted Panji to pour out his heart. Watching her nephew stare blankly at the floor in front of her, Rara Suci covered her face with her hands. She suspected the tragedy that must have already befallen Angreni and tears filled her eyes. Because she didn't want Panji to see her sadness, she rose and quickly walked away, leaving Panji sitting cross-legged, staring at the floor.

Alone in her room, Rara Suci cried. She felt guilty that she could not help her nephew. At first, she had thought she could persuade Panji to take Angreni as his concubine and make Sekartaji his queen. As a concubine, Angreni would be unable to give birth to the future king, but at least she and Panji could be together. But Rara Suci had been wrong. Panji did not waver at all. He wanted Angreni to be his only wife, to be his queen — and thus he made the king angry.

After her heart-wrenching sadness subsided, Rara Suci returned to Panji, who was still sitting in the same position as she had left him. But now, both of his hands pressed the floor forcefully. She could see the muscles in his arms bulge as they tightened.

"Panji, I have heard enough of your reasons for not wanting to take another wife," said Rara Suci in a quavering voice. "I am not telling you to leave, but if you want to return to the palace to meet your father, I will let you go." Her lips continued to move, but not a word was heard. She closed her eyes tightly.

Panji didn't answer. He just bowed his head, stood up slowly, stepped back, then turned and walked quickly towards his horse-drawn carriage.

Rara Suci followed Panji silently. She watched his carriage grow smaller as it moved away until it finally disappeared behind the trees. A glimmer of light began to break through the eastern horizon. Rara Suci closed her eyes again.

On his way back to the palace, Panji thought about his visit with his aunt. He recalled how his aunt had prepared a place for him to rest. He remembered not being able to sleep and walking out onto the veranda, finding his aunt there, ready to listen to his grievances.

The image of Angreni's face blurred the rest of his memory.

Panji felt that the trip back to the palace went much faster than the trip to Rara Suci's residence in Pucangan. The sun was halfway up in the sky when Panji arrived at the palace.

The rattling of his approaching carriage was enough to make the Janggala soldiers who just had their breakfast, scramble. Some welcomed Panji and took care of his carriage and the horses, while others opened the gates. Noticing the soldiers' attentiveness, Panji knew that his trip had become the center of attention in the palace.

Panji hurried through the palace gate. His guess was correct; the king was waiting for his return.

"Didn't your aunt ask you to spend the night, Panji?" King Amiluhur spoke softly, but looked sharply at Panji.

"No, Father." Panji saw the king's hand grip the arm of his chair.

"I hope that what your aunt told you is clear." Amiluhur now folded his hands.

Panji did not respond. Rara Suci had, in fact, not told him anything. It was he who had told his aunt many things. But Panji still nodded and bowed to the king. Then, after the king excused him, Panji left the palace.

⊢—•⊙•—⊣

Panji rode his horse at a gallop out of the palace grounds. Prasanta, who had waited for him at the palace guard post, immediately followed. They rode in silence. They — the master and servant — indeed could understand each other without words. As soon as they entered Panji's estate at the outskirts of the capital, they slowed their horses.

"There's no one around," Prasanta commented. "How unusual."

"Maybe someone is sick." Panji seemed to be reassuring himself rather than answering Prasanta. Both of them were surprised at the odd state of things. They continued on toward the mansion gate.

"Look, Prasanta!" Panji suddenly yelled. "The gate is barred and nailed shut!" He turned anxiously to his loyal aide and pulled hard to rein in his horse. The startled horse reared, blowing and snorting, and tossing its head.

Prasanta dismounted, stunned by the astonishing sight before him.

Ever since King Erlangga had partitioned the Medhang Kingdom into the Kadiri and Janggala kingdoms, both the palaces and the estates of princes required high walls and strong gates for fort-like protection during the bloody battles that waged between the two kingdoms.

"Raden, it appears something terrible happened after you left," Prasanta stammered.

"Let me try the back entrance," Panji said. "Wait here. I'm afraid that rebels have invaded my mansion. Look for me if I don't return soon." Panji raced to the backside of his property while calling out to announce his arrival.

A servant hurriedly opened the back entrance. As soon as Panji stepped into his mansion, the servant immediately dropped himself at Panji's feet, sobbing. A few seconds later, other servants came running in and prostrated themselves before him.

"Where is your mistress, Lady Angreni?" Panji glanced around anxiously, trying to find the person he longed for so much. When no one answered him, Panji ran to his room. But there, he only found grief-stricken handmaids.

"Emban, where is Lady Angreni? Why are all of you crying?" Panji asked the handmaids who were holding on to each other.

"Forgive us," a middle-aged handmaid said, wiping her tears. "Lady Angreni was taken by Raden Brajanata."

"My *brother* Brajanata?" Panji's anxiety soared. Brajanata's involvement meant that whatever had happened was a court affair, most likely related to the wedding planned for him and the crown princess of Kadiri.

"That's right, Raden." The handmaid composed herself. "I overheard Lady Angreni and Raden Brajanata talking when Raden Brajanata came to take Lady Angreni away. I was arranging flowers next to the room where they talked. I overheard Raden Brajanata ask Lady Angreni to accompany him to meet you at Kamal Harbor."

"Me? At Kamal Harbor? That's a lie!"

"That's what Raden Brajanata said. He also told Lady Angreni that they had to leave immediately. There were five soldiers and a carriage waiting outside."

"I was not at Kamal Harbor; I was at Pucangan, visiting my aunt Rara Suci!" Panji's worry turned into anger.

"I was already suspicious," the handmaid continued. "Now I am sure that Raden Brajanata indeed deceived Lady Angreni. I don't know what happened next; we are just servants, we don't know. The gates were closed, barred, and nailed shut from the outside. When we tried to catch up through the back entrance, those who took Lady Angreni were already out of sight. Forgive us, Raden, we are just ignorant and weak servants incapable of acting."

Panji stood still for a moment. A deep melancholy and raging anger tore his heart out. He lurched toward a thick, teakwood pillar and wrapped his arms around it, as if embracing someone he loved.

The servants ran towards him and tried to support his slumping body as it slid to the floor.

Panji now sat cross-legged on the floor, dismayed, his hands tensing and stretching. His lips moved without a sound.

Prasanta came running into the house and immediately noticed the blank look of horror on Panji's face. Quickly, Prasanta gathered all the servants. He sent some of them to notify Panji's closest relatives about his situation. He told the others to watch over their master. Then Prasanta himself mounted his horse and departed for Rara Suci's residence in Pucangan.

Panji started to speak. He spoke as if Angreni were sitting next to him.

The servants sitting cross-legged around him sighed and whispered to one another, "Our master Panji is not himself…"

Panji kept talking to himself.

The members of Panji's household, especially the women, started to cry.

The medicine men who lived near Panji's estate came and tried to heal him. But not one of them succeeded. The Shiva, Vishnu, and Buddhist priests also tried to heal his wounded soul, but their efforts proved fruitless as well.

Panji continued to talk to himself.

Prasanta arrived at Rara Suci's dwelling at dusk.

"I predicted that it would turn out like this," Rara Suci said slowly after hearing Prasanta's account of Panji's mental shock.

Prasanta bowed and begged, "I implore Your Holiness to heal Raden Panji." Rara Suci did not answer immediately. Instead, she showed Prasanta a foreign-looking inscription in the wall.

"Do you know what this is, Prasanta?" Rara Suci asked.

"Honestly, I don't, Your Holiness," Prasanta said, "but it looks like a script similar to the Pallava script that scholars use to write holy books."

"You're correct. One day, our children and grandchildren will use this script to write their stories, the stories they want to pass on to their offspring." Rara Suci stepped closer to the writing on the wall.

Prasanta shifted his seat so that he could see the inscription more clearly.

Rara Suci pointed at the script and recited, "*Ha na ca ra ka* — which means, there were messengers; *da ta sa wa la* — they argued and fought; *pa da ja ya nya* — they are equally strong; *ma ga ba tha nga* — in the end, both of them became dead bodies."

Rara Suci turned to Prasanta. "Do you know the implicit meaning of these verses, Prasanta?"

"Forgive me, Your Holiness, I do not," answered Prasanta.

"The messengers were humans — a man and a woman, to be exact. The man and woman were messengers of Mahadewa, the king of the gods. They were placed on this Earth to proclaim His existence, to teach virtues, and to tell about the existence of the afterlife. That is the implicit meaning of *ha na ca ra ka.*

"*Da ta sa wa la* is the continuation of the story of that pair of human messengers with their noble mission. While carrying out their mission, they fought. The fight was about how to live their lives: Should they follow the rules as commanded by Mahadewa, or should they live by the rules according to their own will? The man chose to follow Mahadewa's command, while the woman chose to follow her own will.

"The woman had the upper hand in the fight. She could force the man to succumb to her will. But she also knew that she would not enjoy her victory if the man felt defeated. She had to invite the man to share in her victory, too. That way, the fight didn't have to end in mutual hostility, but instead would end in mutual pleasure. Thus, the fight between a man and a woman of equal greatness is meant to lead to a climax. This is implied in the meaning of *pa da ja ya nya.*

"*Ma ga ba tha nga* is a result of great lovemaking. *Bathang* means a dead body. After reaching their climax, both participants will lie motionless as if they were dead." Rara Suci briefly closed her eyes before turning to Prasanta. "Can you understand that, Prasanta?"

"Yes, Your Holiness, although not entirely," Prasanta faltered. He hadn't expected to be questioned about some inscription in Rara Suci's wall. "But please excuse me, I came to seek advice for Raden Panji's recovery, Your Holiness."

Ignoring Prasanta's interruption, Rara Suci asked, "If you understand that story, then which part of the verses I just explained to you applies to Panji and Angreni's relationship?"

"Oh..." Confused, Prasanta could only groan.

"Yes, you are correct, Prasanta. Right now, Panji is grieving. You are right."

Prasanta was even more confused. Embarrassed, he lowered his head until it almost touched his knees.

"Panji is groaning because he is at the end of *da ta sa wa la* and has just experienced the beginning of *ma ga ba tha nga.* He had his fight with Angreni and was enjoying the results of the fight. Do not assume that this fight was merely physical, as they struggled spiritually. Like any newlywed, Panji is eager to continue, but the ever-mighty Mahadewa sword severed the thread that held their lives together."

"Oh," Prasanta groaned again. Apparently, he needed to speak more directly to Rara Suci. He was getting nowhere. "Your Holiness, what should we do for Raden Panji's recovery?"

"Let him return to Angreni. If he is unable to find Angreni, his wife, then let him find the Angreni who will be his future wife."

Prasanta groaned for the third time. *Let him find the Angreni who will be his future wife? Wasn't she already Panji's wife?*

Prasanta looked up to ask Rara Suci for an explanation, but the former crown princess — who was once beautiful but was now middle-aged — had disappeared behind the wall with the writings, which now seemed to come alive in Prasanta's eyes.

During his return trip to Panji's estate, Prasanta stopped his horse many times to look at the moon above Penanggungan Mountain. The moon was a torch that guided him through the night. Prasanta was going to help Panji find Angreni's reincarnation.

Chapter 5

SOWING FLOWERS REAPING STORM

The sun was already dropping in the west and was not as scorching hot as it had been when Panji left his residence that morning, heading toward the sea. Walking with long strides, Panji talked to himself. An entourage comprised of his half-brothers, aides, guards, and servants followed him. Wiranata, the coachman, walked amongst Panji's house servants. He acted as if he had no knowledge of the bloody scene he had just left.

Lagging behind was a group of handmaids. They hurried to catch up with the group ahead. All in all, more than a hundred people walked silently behind Panji, the only one who spoke. From a distance, the procession looked like a group of mourners, carrying a dead body to the burial ground.

Whenever Panji saw flowers by the side of the road, he picked them. Holding the flowers close to his chest, he said he wanted to give them to Angreni, his wife. He had collected more than a dozen flowers when they passed a fallen tree with a trunk resembling a snake ready to strike. Panji suddenly dropped to his knees. Singing a love song, he arranged the flowers on the fallen tree. His servants had to finally persuade him to move on.

The procession arrived at the coastal area where the soil was turning into stretches of sand. The western horizon began to glow crimson.

Panji stopped and looked at the angsana trees with their lofty canopies. When the entourage arrived at a field of blooming reeds not far from a secluded beach, he stopped again to look at the reeds. The early evening breeze carried a sweet smell. Panji stopped walking. Closing his eyes, he inhaled the delicious scent and sang another *asmaradana*, love song.

His followers, deciding that Panji had stopped for a while, scattered to find places to sit and stretch their legs. From afar, Panji appeared to be standing alone. The people accompanying him were hidden among the thickets and trees.

When Panji opened his eyes, he noticed footprints in the sand. Curious, he squatted. After tracing the footprints with his eyes, he rose and started to track them. Several of Panji's followers rose to their feet, wanting to know what he was looking for.

The footprints led Panji to a heap of angsana flowers. He stopped next to the mound and looked down at it for a long time before turning his head left and right as if looking for someone.

Wiranata and several other princes ran to Panji to help if needed.

Panji stared at the pile of flowers, then fell to his knees and inched closer. When Panji started to dig into the pile with both hands, Wiranata and another prince helped him move the flowers aside.

Seeing this strange sight, everyone moved closer to Panji, who continued to dig feverishly. Apparently, he thought there was something hidden under the pile of flowers.

Panji suddenly jumped up, then froze. The people straightened in shock. Angreni's corpse, still partially covered with flowers, lay in front of them. Panji covered his face with his hands and broke into heartbreaking howls. But not a single tear fell out of his icy, dull eyes.

Panji picked up his loved one and held her in his arms. Wiranata tucked in her dangling left hand and straightened her lifted sarong.

Panji carried his wife's corpse toward a lush coastal cottonwood tree, growing a stone's throw away.

Unlike the princes and male servants who now followed from a distance, the handmaids stayed right behind Panji. They were eager to clean Angreni's soiled body. Only a middle-aged handmaid dared to walk beside Panji, dusting the sand and dried flowers off her mistress, who lay lifeless in her husband's strong and loving arms. The old handmaid observed the body's stiffness and discolored skin.

Panji stopped under the cottonwood tree and seated himself on a rock. With Angreni's head in his lap, he talked to his dead wife. He tried many ways to engage her into the conversation.

When Panji sang again, all the handmaids bowed and sobbed. The others, unable to bear the sight, looked away, while the setting sun created a veil that covered the mournful scene.

———•◆•———

Prasanta caught up with Panji's group just before darkness blanketed the entire coastal area.

When he saw Prasanta, Wiranata rose immediately to meet him.

"I just returned from Pucangan, Raden," Prasanta told Wiranata.

"Well, what did Rara Suci say?" Wiranata asked impatiently.

"We have to be patient." Prasanta did not feel it necessary to repeat Rara Suci's convoluted words.

"Yes, she is right," Wiranata relented. "We have to be patient."

"Did Aunt Rara Suci give you medicine for Panji?" Wiranata asked.

Prasanta sighed heavily. "No, Raden."

Prasanta was relieved that Wiranata had not asked him to repeat Rara Suci's exact words. Instead, Wiranata asked him to make a bonfire from the dead wood lying around.

While the fire burned and illuminated their surroundings, Wiranata thought about the earlier incident when he and Banyakwulung had left the coast, carrying Sumbita in their carriage. As ordered by Brajanata, they had gone directly to the court physician who had taken care of

Sumbita. After that, Wiranata had immediately gone to the king. No one had ordered him to see the king, but after experiencing so many strange things while accompanying Brajanata, he felt that he had to see the king. As a prince, Wiranata did not have to wait in the audience hall. He was allowed to immediately enter the palace hall and wait there for his father to call him into the inner room.

After prostrating before the king, Wiranata sat cross-legged, waiting for the king's permission to start the conversation.

After his father granted him permission to speak, Wiranata told the king everything that had happened, from the time Brajanata picked up Angreni at Panji's mansion until he saw Sumbita lying in the grass, her body covered with blood.

"This means everything happened according to my plan," Amiluhur murmured, looking into the distance. "Where is Brajanata now?" Amiluhur gave Wiranata a penetrating look.

"I thought that my brother Brajanata had already come to see you, Father." The king's question about Brajanata's whereabouts flustered Wiranata. He added, "I'm sorry if he hasn't, and I don't know where he is now. I took the severely wounded handmaid to the royal physician on Brajanata's orders."

Amiluhur thought: *I didn't expect the involvement of a handmaid in this incident.* "Find Tunggulwulung, the sergeant who helped train Kebotendas, Brajanata's bodyguard," he said slowly. "Tell Tunggulwulung to see me immediately."

"Please, Father, after finding Tunggulwulung and giving him your message, may I go to Panji's residence? I'm worried that something bad will happen."

"That is exactly what I want you to do next, Wiranata. Go and see Panji. Comfort him by fulfilling all his requests. In this case, you must consult Prasanta, Panji's favorite aide." Amiluhur lowered his gaze for quite a while. When he finally looked up, he said, "It may interest you to know what I want to discuss with Tunggulwulung. Kebotendas, who I ordered to hide in Bali after completing his duties, has now become a threat to the dignity and honor of the Janggala Kingdom.

Tomorrow, or the day after tomorrow, at the time you deem proper, please see Tunggulwulung."

After Prasanta, with the help of several others, lit the bonfire, and its light penetrated the darkness of the coastal night, Panji again carried Angreni's body while singing to her. Everyone, including Prasanta, allowed Panji to do whatever he wanted to. Observing Panji's behavior, everyone was convinced that Panji thought Angreni was still alive. They whispered to each other, "Raden Panji has lost his mind."

Wiranata approached another prince in the group and said, "Please return to the palace. Find Tunggulwulung, the drill sergeant, and have him come here with a few soldiers. Tell him we need food and water for about one hundred people."

The prince nodded, bowed, and then quickly left the coastal area. A servant came to Wiranata and asked permission to return to Panji's mansion and tell the others about the discovery of Angreni's body.

"Yes, please prepare everything for Lady Angreni's burial," Wiranata said. "Tell them that cremation will take too much time and will attract the attention of too many people."

Panji continued to caress Angreni. He conversed with his wife's corpse as if she were still alive. The servants around him bowed their heads. Some of them held their necks with both hands, trying to suppress the pain of grief.

It was getting late. Panji's house servants prepared for the wake. They quietly prepared everything needed to ready the body for the burial.

Wiranata had planned to take the body home as soon as Panji put it down. But on the beach, Panji could not be separated from Angreni for even a moment. Now, everyone was silently waiting for what might happen. Prasanta had nodded off while sitting on a coconut tree trunk.

It was near midnight when Panji finally spoke. He asked, "Prasanta, do you feel sorry for me?"

As if hearing the clap of thunder, Prasanta awoke startled, jumped up, and answered nervously, "Of course, Raden, we all feel your suffering."

Then, while still carrying Angreni, Panji turned to all his half-brothers — the princes sitting near Prasanta — and said, "If you pity me, then you will follow me wherever I go."

The princes exchanged glances, then answered almost simultaneously, "Yes, dear brother, we will follow you wherever you go."

"I want to go boating with my wife," Panji said. "But wait and let me ask her first if we should change our clothes."

Tunggulwulung, the drill sergeant, arrived at the coastal area accompanied by a group of fully armed soldiers; some of them led pack horses that carried saddlebags filled with provisions. After ordering his soldiers to distribute food and water to the entire group, Tunggulwulung walked to Wiranata and Prasanta, who were sitting together, talking. While tending to several dying bonfires, he overheard their conversation.

"I figured out what happened to Sumbita," said Wiranata.

"Sumbita?"

"She is Angreni's handmaid, but I could not question her when I saw her, as she had barely regained consciousness. But I did speak to someone who saw Raden Brajanata take Lady Angreni away."

"You already know what really happened?"

"It is still vague, Prasanta, but I will try to clarify the unclear parts. You may disagree with my line of thought."

"Please, Raden."

"His Majesty ordered Brajanata to finish off Angreni. He also ordered Kebotendas to take over if Brajanata was unable to fulfill his duty, because one way or the other, Angreni had to die. Now, Kebotendas, too, needs to be watched, by order of the king. Do you know why Kebotendas has to be watched, Prasanta?"

"Alas, this matter is too complicated for my brain, Raden."

"Kebotendas has to be watched because who can guarantee that he will not disclose this royal disgrace? No one. The person assigned to watch Kebotendas is Kertala, the gardener at Raden Brajanata's estate."

"Oh, my head is going to explode, Raden!"

"Indeed, the best way to protect the honor of the Janggala Kingdom is to kill Kebotendas."

"Oh, no!"

———•◦•———

When they heard that Panji was about to take his dead wife boating, a commotion erupted in the entire group. Everyone thought they would soon be taking Angreni's body home for cremation or burial. Now, things were not going as planned. This latest development was the biggest worry yet for Wiranata and Prasanta.

"I'm ready to take my wife boating," Panji said. "Please find me a vessel."

"All right, Raden," said Prasanta. "Wait a minute, I'll discuss it with your brothers."

Not long after, Wiranata and Prasanta sat cross-legged on the sand, surrounded by Panji's brothers, discussing how they were to fulfill Panji's wish. Horsemen soon rode off in two different directions — some raced towards the palace and others headed for the harbor. The news that Panji was going boating with his dead wife immediately spread to all corners of the palace. The activities during that late night surpassed those on the brightest day. Hundreds of lamps fueled by castor oil illuminated the scene. The brightly lit road that connected the palace and the beach seemed to beckon everyone to travel on it.

Prasanta, acting by the authority the court had bestowed upon him through Wiranata, ordered the soldiers to prepare a ship at Kamal Harbor according to Panji's wishes and equip it with six hundred oarsmen. Another ship at Kamal Harbor, provided by Panji's brothers, was equipped with four hundred oarsmen. They made the two ships seaworthy. By the time the eastern sky turned orange, the preparation for the grand outing on the sea was complete.

Panji's sister, Onengan, and the other princesses wanted to go along, but Wiranata prohibited them. He whispered to Onengan, "I don't know where Panji is going, but I am certain that wherever he goes, this voyage will head for danger. These two ships will be under Panji's command and, right now, his mental condition is worrisome. We will take some handmaids with us, but no princesses."

"Please let us go with him. Maybe there is something we can do for Panji," Onengan insisted, while the other court ladies standing behind her nodded in agreement.

"Apart from what I said earlier, there is another danger." Wiranata responded carefully to the princess. "The harbor master told me that, lately, the weather has been unpredictable."

Despite her unhappiness with Wiranata's explanation, Onengan, accompanied by several bodyguards, reluctantly returned to the palace with the other women.

When the sun was halfway up in the sky, the two ships at Kamal Harbor, fully loaded with Panji and his followers, put out to sea, the oars of the rowers breaking the waves towards the open ocean. Panji sat on the bridge, a raised platform at the stern, holding Angreni's corpse in his lap. The two pleasure ships belonged to the king. The vessels were not only loaded with food, drink, and other supplies, they were also equipped with sets of gamelans.

Panji ordered the musicians to play while he engaged in his one-sided conversation with Angreni's body, as if she were still alive and they were on an outing.

Once they arrived at the open sea, passing fishermen approached Panji's ship in their small fishing boats. They had recognized the royal ships immediately and were approaching to give Panji their best catch of the day.

As the fishing boats kept coming, with fishermen providing fish or simply paying homage to Panji and his followers, Panji continued to converse with his wife, telling her to enjoy the food and beverages they were offered.

When a fisherman presented him with two beautiful garlands, Panji rose with Angreni's corpse in his arms and said, "Fisherman, did you know that my wife and I were going boating today, and is that why you brought us such beautiful garlands?"

The old, weathered fisherman prostrated before answering respectfully, "Yesterday, I dreamed that I would meet Raden and his wife at sea."

"Tell me about your dream, fisherman." Panji's voice was filled with interest.

"In the dream," said the fisherman, "I met an elderly priest who said, 'When you go fishing tomorrow, take the most beautiful flowers you can pick in your neighborhood. Make two garlands to adorn the nobilities you will meet in the middle of the ocean.' So, early this morning, I immediately looked for flowers. Of course, people wondered why. When I told them that I would meet nobilities in the middle of the sea, they laughed at me, but I didn't care. And see? It turns out to be true, I met you and your beloved wife."

After thanking the fisherman and excusing him so he could continue his work, Panji placed one of the garlands around his wife's neck and wore the other himself. Bending closely over her, Panji kept talking to Angreni and continued to caress the lifeless body. From a distance, the flowers seemed to unite husband and wife. The sun, which had started to sink into the west, wrapped them in a warm, red glow.

Noticing how close Panji was bent over Angreni, the gamelan players worried that Panji was having difficulty whispering to Angreni and softened their play. When a gust of wind suddenly whipped away the garlands, the gamelan players stopped altogether.

Black clouds blanketed the darkening sky above Panji's ships, and the gale quickly turned into a raging storm. The waves soared as high as coconut trees. The small fishing boats that did not have time to get home were washed away or tossed like dry leaves. Some bobbed up and down as if being sucked into the sea and then spit back to the surface.

The people on the two large ships panicked. They lowered and rolled up everything that could catch the wind. Anything that weighed down the ship, such as gamelans and food crates, were tossed overboard. Even the soldiers were willing to throw themselves into the sea to reduce the ship's weight, and swim to the fishing boat wreckages they could use as buoys.

Despite being tossed and shifted about several feet back and forth, Panji and Angreni remained on the bridge. When Panji ignored Prasanta, Wiranata, and others who urged him to take cover in the hull, they surrounded him with their bodies to protect him from getting hit by loose wooden and iron objects.

Even though he now had to shout to be heard above the storm, Panji continued conversing with his wife. "The storm is here, my dear," he soothed, "but you don't need to be afraid, I will always be with you. Yes, I know, you're not pleased that the storm took our garlands. But it's not a problem; we can look for them later. And look! I'm not the only one protecting you. Prasanta and Wiranata are also here. And, oh, of course you still remember what I told you a few days ago, that I'm trained not only to become a tough warrior but also to lead soldiers to war."

Panji glanced quickly around him, then continued, "Today, our two ships are manned with a thousand soldiers who are not only skilled in fighting, but also in playing gamelan, cooking, and healing. Among those soldiers, there are one hundred and one elite warriors. Elites, because one of them can beat ten ordinary soldiers in a hand-to-hand combat. One hundred and one elite warriors, my dear. One hundred soldiers and one leader. Yes, I am their leader. Within a year, His

Majesty wants to have a thousand and one strong warriors, a thousand soldiers and one leader — me." Panji held Angreni's swollen, blue face.

Those still on the deck had started to move away from Panji as he held Angreni's body. They were horrified to be so near to a corpse that was beginning to look frightening. If the blowing gales had not been so strong, the stench of the decaying body would have certainly made the situation even more unbearable.

Time stood still. No one could tell if it was afternoon, night, or morning; everything was dark and deafening. The line between life and death was thinner than the scarf stuck to Angreni's skin. Panji and his party were still being tossed about in the middle of the sea. Only the occasional flash of lightning told them they were still alive. While surrounded by a raging sea, they were not in the realm of death. They did not know where the wind would blow the two large ships, which spun like two bird nests circling in a twister. The fierce storm continued to rage.

At early dawn, the wind gradually subsided, and the storm abated. The slowly rising sun allowed the people on the ships to see their true situation. They realized that many of their companions were no longer present. Hundreds of Panji's company had drowned. The ocean currents had swept the two wrecked ships into an unknown bay and beached the two vessels on the sand.

Now, the two ships were only manned by a hundred elite soldiers, including their leader, Tunggulwulung. These remaining elite soldiers possessed such outstanding skills that neither the storm nor the sea had been able to kill them. Including Panji, Angreni, Wiranata, Prasanta, and the one hundred elite soldiers, only one hundred and four people still remained on the ships.

Some of the soldiers and Panji's closest aides had succeeded in swimming to the beach. The swaying welcome of palm trees was their only hope to end their torment of thirst and hunger.

"Prasanta," Wiranata whispered sadly, "the storm has drowned almost a thousand Janggala people. Nearly all of them were soldiers sent by the king to accompany Panji and row the two royal ships.

I'm afraid that the lives of those soldiers were taken in exchange for Angreni's life. The law of nature has demanded the sacrifice of many Janggala people." Wiranata did not want Panji, who sat several meters away, still holding Angreni, to hear him.

"I heard that Lady Angreni was sacrificed to avoid the death of thousands of Janggala soldiers who would die fighting Kadiri soldiers," Prasanta whispered, even sadder.

"Wait!" Tunggulwulung shouted. "Not only the strong men escaped danger." He pointed to a figure lying on the sand, next to the wreckage of a fishing boat. The small, frail body moved and soon sat up slowly.

"That's Angreni's handmaid!" Prasanta cried. "She always stayed near Angreni's body, and she must have sneaked onto the boat!"

Tunggulwulung and Prasanta scrambled off the ship and ran to help the groggy handmaid. "Where is Lady Angreni?" she groaned. "Where is she?" Tunggulwulung carried her thin, drenched body further inland.

The turbulent sea currents had carried the two royal ships to a place known as Mangaran. The shipwrecked passengers came ashore, and the warm morning sun, along with the coconut meat and water, strengthened their weary bodies. Refreshed, the group began to leave the beach. The day was growing warm.

Panji still carried his wife's corpse, talking to her. When he started to sing to her, the storm survivors looked at each other silently.

"Prasanta, we have to do something." Wiranata looked at Panji sitting with Angreni's body on flat stones under a tamarind tree. "Lady Angreni's corpse has started to decay and reek."

"You're probably right, Raden, but I don't know what to do," Prasanta replied.

"Prasanta, you're the closest person to Panji. Even Her Majesty the Queen is not as close to him as you are."

"Maybe that's true, but I am only a servant. My closeness to him is only caused by frequent encounters, not by the heart and feelings. Compared to me, Her Majesty the Queen is much closer to his heart and feelings."

"Did Panji ever tell you about his mother?"

"Many times, Raden. What I remember most is his fascination with the stories she told him when he was a child."

"Could you tell Panji one of the stories that you think fits his current situation?"

"Certainly. I think this is a good idea. It's better than us doing nothing to lessen Panji's suffering."

"Hopefully, our efforts will produce results. If that story can comfort and calm Panji, then you can ask him if we can bury his wife's body properly."

Prasanta thought for a moment before approaching Panji, but when he was a few feet behind his master, his mouth went dry. Only after swallowing his bitter saliva several times, Prasanta spoke with a trembling voice. "Raden, please forgive my impertinence to approach you without being called."

"Is that you, Prasanta?" Panji stopped singing but did not turn.

"Yes, Raden, it is me. Will you allow me to console you, Raden?"

"Please, Prasanta," Panji answered without taking his eyes off his wife, whose face had grown paler and more swollen. "But I'm not the only one who needs to be consoled. Angreni also needs someone to cheer her."

"Let me tell you a story, about a king and a queen, that might entertain you," Prasanta said, now facing his master.

Panji shifted his eyes from his wife to Prasanta, who was still nervous.

"The king was Aji Dharma," Prasanta began. "He lived at Urawan Palace, in an ancient kingdom on the island of Java. The king was so in love with his wife that he could not think of having any other woman in his life. He was indeed different from the other kings of his time, who mostly had dozens of wives. But, as tragedy unfortunately cannot be avoided, he lost his beloved wife soon after their marriage.

"After that terrible incident, Aji Dharma became a wanderer. Because it was believed that the most noble way to die was to die while destroying evil on the battlefield, the king became a warlord, hoping to hasten his death. His hope was that after leaving this mortal world, he would be reunited with his wife in the afterlife. Indeed, after his death on the battlefield, Aji Dharma ascended to heaven, where he was reunited with his wife, and they were able to live happily together again."

"Prasanta," Panji said with a faint smile, "I think I have heard that story before."

Wiranata and the people watching Panji and Prasanta were relieved when Panji remembered his mother's story. It meant that he was still able to reason.

"That's right, Raden. Her Majesty the Queen once told you this story."

"Oh, yes! I remember now. Aji Dharma was certainly a wise king, but what am I?" Panji asked Prasanta. "What should I do?"

"If you wish to find happiness like King Aji Dharma, who reunited with his wife in heaven, then you must let Lady Angreni rest here. That way, you can go fight against evil and join her in heaven when you die."

"All right, Prasanta," Panji said slowly. "Please prepare a resting place for my wife, Angreni."

Prasanta bowed and immediately hurried back to Wiranata to tell him the news that Panji was willing to let go of his wife's corpse.

"Emban," Wiranata said to a handmaid roasting cassava roots. Seeing the scattered cassava peels and charred remains on the corners of her mouth, Wiranata knew that she had just eaten some of the filling roots. "Ask Raden Panji for Lady Angreni's body. After you have the body, carry it to that boulder. Place the body right behind the boulder so Panji cannot see it. Do you understand, emban?"

"Yes, Raden. I hope that my small, wrinkled hands are strong enough to carry my mistress's body," the handmaid said, looking at Panji.

Wiranata, Prasanta, and Tunggulwulung watched apprehensively from a distance while Panji handed Angreni's body to the handmaid. Staggering, she carried the corpse to the boulder and placed the body behind it. The three men watched the handmaid fall backward after she put the body down.

While Wiranata and Prasanta stood witness, the handmaid removed Angreni's earrings, necklace, and bracelets. She wrapped the jewelry in Angreni's scarf and handed the small bundle to Wiranata, because he was Panji's younger brother. But Wiranata refused. "Let Prasanta keep it," Wiranata said. Then he muttered softly, "Panji has been carrying the body for almost two days."

Meanwhile, Tunggulwulung had ordered a dozen soldiers to quietly dig a hole with available tools. He ordered other soldiers to remain next to Panji and to wait for his orders.

Wiranata had already guessed what Panji would do next.

As soon as he had handed Angreni's corpse to the handmaid, Panji lined up the soldiers who had survived the storm. In a steadfast manner and loud voice, Panji laid out his plans. The story of King Aji Dharma's reunion with his wife in heaven seemed to have greatly affected him.

Some twenty meters away from where the soldiers lined up under Panji's command, several other soldiers silently hurried to finish digging Angreni's grave.

The handmaid carried Angreni's prepared body, neatly wrapped in Angreni's own sarong and Wiranata's, to the gravesite, where four soldiers stood in the pit ready to receive the body.

They used stones that were unearthed during the digging to neatly arrange a grave marker beside the mounded soil, beneath which Angreni now peacefully rested. Scattered, colorful blossoms adorned the final resting place of the girl who had been the kingdom's most beautiful flower.

———•———

When King Amiluhur of Janggala heard that his son had taken Angreni's dead body on a sea excursion, along with his closest companions and one thousand crew mates, the king, accompanied by the court priest and several soldiers, went by carriage to the beach where the ships wrecked to meet Panji. But when he arrived at the seashore, the king only found hundreds of corpses that had washed up on the sand, along with the wreckage of fishing boats. Most of the bodies, judging from their clothes, belonged to the soldiers assigned to accompany Panji.

Struck by the numbing sight, Amiluhur gazed blankly into the distance for a long time while clasping his hands. Everything he saw saddened him deeply. He feared that Panji, his son, had also drowned in the violent storm.

"Your Holiness, I didn't think this would happen," Amiluhur moaned, turning to the court priest. Unable to comment, the priest could only pray.

"Seeing all of this, I feel I have failed as a king and a father." Amiluhur moaned again. He removed his crown and all his jewelry and placed the items in the carriage.

"Return to the palace, Your Holiness," the king ordered. "Give my crown and jewelry to Brajanata."

"Where are you going, Your Majesty?" the priest stammered, watching Amiluhur walk away.

"I am going to Pucangan. Go, and let me walk there by myself."

The court priest knew that the king was disturbed and wanted to punish himself, so he let him walk away. But the priest immediately ordered four of the soldiers to secretly follow the king, far enough behind him so that he would not notice. In the king's current state of mental shock, he would not be as vigilant. He had to be protected from wild animals and other dangers during his travel.

Back at the palace, the court priest immediately ordered a servant to gather a sarong, belt, and *kudi*, a small machete. Then, the priest ordered the servant to deliver the items to Rara Suci's residence in Pucangan. He was certain that the king would remove his regalia and change into a priest's robe for at least one full moon.

Chapter 6

KELANA JAYENGSARI IN BALI

While the storm was destroying Panji's ships, Kebotendas found a hiding place in Bali. Reclining on his bamboo cot with food and drink next to him, he thought about all the recent events he had experienced.

Yes, he had indeed received a direct order from the king to kill Angreni if Brajanata hesitated or did not have the heart to do it. Yes, he had indeed been ordered to flee to Bali afterwards and go into hiding to avoid unwanted attention.

Panji's wrath, as well as the wrath of the prime minister, Patih Kudanawarsa, might cost him his life. His situation was far grimmer than Brajanata's. The son of the king could immediately hide behind the king's back, while he, Kebotendas, was only a soldier. Behind whose back could he safely hide?

Holding his kris and a bag of silver that King Amiluhur had given him, Kebotendas headed for Bali after the murder of Angreni on the beach. The kris he carried would prove that he was a royal envoy, hiding in a friendly country. While at the harbor in Banyuwangi, waiting for a boat to take him to Bali, he noticed someone hurriedly approaching him.

"Tendas! Wait!"

The voice sounded familiar, but because he was on the run, Kebotendas had to be extremely careful. He waited for the caller to come closer.

"Kang Kertala?" Kebotendas now recognized Brajanata's gardener, who had disguised himself as a common peddler.

After the two exchanged brief greetings, Kertala said, "So you have carried out your orders from the king, but now you must face the issues related to your own personal safety."

"I have to report to the king of Bali," Kebotendas explained. "His Majesty King Amiluhur of Janggala had already expected this to happen."

"The king of Bali doesn't know you," Kertala pointed out. "He's never seen your face. Just carrying the kris from His Majesty is not enough. I will accompany you to see him."

"Thank you," Kebotendas said gratefully. "The king gave me enough silver coins for the journey. I spent some to buy a horse to ride here. We need to be dressed like the Janggala king's envoy when we see the king of Bali."

"You are right," Kertala agreed. "Let's find a place to stay and get some clothes first."

———•◦•———

During his travel with Kertala, Kebotendas could not forget the incident on the beach not far from Kamal Harbor. Angreni's and Sumbita's faces alternately blurred his vision. When he closed his eyes, the two faces seemed to appear right in front of him.

Even after he and Kertala found lodging, Kebotendas was afraid to close his eyes, let alone sleep. As it was during his travel to Banyuwangi, his sleep was always filled with chaotic dreams of his fight with the two tough women. In his dreams, he was always their target.

When the images of the two women made him too anxious, Kebotendas forced himself to think of another woman who used to appear in his dreams often. She was Mirah, his brother's lover.

He remembered saying to her, "I have already prepared a house for us to stay, Mirah." When, unexpectedly, the girl did not answer, he had continued, "Shall I take you to see our house? It is very simple, but in the mornings, you can smell the flowers and hear the water gurgling."

Ignoring Kebotendas's words, Mirah asked about Tandang's whereabouts. "Where did your brother go?"

"Didn't he tell you that he was on royal duty?" Kebotendas asked, indifferently. He knew Mirah was more interested in his brother, but he also knew that his brother did not really care about her. Instead, Tandang was determined to fully devote himself to a military career. Without Brajanata's help, Tandang could not have enlisted. After all, he was still Siwur's son, an outcast.

"Yes, he told me that," Mirah said without looking at Kebotendas. "What he didn't tell me is where he went."

"Don't you want to see our house?"

"Our house? It is your house, Tendas, not mine."

Kebotendas felt that Tandang's status as a soldier had captivated Mirah. He wondered now if his decision to become a soldier like Tandang was caused by his disappointment at being rebuffed by Mirah, whom he loved. Kebotendas did not dare answer his own question.

———•◦•———

Two days after Angreni's murder, Patih Kudanawarsa heard the rumors about his daughter's death. The information undoubtedly came from Panji's house servants.

Although the death had not been confirmed, Nyai Patih, the prime minister's wife, was deeply saddened. She tried to extract the truth from her handmaids, and their whispers made her fear that the rumors were true indeed. Patih Kudanawarsa tried to hide his own sadness by consoling his wife.

Three days after the disappearance of Angreni and Sumbita, there still was no news about their return. The prime minister felt that, true to tradition, he should hold a ceremony to pray for his daughter, who he now believed had died. The handmaids had told him that Angreni was taken by one of the king's sons. Therefore, there was nothing the prime minister could do about it. He tried to overcome his restlessness by visiting the secluded holy men and giving them alms.

Patih Kudanawarsa was certain that if Angreni had in fact been taken away by a Janggala prince, the incident had to be related to the problem that had troubled the king a few days ago — that Panji wanted Angreni to be his only wife and refused to marry anyone else. Kudanawarsa was convinced that Panji's stubbornness had brought bad fortune to Angreni.

Almost every night, Nyai Patih went alone to the prayer hut in the corner of the garden. The prayer she sent to the gods was always the same: She asked that her daughter Angreni, who had been killed at such a young age, would be remembered. That even long after her death, people would continue to say her name with great respect and affection.

——•◆•——

After Brajanata returned from his bloody assignment on the coast and had been unable to face the king to report everything that had happened, he headed for Rara Suci's residence in Pucangan. Apart from wanting to see his aunt, he also wanted to see his best friend, Kusni. He knew that Kusni visited Rara Suci every week to talk about mysticism. Kusni considered Rara Suci his teacher, while Rara Suci considered Kusni good company for conversation.

When he arrived at Rara Suci's, he tethered his horse under a shade tree. "Where did Rara Suci go?" Brajanata asked Kusni.

Kusni paused from splitting the logs for firewood. He pointed into the distance. "She went to the village down there. One of her disciple's parents is seriously ill." Resuming his work, he added, "Just wait inside.

Let me finish chopping this wood." Kusni enjoyed helping his teacher. When he was not chopping wood, he was drawing water from the well. He happily performed the chores that Rara Suci usually assigned to the disciples who lived in her house.

Kusni walked into the inner room, carrying water in an earthen jug, and boiled a few taro roots for refreshment. Even though the owner of this home was the sister of the king of Janggala, everything, including the food and beverages, was simple. This was one of the reasons Kusni believed that Rara Suci was indeed a holy woman.

Kusni immediately sensed something was wrong. Brajanata was not his usual self. He was withdrawn while visiting with his best friend. "What is bothering you, Raden?"

"What do you think a godly king is?" Brajanata asked in return.

"A godly king is the embodiment of a god in a king," answered Kusni, who had read many books that belonged to Rara Suci. "The god I mention here, of course, is a benevolent god."

"I want to hear your opinion: Am I correct in following all of my father's orders because his majesty is also a god?" Brajanata articulated his words carefully. He didn't want Kusni to misunderstand the meaning of his question.

"From my conversations with Her Holiness Rara Suci, I conclude that gods are none other than angels," Kusni answered. "The difference is that while angels are always benevolent, gods — according to Her Holiness's belief — are not. There are gods who are evil. As far as I know, the evil angel is called the devil, and that's why we never call the devil an angel anymore. On this island of Java, gods who are not benevolent are still called gods. In *wayang,* puppet, stories, for example, Kala is still called Dewa Kala, even though he always fights the benevolent nobilities. If the godly king symbolizes a good king of a divine nature, you have to obey his orders, especially if he is your own father..." Kusni could not finish his sentence. He scanned Brajanata's face.

Brajanata bowed his head and stammered, "He ordered me to —"

"Raden, you don't need to say anything that bothers you." Kusni could guess what his friend was about to say.

Both of them fell silent again.

"I guess you no longer believe that your father is really a godly king," Kusni said.

"It isn't that I no longer believe that, it's just that the orders of a godly king are confusing." Brajanata was unable to tell Kusni that he had just been *forced* to execute the orders from a godly king. The decree had required him to kill his own brother's wife. It stated that if his brother's wife was not killed, there would be war between two kingdoms reigned by sibling kings. Brajanata wanted to end the conversation, but Kusni still wanted to continue it.

"In a book about the history of Arabia, there is a story about a messenger whose wife fought against the messenger's nephew," Kusni said. "According to my faith, 'messenger' is the highest title for a human being. Both the wife and the nephew were good people who studied directly under the messenger, so the battle between the two good people confused me. Why did something like that happen? Why did two good people fight about something as futile as power?"

"You said he was a messenger. Who sent him?" Brajanata asked.

"The king of gods."

"You mean that the king of gods is also the king of angels and devils?"

"Yes, that's right." Kusni nodded. "You seem to be dealing with a problem that is closely related to the issue of power."

"Is your king in the Perlak Kingdom also a god?"

"A godly king? Only someone who is a messenger is capable of becoming a godly king. One of the reasons I left Perlak was to avoid bloodshed caused by a struggle for power."

They now noticed Rara Suci, in the distance, walking home with two disciples. When the wise noblewoman saw Brajanata, she immediately knew that his visit was related to the crisis taking place between the king and Panji.

Knowing his position, Kusni immediately excused himself and went back to splitting firewood.

Rara Suci and Brajanata remained in the inner room.

After about an hour, Kusni saw Brajanata standing in the doorway. One of his hands held on to the door frame, while he ran the fingers of his other hand through his hair. After a while, Brajanata slowly walked toward his tethered horse.

"Raden!" Kusni put his ax down and ran after Brajanata.

Brajanata, standing beside his horse, was surprised to see his best friend approach him. For a moment, they looked at each other silently. Then Brajanata turned his gaze to the scattered pieces of firewood Kusni had just split.

Kusni followed his gaze to the pile of logs in Rara Suci's side yard. "If only I could ease your burden…"

"Unfortunately, I'm the only one who can lighten my burden," Brajanata said in a husky voice. "That's what Aunt Rara Suci said."

Indeed, when it came to dealing with hurt, only he could heal himself, Kusni thought. But aloud, Kusni said, "Be patient, Raden."

Brajanata mounted his horse, his eyes brimming with tears. He choked on his words when he said goodbye before slowly riding away.

Judging from the direction he was heading, Kusni assumed that Brajanata was returning to the palace.

Rara Suci remained seated on the veranda, deep in thought. The spacious room was usually used to receive guests, who mostly came asking for solutions or simply trying to find a little enlightenment about the problems they were facing.

Kusni felt that it was the right time to approach the priestess. "Excuse me, Your Holiness." Kusni seated himself cross-legged in front of Rara Suci. "Didn't Your Holiness promise to tell me today about a book that shocked all the priests and religious leaders in Java?"

"You mean the Book of Kudasrenggara?" Rara Suci reached for a cup of water and took a sip.

"I am not sure," Kusni said. "I forgot the title. I only remember that the book warns against the dangers of becoming a clergyman, which sounds strange to me."

"I lent the book to the Janggala royal priest," Rara Suci said. "When it hadn't been returned for more than a year, I asked about the book's whereabouts. The priest said that the book had been borrowed by a priest at the court of the Bali Kingdom."

"So the book is now in Bali?" Kusni sounded disappointed. He had come all the way from Perlak with the ultimate goal to study from the Book of Kudasrenggara, which, according to his teacher, discussed how to reconcile all religions in the world. Thus, the book could be used to unite all humans in a world where fighting was caused by a difference in belief, more than any other reason. He was really eager to study the book.

"According to Tandang, a Janggala soldier I commissioned to find the Book of Kudasrenggara, the book is now in the hands of the Bali's crown princess. I can ask my brother, the king of Janggala, to assign Tandang to escort you to look for the book in Bali."

"Thank you, Your Holiness," Kusni bowed. "I will wait for Tandang, the soldier Your Holiness mentioned earlier.

By the time King Lembu Amiluhur, who had walked the entire way from the shipwreck site, arrived at Rara Suci's residence, Kusni had already left to buy his daily supplies from his merchant in Janggala.

When Panji and his troops were ready to go to war, Wiranata remembered his relief when Panji finally let go of Angreni's body. He and Prasanta had just finished discussing the plans to heal Panji's heart when the handmaid had managed to walk away from Panji with Angreni's body. He remembered secretly ordering a dozen soldiers to quickly dig a grave and bury her, and he could still see in his mind those soldiers who could not stand the odor and vomited. By the time the sun was halfway up in the sky, they had buried Angreni. Wiranata,

Panji's half-brother, sighed with relief. Panji had carried the lifeless, decaying body around with him for almost two full days.

Now, after lining up and inspecting his troops, Panji paced back and forth.

Prasanta approached him. "It is time for you to be reunited with your beloved wife," he said. "The way to accomplish this is by going to war against Bali." Prasanta chose to attack Bali because Wiranata had told him that Kebotendas, who was now a thorn in the flesh of the Janggala kingdom, was hiding out in Bali.

Following Wiranata's suggestion, and fearing that Panji would suddenly remember his wife again, Prasanta proposed to attack Bali immediately. It hadn't taken much for Wiranata to connect Angreni's death to Brajanata and Kebotendas. He was quite certain that the king was the source of all the unfortunate incidents. The king had assigned Kertala to find and follow Kebotendas.

So they chose to go to war against the king of Bali so that Panji would forget the bitterness of Angreni's loss. Another consideration was that Bali was weak. The current king overindulged in amusement and the army was untrained. With his one hundred elite warriors, Panji would be able to conquer Bali easily.

Kebotendas must have arrived in Bali by now, Wiranata thought. He had already told Prasanta that if they could kill this Janggala fugitive during the war, then the king's indiscretion was safe, and no one would ever know about it.

"All right, Prasanta, we will conquer Bali." Panji walked back to his soldiers, who still stood in a neat line. Among the hundred soldiers who had survived the raging storm, nearly a third were Panji's siblings, born from more than a dozen of the king's concubines.

"Emban, get ready," Wiranata said to the handmaid. "We are going to Bali."

"Please, Raden, allow me to stay here and take care of Lady Angreni," the handmaid pleaded, sitting on her knees beside the burial mound.

Wiranata could only nod. He took out a few coins from his cummerbund and handed them to the loyal handmaid.

———•—•———

By the time Brajanata returned to the palace from his visit with Rara Suci, only the prime minister and court priest were there to meet him. The prime minister said that the king had assigned him, Brajanata, to temporarily take care of the kingdom's affairs. As a token of proof, the prime minister handed him the king's crown and jewelry.

Brajanata didn't need to ask for an explanation. He could easily guess how mortified the king was after learning of the recent tragic events.

As the interim king, Brajanata did not feel out of place, let alone confused. Even though he was not the crown prince, he was the king's eldest son. He had represented the king several times at state functions when Panji was still too young to lead events that demanded wisdom rather than rank.

On the fourth day of Brajanata serving in the king's stead, two envoys from Kadiri came to visit. Brajanata and court officials welcomed them. As was custom, they held a modest banquet as a forerunner to the main event.

After Brajanata seated the royal emissaries across from him, he said, "Please forgive me, His Majesty is currently taking a leave and staying at my Aunt Rara Suci's residence in Pucangan."

"That is no problem, Raden. We just want to confirm some news we heard." The envoy lowered his eyes and bowed his head before asking, "Is it true that Raden Panji has married the daughter of Patih Kudanawarsa?"

"Yes, indeed. It happened two weeks ago."

The two royal emissaries glanced at each other before one of them continued, "Does Raden Panji no longer intend to marry the crown princess of Kadiri, Sekartaji, his fiancée?"

"Yes, that's what the king told me. However, I must tell you that Raden Panji and his wife both died when their ships were caught in a storm. Hundreds of soldiers who accompanied him also died in the disaster."

The two royal emissaries exchanged glances again before they lowered their heads. For a long time the envoys stared at the shiny floor of the Janggala palace.

One of the royal emissaries broke the silence. "On behalf of King Amerdadu of Kadiri, we express our condolences, Raden. After all, Raden Panji is still Princess Sekartaji's fiancé. We will, of course, hold a ceremony to observe Raden Panji's passing."

Without touching any of the refreshments that had been served in the meeting room, the two envoys said goodbye. Followed by several guards, they returned to their waiting horse carriage and rode back to Kadiri.

After hearing the news of Panji's death, Sekartaji, the crown princess of Kadiri, decided to leave the palace for a while. Her mother telling her to wait patiently for another suitor had hurt her, although she had kept her feelings to herself. *Now is the time for me to escape from the painful stares of the people in the palace*, she thought.

While packing, Sekartaji thought about the problem that her younger brother, Gunungsari, had told her about a few days ago. The problem involved Gunungsari's argument with Sarag, his wife. Sarag was the daughter of a rich merchant from Perlak, who people often referred to as Bagong, because his portly and short stature resembled his namesake in the wayang story.

Gunungsari told Sekartaji that recently he had returned home from an audience with the king and had immediately taken a seat on the rug on his veranda, to be by himself. Normally, he would have called out to Sarag to tell her he was home; but this time, he did not.

When Sarag noticed that her husband was home, she rushed to meet him with a tray of his favorite finger food. Sitting down right next to him, Sarag offered Gunungsari the delicacies, only to be ignored.

"Are you angry at me?" Sarag looked at Gunungsari's grim face.

When her husband remained silent, she probed, "What did I do wrong?" Sarag took Gunungsari's hand and stroked it. "Please, tell me, don't just keep silent."

"Leave me alone!" Gunungsari jerked his hand free. "If you don't, I'll hit you on the head with a rock! Get a mirror. Look at your pig-like face! Your nose looks like a potato, and your hair makes you look like a ghost!"

"What are you talking about? It's as if you've never seen my face before. You've never said anything like this. Didn't you know from the onset that I am not pretty?" Sarag ran to her room and slammed the door. From behind the closed door, she shouted, "Why did you marry me? Why did your parents propose to me?"

The loud arguing between the childless couple continued. Gunungsari stood on the veranda shouting at Sarag, and Sarag screamed back at him from inside her room. It was impossible that either could hear the other.

The sound of glassware crashing to the floor made handmaids run to Sarag's room, only to sit down in front of the locked door.

During the following days, Gunungsari avoided his wife. He preferred to linger near the gates alone and lounge on the long bench there. Or sit on the flat rock under the orange jasmine tree and enjoy the breeze.

He knew very well the reason he had married Sarag. The wedding had been celebrated with a big feast. They slaughtered ten cows and hundreds of chickens. Six puppeteers took turns performing for three days and three nights, and dozens of gamelan musicians were hired.

Bagong, Sarag's rich merchant father, was related to Kusni. When Kusni had first arrived in Janggala, he lived at Bagong's house, which the villagers referred to as the Bagong Palace.

Bagong and Kusni were spice merchants and friends of the court priest from Kadiri. They worked together in the spice trade and sent the spices to be sold in Malay and the surrounding region. Bagong dared to buy his spices from Kadiri's and Janggala's farmers at a higher price than most local traders because he could sell them to Arab merchants in Perlak and Malay. The trade not only benefited the Kadiri court priest, but also improved the welfare of many spice farmers.

Amerdadu, the king of Kadiri, was very pleased that his people prospered because of the cooperation between the court priest and Bagong the merchant. Therefore, the king agreed when the court priest proposed to marry the king's son, Gunungsari, to the merchant's only daughter, Sarag.

Their marriage, based on trade interests, did not make Gunungsari happy. Even though the marriage made Sekartaji's younger brother the richest Kadiri prince — his home was no less beautiful than the king's own palace — he was undoubtedly the prince who suffered the most in matters of romance. At every royal event that had to be attended by the princes and their wives, Gunungsari became the favorite subject of ridicule because his wife's appearance so closely resembled her father's, Bagong the merchant.

Gunungsari's anger at Sarag exploded the day he overheard his wife loudly rebuking the princesses, who had laughed at her appearance. Sarag told them that Gunungsari was no more than a parasite, and that despite her grotesque appearance, at least she was able to support a king's son, a shameless leech. Sarag hadn't realized that Gunungsari was standing behind her, and, of course, the princesses saw the flushed face of the angry prince.

On the fifth day after this incident, Sekartaji arrived to tell Gunungsari about her plans to leave the palace. Gunungsari now felt more comfortable under the orange jasmine tree than he did at home. When Sekartaji noticed the change in her brother's behavior, she asked what was wrong, and Gunungsari told her everything.

"Why don't you just leave the house?" Sekartaji suggested. "When you feel better, you can go back home to see your wife."

"I have already planned on leaving, dear sister. I just haven't found the right time."

"How about tomorrow? We can leave together."

"Are you leaving because of the death of Panji, your fiancé?"

Sekartaji did not answer. Instead, she looked closely at her brother and ordered, "Prepare two horses, wear peasant clothes, and meet me later tonight."

⊷•⊶

Prasanta had proposed the war against Bali only after discussing it with Wiranata, who acted as Brajanata's representative in regard to Panji's care. Wiranata, of course, was also well-prepared.

Under Panji's command, the hundred elite soldiers became a strange battle-ready force — without sufficient weapons, proper uniforms, or colorful war banners. They had lost their weapons in the violent storm, along with all the other valuables they had brought from the palace. Everything had been tossed overboard and swallowed by the raging sea. Each soldier now only had a kris, which was attached to his body like the clothes he wore, and a box of gunpowder, the raw material for making their main grenade-like weapon, which they referred to as *kepel*. At a glance, the weapon looked like the kepel fruit. The size of a small apple and useful as a deodorant, the kepel fruit was a favorite among the princesses. The kepel weapon, smashed or thrown to the ground, would explode, injuring or killing people near it. The weapon was a combination of Javanese ingenuity and Chinese technology. The first kepel weapon was developed during the reign of King Erlangga, Panji's progenitor, who lived decades ago.

"Raden, the soldiers' drill sergeant, Tunggulwulung, suggested we not approach the Bali palace from the port," Prasanta told Panji while preparing for the Bali attack.

"Tunggulwulung? I haven't talked to him for a long time. Tell him to see me." Panji had known Tunggulwulung for five years. They once

108

lived in the same barracks at a *bandayuda,* a special training camp for close combat.

Tunggulwulung had been waiting for Panji to call him to discuss his strategy. But he knew that the present Panji was different from the Panji he'd known in the past. "Go ahead, Tunggulwulung. I'm giving you the opportunity to tell me your strategy." Panji was playing with the guava fruit he had just picked.

"Thank you, Raden." Tunggulwulung folded his hands in front of his chest before continuing. "I intend to propose where our troops should land. In my opinion, landing at the port is not quite right. The Balinese aristocrats and guards will intercept us. Even if we could easily defeat them, I'm afraid the encounter would reduce our strength too much before we reached the palace gate."

"Where should we land then?" Panji asked, chewing on the guava.

"I ask that you give me two or three days to find a good landing spot, as well as the most secure route to the palace," Tunggulwulung replied. "I have friends in Bali who I can ask for help."

"That is too long to wait, Tunggulwulung. We have to fight tomorrow." Panji spat out the guava pit. He looked into the distance as if he were contemplating something.

"But, Raden…" Tunggulwulung turned to Prasanta. Prasanta immediately shook his head and signaled him to leave. Tunggulwulung bowed, then left.

"Wait, Commander!" Panji called after Tunggulwulung, who stopped and turned. "The more danger that confronts us, the more I like it!"

Tunggulwulung immediately bowed and turned away again. Deep in his heart, he pitied Panji.

Prasanta rushed over to see Panji. "Raden, we better not use our real names as long as we are at war."

"Good idea, I agree," Panji answered happily. "From now on, my name is Sweet Guava."

Prasanta glanced at Panji's right hand holding half of the remaining guava. "Pardon me, Raden, shouldn't you use another name? May I suggest that you change your name to "Kelana" or traveler, since you are about to travel?"

"All right. From now on, my name is Kelana Jayengsari. Now, what is my name, Prasanta?"

"Kelana Jayengsari."

"Come, Prasanta. Let's walk along the beach before crossing to Bali."

Chapter 7

THE RADIANT BALINESE PRINCESS

Panji and his troops crossed the Bali Strait with ten boats rented from fishermen along the Banyuwangi coast. Except for Panji, Wiranata, and Prasanta, all the soldiers were dressed like locals. They had sold what little jewelry they still had to purchase food and the clothes they wore now. When Wiranata and Prasanta tried to persuade Panji to change his clothes to those of a commoner, he only laughed.

The arrival of ten boats, complemented by a crew of strong men, drew everyone's attention at the port of Bali. As soon as Panji's men started to disembark, suspicious Balinese harbor officials met them. But the disguised soldiers kept moving and did not appear to have any intention of talking to the officers in charge of inspection.

"Wait! Where are you going?" one of the officers yelled when he saw Tunggulwulung leaving the boat dock followed by his shipmates.

Tunggulwulung halted and replied calmly, "We want to sell our merchandise at the Gianyar market."

The officer approached Tunggulwulung. "We have to check your merchandise."

"We do not carry any prohibited merchandise. Please excuse us, we're in a hurry." Tunggulwulung turned and walked away. His shipmates had continued walking and now were up ahead, waiting near a forest in the distance. Panji, Wiranata, and Prasanta, who sailed on the last boat, were still onboard.

"Stay there!" shouted the officer, who appeared to be the harbormaster. "You are all under arrest for further inspection!" And in an instant, Tunggulwulung was surrounded by six men trying to arrest him. But six men were no match for Tunggulwulung. Punching, kicking, and ramming, Tunggulwulung quickly knocked four of them down. The other two fled without looking back. The harbor master, a tall, bearded man, felt belittled. He quickly pulled his kris from its sheath and attacked Tunggulwulung.

Expecting this to happen, Tunggulwulung immediately jumped back and drew his kris.

"Tunggulwulung, please step back." Panji had disembarked from his boat and jumped between Tunggulwulung and the harbor master.

"Raden?" Tunggulwulung stuttered.

"Take care of your men and continue your journey," Panji ordered.

Tunggulwulung nodded and ran to join his men in the forest.

Seeing the escalating commotion, a worker at the port left quietly to report the incident to the king of Bali, whose court was seated in Gianyar.

"Apparently, you are the mastermind of all this trouble," snarled the harbor master, consumed with anger. Aiming for Panji's chest with the tip of his kris, he shouted, "Die!"

Panji, instinctively remembering his training in avoiding kris stabs and sword blows, merely shifted his body, and the kris hit empty air. "Don't be reckless, Beardman," Panji said calmly. "I also have a weapon."

The harbor master, although much older than Panji, launched another attack. But seeing that Panji had drawn his kris, he was more careful. When his second thrust, aimed at Panji's stomach, missed again, Panji's empty left hand punched his opponent in the ribs. As the harbor master faltered, Panji kicked him in the chest. The harbor master fell, sprawling on his back. His kris was flung to the ground near his head.

For a moment, Panji stared at his diamond-studded kris. Slowly, he slipped the kris back into its sheath, decorated with golden dragons, then casually walked away from the harbor master, lying still on the ground.

Seeing Panji's back turned toward him, the harbor master pulled out a knife. But before he could throw it, a rock as big as a fist hit his head, cracking his skull. Prasanta, unwilling to remain a passive bystander while Panji's safety was threatened, had thrown the rock.

Suddenly, some two hundred Balinese army soldiers appeared at the harbor, led by General Kretabasa.

"We're surrounded!" Wiranata shouted at the disguised soldiers who were still at the port. "Where's Tunggulwulung?" Without any insignia, they now were better described as Panji's company.

"Commander Tunggulwulung predicted this encirclement," replied a soldier, assigned by Tunggulwulung to report to Wiranata. The soldier pointed to the forest, and said, "He took twenty soldiers to that forest."

The remaining eighty of Panji's men were now surrounded at the port by two hundred Balinese soldiers. Wiranata immediately organized the eighty men and ordered an attack. At the end of the encounter, Panji's men had taken many Balinese soldiers prisoner, including the harbor master's crew, porters, and fishermen.

Indifferent to Wiranata's strategies to safeguard the group, Panji said to Prasanta, "Why bother avoiding an encounter? Aren't we here to fight?"

Prasanta did not answer right away. He pointed at the banners of the Bali kingdom, showing their colors everywhere except at the beach around the harbor. "You're correct, Raden," he said. "We're here to fight, so we are not going to retreat back to the sea. We have to keep advancing to the capital of the Bali kingdom."

"Who wants to retreat to the sea? We will march on!"

"If they shower us with arrows, we would have no choice but retreat to the sea," Prasanta explained. "Therefore, we must do whatever it takes to not allow that to happen."

Panji looked thoughtful for a moment, then nodded.

Prasanta was pleased that Panji seemed to understand everything he had said. Prasanta was now even more convinced that warring would heal Panji's wounded soul.

Before the two could take cover at the harbor, someone shouted, "You are surrounded! Come out of your hiding! Surrender!"

"We have more than ten of your people in custody," Panji shouted back "They will die as soon as you attack us!"

"We don't care about those people's lives! We have been ordered to put all of you in chains or kill you."

"Fine, I await your attack!"

A deep silence followed. Even the wind seemed to stop blowing. Then dozens of arrows filled the air, making thudding sounds as the arrowheads hit wood and other hard surfaces. Then, everything was quiet again.

Suddenly, from the direction where Panji and his men had taken shelter behind a wooden wall of the fish market, the severed head of the harbor master sailed through the air, dropped to the ground, and rolled a few meters before it ran into a piece of wood and stopped.

The long silence that followed seemed to swallow the sand, the soil, and the people standing on it.

Panji could not bear the uncertainty that the long silence created. He drew his kris and ran out from behind the wooden wall of the fish market. Realizing the great danger that could befall their leader, Panji's men ran after him, but the barrage of arrows they expected never came. Instead, they heard chaotic shouts coming from the direction of the besiegers.

"Tunggulwulung has made his move!" Wiranata shouted. "Leave two soldiers here. Storm the enemy with the others!"

Panji's troops stormed ahead, spreading to the left, the center, and the right.

Wiranata, Prasanta, and two soldiers remained with their captives. Prasanta shouted, "You, Balinese people, escape to the sea. Take the remaining boats or swim away. A big battle is about to be fought here." The hostages immediately fled in a disorderly haste toward the sea.

Panji's troops, despite being far outnumbered with fewer weapons, clearly controlled the territory and situation.

The Balinese soldiers, confused by the attack from behind, were now also being attacked from the front by Panji's men using makeshift shields, such as the four men who carried a boat as cover while advancing towards the besiegers.

The Balinese soldiers tried to shoot arrows at their frontline attackers, without any results.

Panji reached the enemy line first and immediately attacked madly with accurate and deadly thrusts. In a short time, he brought down a dozen Balinese soldiers with gaping wounds in their necks and chests.

The other soldiers followed Panji, including those led by Tunggulwulung, in attacking and taking the lives of the Balinese soldiers without mercy. Panji's company of nearly one hundred soldiers had no difficulty defeating the two hundred Balinese soldiers. When the Balinese troops had dwindled to only one third, they fled to save their lives. General Kretabasa, their leader, was among those who ran away.

"Don't chase them!" Tunggulwulung stopped the soldiers from chasing the enemy.

"But they will report to the palace, Commander!" The soldiers had taken to calling Tunggulwulung "commander" after hearing Panji address him that way.

"Let them!" said Tunggulwulung. "We have more important things to do now." Tunggulwulung ordered the men to collect the scattered weapons — spears, swords, shields, bows, arrows, and krisses — as well as war horses that roamed without riders.

Twenty Balinese soldiers appeared to still be alive.

Wiranata, Prasanta, and the two soldiers on the dock had joined the others after their captives fled. Wiranata ordered the men to gather the survivors and provide them with help.

"We need to save energy and supplies to attack Gianyar, the capital,"Tunggulwulung said to Wiranata. "Why should we help these Balinese soldiers who shot their arrows at us?"

"Because when we enter the capital," Wiranata replied, "we are going to use them as human shields."

"We don't need shields," Tunggulwulung countered. "We only need speed. I suggest we split the troops in two. The ones I lead will circle around and attack from behind; the ones Raden Panji leads will attack from the front."

"I agree with you, but don't forget, we're fighting this war not only to win; we are fighting this war to heal our crown prince." Wiranata looked at Panji, who sat singing under a blooming frangipani tree.

"What do you mean, Raden?" Tunggulwulung raised his thick eyebrows.

"I'm sure Panji will want to lead the troops. He'll be in the front line riding to the capital to siege the palace. He will not care about his own safety under such conditions." Wiranata turned again to Panji, who now was dancing with frangipani flowers tucked behind his ears. "Raden Panji needs a shield."

"We are going to use the captured soldiers as a human shield for Raden Panji?"

"That's right, Tunggulwulung. We will have them mount their horses, then tie them to their horses. They will be at the head of the formation when we march to the city. We are going to ride in a horseshoe formation, with Raden Panji in the middle. The prisoners will act as a shield for Panji while our troops will be right behind him."

"All right then."Tunggulwulung nodded in agreement. "Today, we will stay here. We will start moving tomorrow."

"It would be better if you and your company leave near midnight. I'm sure Bali has sent scouts to spy on us. They probably know by now that we are here." Tunggulwulung and Wiranata surveyed the surrounding area with utmost caution.

Panji had covered his face with his hands, sobbing.

All of Panji's soldiers now possessed horses and weapons, confiscated from the dead Balinese soldiers. Near midnight, forty of Panji's soldiers wearing Balinese soldiers' uniforms, led by Tunggulwulung, separated from the others to head for the capital, where they would circle to attack the palace from behind.

The next morning, the captured Balinese soldiers mounted their horses and were tied. Panji was hidden behind the human shield of captured Balinese soldiers.

As Prasanta expected, Panji did not want to be seen as a coward and wanted to ride in front. Only after explaining to Panji that riding in the front line could be seen as an act of arrogance, and therefore be less honorable, did Prasanta succeed in convincing Panji to maintain his protected position. And now Panji's company moved forward towards Gianyar. With soldiers dressed in Balinese uniforms leading the formation, the people along the journey thought that Balinese military were escorting foreign soldiers to meet Bali's king.

⊢—•⊛•—⊣

When the king of Bali received the news from General Kretabasa about an invasion of foreign troops, he ignored it after he learned that the attacker's army only numbered one hundred men. He was convinced that his soldiers could easily eliminate the intruders. Besides, the king was busy planning his thirtieth — or fortieth — marriage, this time to the daughter of a regent.

The king's countless marriages had slowly but surely weakened the kingdom. The kingdom's resources were almost depleted from expenditures that only benefitted the king and his immediate family. Fortunately, Bali was blessed with fertile soil and peaceful people, who liked to spend their money and energy on performing religious ceremonies, such as making offerings to their gods and ancestors. The kingdom had never gone through any upheaval.

"The latest report mentioned that the foreign troops managed to capture and enslave our soldiers, Your Majesty," General Kretabasa said nervously.

"So send more soldiers, General," the king answered, dryly.

"Please forgive me, Your Majesty. The intruders are already heading for the capital. I recommend that we deploy our entire army to defend the palace rather than trying to stop them."

The king raised his voice. "Don't disobey my orders, General. Send soldiers to intercept and destroy those intruders. You said there were only about a hundred of them, right? It will be easy to crush them."

"Yes, Your Majesty," Kretabasa responded with an unsteady voice. He felt a great turmoil inside his chest. Those one hundred enemy soldiers had defeated his two hundred best soldiers with ease. Kretabasa was certain that his remaining one thousand soldiers would not be able to defend the palace. Most members of his troops had become soldiers only because they claimed to be the son of a concubine or some distant relative of the king. They did not have any combat skills, let alone the courage to fight. Too many of the royal officials preferred to indulge in delicious food and pretty women than study the intricacies of war tactics and the complications of governance. Despite his repeated warnings to his king that the defense of the Bali kingdom was very weak, Kretabasa knew he was only the king's subordinate, a general of the army.

Kretabasa did not want to waste more time. He ordered five hundred soldiers to guard the palace and took the other five hundred to intercept and block the invading army from advancing. He reinforced the infantry and cavalry with a battalion of war elephants.

Panji's small army sensed an ambush. Before entering the city, Wiranata ordered three men to climb into the tops of the three tallest trees near them. One of the men gave a warning signal from the treetop. The troops spread out to span the road.

"We spotted war elephants, followed by cavalry and infantry," the scouts reported to Wiranata.

"Very good!" Panji screamed, joyfully. "I will have a good chance to fight to my death!"

"You're correct, this is a great opportunity." Wiranata wanted to calm Panji. "But to make the battle even more exciting, we need to have a strategy."

"I'm leaving everything for you to decide," said Panji nonchalantly, still riding his horse in the middle of the road with his arms folded across his chest. "The most important thing is I'm ready to die here."

Wiranata rode away from Panji and approached Prasanta and a soldier who Tunggulwulung had selected to represent him while he and his 40 soldiers stationed themselves at the back of the palace.

"We may not win if we attack them directly," Wiranata said quietly.

"I estimate they are ten times our number," the soldier agreed.

"We are already too close," Prasanta added. "We can't turn around."

"Right now, it will be impossible to move Panji," Wiranata said. "Let's stick to the original plan. We will use the captured Balinese soldiers as a shield and strengthen that human wall with our soldiers."

Both the soldier and Prasanta nodded.

The ten captured Balinese prisoners were taken off their horses and lined up across the road, where they were forced to kneel. Both their feet and hands were tied to join them to one another with a rope. The line of tied Balinese soldiers was placed directly in front of Panji, still sitting on his horse in the middle of the road. Thus, the ten prisoners became a human shield, ready to be crushed by advancing Balinese troops.

"By the time the enemy's troops are close enough to see the prisoners, they will either stop or continue to advance and trample them," Wiranata said. "I'm sure Panji will rush forward as soon as he sees the enemy's troops approaching. When he advances to attack, we fire arrows at the Balinese troops."

Indeed, when the forerunners of the Balinese army saw that their path was blocked by the captured Balinese soldiers, their leader signaled them to stop. Panji immediately jumped off his horse and over the prisoners kneeling on the ground. Shouting and brandishing his sword, Panji ran to meet the enemy troops.

While the Balinese army forerunners stopped still, confused by the strange sight of a row of people kneeling on the road and a man jumping wildly over them, a volley of arrows suddenly pierced their front line. The soldiers hit by the arrows toppled from their horses and elephants.

The sixty archers then dropped their bows and joined Panji, engaged in battle and wielding his sword wildly. Some of them advanced by brandishing their swords; most of them hurled kepel toward the remaining enemy. When the kepels hit the ground — or were stepped on in the chaos of soldiers, horses, and elephants — they exploded, creating a thick, suffocating smoke. The deafening noise and acrid smell quickly destroyed the morale of the Balinese soldiers — most of whom had never fought in a battle before.

Exploding kepels typically injured soldiers rather than killed them. Wounded and immobilized, many Balinese soldiers lay helplessly on the ground, while Panji's men — armed with swords — killed them. In a short time, half of the Balinese army had lost their lives, while the remaining inexperienced recruits fled the battlefield.

Panji, dirty and dripping with sweat and blood, seemed calmer. Puffing out his chest slightly, he strutted around for a bit before jumping back on his horse. Occasionally, Panji's horse reared.

Riding the elephants and horses left behind by the defeated Balinese army, Panji and his company advanced to Gianyar, accompanied by more than a hundred prisoners of war lined up in front of Panji's troops.

Meanwhile, Tunggulwulung and his platoon were positioned about one mile behind the palace wall. The group paced restlessly, waiting for Panji to attack the palace from the front. After a while, Tunggulwulung sent two of his men, disguised as Balinese soldiers, to investigate the situation at the front. When the two scouts got close enough to hear the screams that indicated Panji's troops had attacked, they immediately reported back to Tunggulwulung.

Tunggulwulung quickly split his small platoon into three groups to execute a squeeze maneuver by striking from behind, from the left, and from the right of the palace, all at the same time. Using fire arrows and kepel as their main weapons, the three groups advanced to the rear gate of the palace, now just a stone's throw away. As shouts from the front gate grew louder, fiery arrows pelted the palace from three directions. The soldiers who carried kepels immediately ran forward, armed with strings of the grenade-like weapons around their shoulders.

Taken totally by surprise, the Balinese palace guards ran frantically from the guardhouse.

In the front, Panji's troops had arrived at the palace wall's gate.

The terrified Balinese army tried to protect the king's sovereignty, but was unable to put up much resistance.

From the rear and sides, Tunggulwulung's platoons continued throwing deadly kepels and shooting fire arrows at the palace. Tunggulwulung's platoon had succeeded in destroying the palace's rear defense with a firestorm of arrows and explosions.

At the palace's front wall, swinging his sword wildly, Panji jumped on and off his horse each time he brought down a Balinese soldier. He fought with no regard for his own safety. He fought like a madman and, by standards of good combat strategies, far too carelessly.

Fortunately, Panji's skilled soldiers protected him from being killed, although the enemy managed to inflict small wounds all over his body. But Panji seemed unaware of his bleeding wounds. Instead, he appeared frustrated that no opponent could match his fury.

With parts of the palace roof burning and dead bodies sprawled everywhere, the Balinese soldiers under the command of General Kretabasa quickly lost their courage. Dozens of Balinese officials were killed. Most of those dignitaries did not know war tactics; they had arrived at their positions only because of kinship to the king. General Kretabasa, who had survived the invasion of Panji's company, was among only a handful of Balinese leaders who had been willing to do the work of learning about warfare.

After observing the situation on the battlefield and seeing no chance of winning, General Kretabasa decided to end the resistance. He hurried into the inner halls of the palace. "I humbly apologize, Your Majesty, for coming to you without being summoned." Kretabasa bowed respectfully.

"I told you that I left all the decisions about the war to you, General," the king said curtly. He was busy trying to calm his wives, who had panicked at the sight of flames and the sound of screaming, wounded soldiers.

"I apologize, Your Majesty," Kretabasa stammered, "but to avoid even more casualties, I suggest that we surrender to the invaders."

"Repeat what you just said, General!" the king barked.

Kretabasa took a deep breath. "I suggest we surrender, Your Majesty."

"Surrender?" the king shouted incredulously.

"Yes, surrender, Your Majesty," Kretabasa almost whispered.

The king jumped up from his throne. For a moment, he stood silently, his chest heaving and fists clenching.

Several dignitaries standing in the royal audience hall bowed their heads deeply. The servants kneeling behind the king bowed even lower, their foreheads almost touching the floor.

The king snorted. "I want to meet the leader of these rioters, Kretabasa. Bring him to me."

Stunned, Kretabasa said haltingly, "Very well, Your Majesty."

Kretabasa rode away from the palace filled with anxiety. When he arrived at the battlefield outside the palace gates, he shouted his request to meet the leader of the invaders. Kretabasa's words echoed and reverberated throughout the battlefield until they finally reached Panji's ears.

Panji squinted when he saw Kretabasa, searching for him.

"You want to see me?" Panji put his hands on his hips and leaned forward.

Kretabasa looked at Panji, baffled at his changing expressions. Sometimes Panji glared at him wildly, his lips curved in a sneering grin; the next moment, his eyes filled with melancholy and his mouth settled in a shy smile. Kretabasa asked, "Are you the leader of these rioters?"

"I am the leader of this army," Panji taunted. "Do you want to have a one-on-one duel with me?"

"The king of Bali wants to meet you," Kretabasa replied calmly. "Please follow me."

"Did you think that I would just leave my brave soldiers in the middle of a battle? No! I must fight even more valiantly than they do!"

"Do you think the king's invitation is for a social visit?"

"That is your king's business! But I'm not going to stand idle, while my soldiers are in combat, wielding their swords!"

Kretabasa, discerning Panji's point, shouted orders to the Balinese army to stop fighting. His order was heeded by both sides of the warring forces. The two opposing sides broke away from one another and retreated to join their respective leaders.

Panji's company gathered under a tree about a stone's throw away from the palace gate, where they could observe the crowd from a distance.

The Balinese army gathered in front of the palace audience hall in anticipation of Panji's arrival to meet the king, but it turned out that the king was already waiting for the attackers' leader by the palace gate, guarded by three lines of guards.

Panji jumped off his horse and slowly approached the king. When he was a few yards away, Panji bowed respectfully.

Panji's good looks and comportment took the king by surprise. He relaxed and said, "It seems that you still have manners." Panji's courtesy puzzled the king. He asked, "What's your name, and where do you come from?"

"My name is Kelana Jayengsari, and I come from nowhere," Panji answered and bowed again.

"Why do you attack my kingdom?"

"I want to fight, Your Majesty. Hopefully, you will take my life."

Perplexed, the king studied Panji. He had never met a young man who was so polite, yet so threatening.

"Very well, young man," the king said, shaking his head, "I accept your challenge. Get ready!"

The men in the king's guard had listened attentively to the conversation between Panji and the king. They now formed a circle around the two men who were preparing to fight.

Likewise, Panji's men formed a second circle, about a meter or two behind the first.

The rest of the soldiers from both sides who had been watching from a distance, walked closer towards the fighting circle.

Several brave Balinese commoners, who had not fled the city during the invasion, climbed trees to better watch the fight between their king and the invader. They seemed to regard the contest like a cockfight, a favorite pastime. In the middle of the circle, the two fighters stood ready to compete.

"Do you choose to fight barehanded or with a weapon, young man?" the king asked.

"I will leave that for Your Majesty to decide," Panji replied and bowed again.

"All right, we will fight barehanded. If I lose, you can take control of this kingdom. But if *you* lose, we will strip you and your men and parade you to the town square to be stoned. Do you agree?"

"I agree, Your Majesty."

Then, the two men of equal stature but unequal age started to fight.

Although the king was no longer young, he was still quite agile for his age. His punches were fast and targeted. His kicks were often quick and unexpected. But finally, his age did catch up with him. After throwing more than ten punches, only one blow grazed Panji's forehead. The ring on the king's finger scraped Panji's brow, drawing blood. Of the five kicks he executed next, only one hit Panji's arm. The king's anklets scratched Panji's arm and a few blood droplets splattered.

Prasanta watched closely and saw Panji's wounds. He studied the king's ring and anklets, which seemed too large to be mere jewelry. Prasanta worried that the ornaments might be weapons and very well contain poison.

Watching how Panji simply dodged the king's attacks without ever countering, Prasanta became even more concerned. The longer the fight lasted, the more dangerous it was for Panji. If the ring and anklets were indeed poisonous, the poison would have time to spread throughout Panji's body.

Prasanta pushed into the front row. After making sure that Panji saw him, Prasanta pulled out Angreni's scarf, the one the handmaid had wrapped Angreni's jewelry in. Prasanta had kept the scarf after giving the jewelry to her parents. Prasanta now tossed the scarf into the circle. It fluttered for a moment before gliding to the ground.

Seeing the scarf, Panji's expression immediately changed. His desire to die nobly on the battlefield awakened. He now attacked the king fiercely. Without considering his safety, Panji's repeated quick punches and kicks were too difficult for the king to avoid. When Panji rammed his head into the king's chest, the completely unexpected maneuver made the king stagger and fall. The dust rising from the ground celebrated his fall.

Thundering cheers from Panji's company filled the air.

Prasanta ran to Panji, who was picking up Angreni's scarf. His eyes brimming with tears, he kissed the piece of silk. Then, his body suddenly stiffened, and he fell sideways with his arms stretched out. Prasanta was now certain that Panji had been poisoned, and that the poison had spread through his body.

"Tunggulwulung, hurry!" Prasanta shouted. "Find the medicine man! Panji has been poisoned!" When he tried to lift Panji, two soldiers rushed to his aid. The three of them carried their leader away from the crowd. They rushed Panji to the closest house and lay him on the bed. A moment later, several of his men were gathered around him.

One of Panji's soldiers well-known for his medical skills arrived. The medic's own wounds did not prevent him from helping the prince.

He checked Panji's eyes, tongue, and wrist, then sank into silence, shaking his head in despair. The anxious people surrounding Panji lowered their gaze, dismayed.

The battle in front of the palace had flared up again. Even though the Balinese king had been carried into the palace unconscious, a few of his soldiers refused to hand over the palace to the invaders and continued the fight.

But the majority of the Balinese soldiers honored the king's pact: "If I lose, you can take control of this kingdom." These remaining Balinese soldiers sat cross-legged, facing the palace, waiting for the king's orders, while the dead soldiers were removed to nearby residents' yards or carried home by their relatives.

Only two of Panji's soldiers had been badly injured and were being treated by their comrades.

Panji's condition had not changed; he lay still, beyond help. Only his breathing indicated that he was still alive. Wiranata closed his eyes and pressed his lips tightly together as he repeatedly dropped his head into his hands. Everyone sat in silent bewilderment.

Suddenly, a middle-aged woman who looked like a handmaid entered the room. She bowed and said, "My Lady sent me to give you this." She handed Wiranata a cup of thick green liquid. "My Lady said to rub this liquid all over your leader's body, but reserve a little. Add some water to the reserve and have your leader drink it once he regains consciousness." The handmaid bowed. "May your leader be well soon."

Wiranata studied the middle-aged woman carefully from head to toe. "Thank you, emban, I accept your lady's gift. Please give her our greetings and gratitude."

"Yes, Raden, I will convey your message to Her Royal Highness Princess Andayaprana."

"Andayaprana." Wiranata repeated the name out loud, and the others repeated it silently in their hearts.

Wiranata gave the cup to the medicine man.

The man studied the cup for a moment, then dipped his finger into the liquid and licked it. Then he nodded. He smeared the thick green liquid all over Panji's body, especially on his chest and stomach. The liquid smelled strong and had a warming effect. Panji's face slowly regained its color. When Panji regained consciousness, the medicine man diluted the remaining liquid and gave it to Panji to drink. Then he asked Panji to lie down again.

Panji began perspiring profusely. Sweat poured from his face, neck, and underarms. Seeing that Panji was getting better, Wiranata, Prasanta, and Tunggulwulung almost simultaneously heaved a sigh of relief.

"His Majesty the All-Wise King does not break promises!" someone shouted from outside. "Please gather in front of the palace!" The hawker repeated the announcement three times. After exchanging glances with Wiranata, Tunggulwulung said, "I will take half of our men and go to the palace."

In front of the palace, General Kretabasa and some hundred soldiers were waiting for their conqueror. When Tunggulwulung, escorted by fifty soldiers, approached him, Kretabasa said, "You are not the leader of this army."

"I am not. I represent him. Your king's ring and anklets are great weapons indeed." Tunggulwulung did not hide his anger.

"Is your leader still alive?"

"Of course he is still alive," Tunggulwulung retorted. "He is now busy thinking about what to do with all of your king's wives."

Silence enveloped the palace's front yard.

Finally, Kretabasa said, "I can only discuss kingdom matters with your leader."

"Do you think our men are tired of fighting? We're not, not at all. We're still ready to destroy the palace."

Another moment of silence ensued.

"I am the leader of the attack." Panji suddenly appeared at Tunggulwulung's side. He was pale, but otherwise recovered.

"Yes, I remember you," said Kretabasa. "As a representative of His Majesty the King, I am to hand over the kingdom to you."

"What proof will you give that Bali has surrendered to me?"

"Aren't my words enough?"

"Of course not!" Panji snorted. "As proof of your kingdom's concession, I demand that you hand me the most beautiful flower in the kingdom."

"The most beautiful flower?"

"Are you so ignorant that I have to explain what I mean by the most beautiful flower?"

During another thick silence that cloaked the surroundings, Kretabasa turned and walked towards the palace gate.

Panji shouted after him, "The most beautiful flower in the kingdom is named Andayaprana!"

Kretabasa paused briefly, then quickly continued through the palace gate.

Panji's entire army of one hundred men was now on the scene and, without further delay, began to disarm the defeated Balinese army. The Balinese soldiers handed over their weapons without saying a word. Panji ordered them to leave, and they moved in groups out of the palace courtyard, empty-handed.

Kretabasa appeared in the company of Andayaprana, the crown princess of the Bali kingdom. He said, "I hereby hand you the crown princess as proof of the Bali kingdom's capitulation."

Panji walked over to Andayaprana. Standing in front of her, Panji said softly, "It is a great honor to take with me such a beautiful and virtuous crown princess."

For a long time, the silent Balinese princess looked down. When she finally raised her head, she said, "Are you taking me with you, Raden?"

"Yes, I'm taking you with me, my dear," Panji answered. "You saved my life, so I want you to always be with me."

"You don't owe me anything," Andayaprana said. "I gave you the antidote because you deserve it. All I want is for you to forgive my father, the king."

"I would like to check on the king's condition," Panji said. "Please take me to your father, dear." Both of them entered the palace, followed by their guards. Panji said to his men, "Everything here is now ours. Don't destroy what belongs to us."

Outside the palace, Kretabasa stood in deep thought with his arms crossed. He truly hoped that Andayaprana would capture Kelana's heart. If Kelana married her, the situation in the Bali kingdom would improve. As an experienced commander, Kretabasa had noticed the invader's potential. If he became the king of Bali, with Andayaprana as his queen, the kingdom would prosper.

Kretabasa was still pondering when Prasanta and Wiranata entered the gate. As someone who was now a member of a conquered kingdom, Kretabasa bowed respectfully.

"Where are Raden Kelana Jayengsari and Her Royal Highness Andayaprana?" Wiranata asked.

"Please go to the inner room." Kretabasa pointed with his thumb toward the palace hall. "The servant who is posted there will show you to the king's royal chamber. I'm sure that Raden Kelana and Her Highness will be there."

Inside the palace, the princesses had burst into sobs when they heard that their king had been defeated. They realized that they would soon have to endure their conquerors' brutality. The king's wives gathered in one room on their own initiative. The forty beautiful women embraced each other, crying.

Tunggulwulung, accompanied by fifty soldiers, found the palace's storehouse and some of the king's treasure rooms. The other soldiers, who wandered around the palace, happened upon the room where the king's wives were hiding.

"It looks like we are going to have some fun soon enough," said a soldier, pointing at the closed door. "It sounds like this is where the king's wives are."

"Raden Panji — I mean, Raden Kelana Jayengsari — warned us not to destroy our own property," said another soldier, tilting his head, trying to discern the voices behind the closed door.

"Ah, we won't hurt them," the first soldier said, grinning and flaring his nostrils. "We will caress them with great tenderness." His long face made him look like a horse.

"Your hands are rougher than jackfruit skin; how can you be gentle?"

"My hands are rough, but my 'third hand' is smoother than a cucumber!" jeered the horse-faced soldier.

"I don't believe you have a smooth cucumber."

"Why are you being so annoying?"

"You started the argument!"

"All right, all right."

"I don't want to join in," said his comrade, looking at himself in a mirror on the wall. "Either soft or rough, the wives won't like sweaty bodies smelling of blood. We have to clean ourselves first." His words were enough to suppress his companion's growing lust.

The two soldiers cleaned themselves and had their wounds treated. They were very hungry and thirsty. Since their arrival in Bali, they had only eaten the provisions they had brought from across the strait. After they ate, drowsiness followed, and the two fell asleep.

Waking up refreshed, they remembered what they had set out to do. "Aren't we entitled to enjoy what is ours now?" asked the horse-faced soldier.

"You are right, let's go!" his comrade agreed, excitedly.

The two soldiers hurried to find the room where the king's wives were hiding. Other soldiers, who had overheard their conversation, followed them. Soon, some twenty soldiers were headed in the same direction. But when they reached the door and tried to open it, they found it locked. A soldier climbed up on the windowsill to peek inside. "It's empty! There's no one in there!"

Their disappointment turned into embarrassment when Wiranata and Tunggulwulung suddenly appeared.

Looking at his men's sheepish looks, Wiranata asked, "Are you lusting for the king's wives? Well, I've gathered them in the front room. Only half of them are there; the rest have left the palace."

Wiranata could see that the soldiers clearly didn't understand what he was talking about, so he filled in the story. "I told each wife: 'If you give us the jewelry you wear, you can go anywhere you like. But, if you want to keep your jewelry, you are obliged to serve our soldiers in the same manner you served your king.' Half of the wives gave us their jewelry and left the palace, while the other half chose to keep their jewelry and remain here. I then secretly returned the jewelry to those who had chosen to give it to us and leave the palace. They are good women who deserve to live well outside the palace."

Wiranata continued, "The king's wives who chose to keep their jewelry and stay here are women who love their property more than their honor and freedom. Women like that deserve to be used for your entertainment. But remember, you must not hurt them; on the contrary, you must please them. If I hear a cry of pain or a shout of anger, I will punish you by discharging you from our force. Finally, I say: Before you decide whether to satisfy your lust by having fun with them, or restrain it by doing something more beneficial, please ask guidance from the gods who protect us."

Wiranata's words were enough to discourage half of the soldiers. The other half insisted on having fun with the king's wives, who seemed eager to entertain anyone, as long as they could keep their jewelry and possibly add to it.

Wiranata muttered, "Such women deserve to be treated as an object of entertainment by the soldiers."

Chapter 8

BEHIND THE SILENT ORANGE JASMINE TREE

In his royal chamber, the deposed king of Bali and Panji discussed the kingdom's surrender.

"If Your Majesty does not feel well, we can wait until you are fully recovered." Panji sat next to Andayaprana, while Tunggulwulung and Prasanta were seated a little behind them.

"I feel much better," the king said calmly. He noticed that Andayaprana did not show the slightest fear. The presence of Kretabasa and a few other trusted officials also calmed him. "We can discuss the matters concerning the handover of the kingdom now."

Prasanta, knowing that Panji's mind was still feeble, inched toward him. Whispering, he suggested that Panji delegate the surrendering process to Tunggulwulung.

"I have entrusted this matter to my general," Panji said, inviting Tunggulwulung to step forward.

"All right, then," said the king, "I will direct my question to you, General. What will you do to me and my family after I hand over my kingdom?"

"We will do nothing to you and your family, Your Majesty," Tunggulwulung said.

The king looked at him, puzzled. "I don't understand what you mean."

"You keep your throne, and we will continue our journey to conquer another kingdom," Tunggulwulung explained.

The room became silent. No one dared to speak.

Tunggulwulung's explanations were based on an earlier discussion with Prasanta and Wiranata. When Andayaprana was handed over to Panji as a token of submission, Wiranata immediately ordered several soldiers to quickly gather information about the king's allies. The scouts told Tunggulwulung that the rulers of the northern regions were strong and loyal allies and were currently assembling forces to retake Bali. Tunggulwulung did not want to complicate matters, so he did not convey this information to Panji. Tunggulwulung knew Panji would be only too happy to fight Bali's allies.

Wiranata and Prasanta agreed with Tunggulwulung. They did not want to fight a losing battle. After defeating Bali, they wanted to conquer other weaker regions. Unlike Panji, who fought to die, his three companions fought for a better, more peaceful life on the island of Java, the land they loved.

This peace could be realized by maintaining harmony between Janggala and Kadiri. For the time being, the "disappearance" of Panji and Angreni had reconciled Java's two major kingdoms.

"Thank you, Kelana Jayengsari." The king was sad that he'd lost the battle as well as his daughter.

But Panji's attention was directed to Andayaprana. Feeling Panji's eyes resting on her, Andayaprana turned to him. Their eyes met. Andayaprana's eyes reminded Panji of Angreni's. He rose brusquely and strode out of the room. Andayaprana followed him. She had started to feel comfortable in Panji's presence, and she wanted to know why Panji had suddenly left her.

"Kretabasa," said the king of Bali, "announce to all the people in the Bali Kingdom that I am still their king."

The general nodded excitedly then prostrated. But he was not going to make the announcement to the people just yet. It was more important to first inform the king's loyal allies in the northern regions and ask them to cancel their plans to attack the conquered Bali Palace.

———•———

Wiranata and two soldiers had set about investigating Kebotendas's whereabouts in Bali. They started with a clue that the palace gatekeeper had given them. From the gatekeeper, they learned about an envoy sent by Janggala's king. At the time of the battle, Kebotendas was living on the outskirts of the capital. But by the time Panji had conquered the Bali kingdom, Kebotendas had moved.

"When did your guest leave?" Wiranata asked the woman in charge of the inn where Kebotendas had stayed.

"When the news broke that the king had handed over his daughter to the invaders, my guest paid his bill and left," said the woman. "He didn't tell me where he was going, sir."

"Did he have any visitors?" Wiranata probed.

"I never saw any of his friends. But sometimes, he did spend time at the food stall at the end of the road." The woman gestured with her thumb.

After thanking her, Wiranata and the two soldiers visited the eatery. The owner did not add anything to their knowledge and did not know where Kebotendas had gone.

Wiranata and the soldiers were about to leave the food stall, when a boy approached them. "Sir, are you a friend of Tendas?" When Wiranata nodded, the boy continued, "He once showed me his kris. He said the king of Bali and the *adipati*, regional governor, of Blambangan were familiar with it."

"Did you say the adipati of Blambangan?" Wiranata raised his eyebrows. Blambangan was an autonomous region within the kingdom of Janggala.

"Yes, sir, the adipati of Blambangan, who is ruling the eastern coastal region of Java. I'm sure I heard him correctly."

"Thank you, that's very valuable information." Wiranata and the soldiers turned to leave.

"Pardon me, sir," said the boy. "Tendas always gave me a few coins whenever I gave him valuable information."

"Oh!" Wiranata gave the boy some change, and the boy happily scurried away.

"Do you believe him?" asked one of the soldiers skeptically.

"No, but since we have no other information, we have no other choice but to check out what he says. We will try to find Kebotendas in Blambangan."

⊢—•—⊣

The news that Panji would not occupy Bali quickly spread throughout the kingdom, causing the king's allies to respect the conqueror and discouraging them from defending the king. The king's allies also knew that it was the king's behavior that made the kingdom weak. The king's sons and daughters were also critical of their father's behavior.

Contrary to the belief of most Balinese, Andayaprana did not feel repressed as a captured princess; instead, she pitied her captor, Raden Kelana Jayengsari.

The first time Andayaprana felt pity for Raden Kelana was when she tried to follow him after he had left the king's chamber so suddenly during the conversation between the king and Tunggulwulung. Unable to find him, Andayaprana instinctively went out to the garden to breathe some fresh, evening air after being in her father's stuffy chamber for such a long time. In the garden, the fragrance of the orange jasmine tree lured her.

But under the orange jasmine tree, she saw Raden Kelana with his head bowed.

Slowly stepping closer, Andayaprana first heard him talking. Then she heard him sing. His voice was filled with deep sorrow.

The pale moon lit the hills behind the palace and added to the sorrowful mood. Andayaprana remembered sad moments in her own life. The saddest one was when her mother left her forever. She knew that her mother had suffered greatly before she died. Her mother could not bear the pain the king inflicted upon her almost daily by sleeping with beautiful girls in the room that was supposed to be used only for their marital bed.

The memory made Andayaprana weep.

"Don't cry, my dear Ndaya," Panji suddenly appeared before Andayaprana. "Let all the sorrow be mine."

Ndaya. That was the name her mother had affectionately called her. Startled, Andayaprana hurriedly wiped her tears. "I apologize for bothering you, Raden," she said anxiously.

"You didn't bother me at all, absolutely not. But you did make me sad."

"I've made you sad?"

"Your face, especially your eyes, remind me of my wife, who —" Panji's voice faltered, and he wept.

"Shh, Raden." Andayaprana held him in her arms, trying to calm him. Panji wept for a long time in Andayaprana's embrace.

Kretabasa, out searching for Raden Kelana in the garden, caught sight of the two, comforting each other in their sorrows. The general paused, then turned and walked away with a faint smile on his lips.

The reports about Raden Kelana refusing the Bali throne and his close relationship with Bali's crown princess, Andayaprana, became the talk of not only the entire palace but also of the entire kingdom.

One morning, Panji entered the chambers of the Bali king, who was still recovering and resting. Panji said, "Along with my brothers and soldiers, I would like to say goodbye."

"I have no right to prevent you from leaving, Raden." By now, the king considered Panji more a son than his conqueror. "Where are you going?"

"I am going to Blambangan," Panji said. "I ask your permission to take Ndaya with me."

"Andayaprana is yours," said the king. "Of course you must take her wherever you go. True to our custom, tomorrow, I will send you off with a royal procession."

"If so, we will be waiting at the city square for the Balinese royal procession, Your Majesty," Panji said and left the room.

———•◦•———

As planned, the following day, Panji's troops were in the city square preparing to leave Bali, the kingdom they had conquered but not overthrown. One hundred horsemen, dressed much more elegantly and smartly than when they first arrived in Bali, were neatly lined up.

Tunggulwulung was in the front line, with Prasanta, Wiranata, and Panji behind him. The Balinese people congregated around the grassy field of the town square to hail the conqueror whose greatness and wisdom they admired.

In the distance, they could see the approaching procession with Andayaprana inside the royal carriage. As was custom when honoring a royal guest, an elegantly decorated elephant followed the carriage. Kretabasa gracefully rode the elephant.

"Raden Kelana Jayengsari," Kretabasa said when he arrived in front of Panji, who welcomed the procession. "On behalf of the king of Bali, we hereby hand over Her Royal Highness Andayaprana to you as a sign of our trust in your wisdom and your accompanying army. We also hand over the royal carriage she rides in and the elephant guarding it."

Panji bowed. "General Kretabasa, I hereby receive my dear wife Ndaya along with the royal carriage and the elephant escorting it."

"We also entrust you with her younger brother," Kretabasa added softly, "who could not be separated from his sister after their mother died."

Panji beckoned to a young teenager standing next to the royal carriage. "Young man, what's your name?" Panji asked kindly.

The teenager approached Panji. "My name is Kudanatpada, Raden Kelana," he replied shyly.

Panji said, "Perhaps you'd prefer to take care of your father, who is not very well, instead of joining me in war."

"No, Raden, I want to accompany my dear sister Ndaya, even if I have to go to war," Kudanatpada answered.

Panji thought for a moment, then said, "Well, if that's what you want, and as long as you're ready to live a hard live, you can come along, young man."

Kudanatpada grinned, bowed, and cheerfully ran back to his sister waiting in the carriage. Panji saw Kudanatpada hand his sister a box wrapped in white cloth. Panji had seen that box before, in Andayaprana's room. When she took a book from the box, he had glanced at the letters on the cover: *Kudasrenggara*, it was a religious book written on lontar leaves.

The coachman, Kretabasa, and their convoy of two hundred horsemen returned to the palace after watching Panji's departure to Blambangan.

Panji's small army now looked more powerful. His soldiers sat straight, mounted on gallant war horses. Tunggulwulung rode the elephant. Panji sat next to Andayaprana in the royal carriage. Prasanta became the coachman, accompanied by Wiranata, while Kudanatpada rode Prasanta's horse right behind them.

After crossing the Bali Strait for the second time, the convoy traveled to Blambangan on a route not commonly used by merchants and travelers. By taking the alternative, less-traveled route, the journey would become much longer, but they deliberately chose to go this way to avoid attention.

The small army was also waiting for the return of the two scouts they had sent to Blambangan over the more common, faster route. The two scouts, after changing from their uniforms to commoner's clothes, had been sent to observe and determine the right time and place to attack. The scouts knew not to ride side by side, but rather to follow each other at a distance so they could help one another if trouble arose.

Andayaprana sat next to Panji as befitted a wife who served her husband. She had begun to think of herself as Panji's wife not when she was handed over during the procession at the city square, but earlier, when Panji had wept in her arms. After the intimate incident in the garden, they had gone into Andayaprana's room, holding hands and Panji had spent the night with her.

Andayaprana had never been in a relationship with a man. When she fell asleep next to Panji that night, it didn't feel any different than when she fell asleep beside Kudanatpada, her younger brother. She expected that she and Panji would sleep soundly until the morning light woke them up. Instead, she had been awakened by a caress. When she opened her eyes, Panji was sitting up next to her, stroking her long black hair.

Andayaprana sat up and faced Panji. Holding her eyes with his, Panji gently took off her necklaces and pendants. Andayaprana's now unadorned neck and chest revealed her radiant skin.

Panji was about to remove the cloth covering her lower body, when Andayaprana gently took his hand and said, "I will surrender my chastity to Raden alone." Trembling slightly, she added, "but not now."

Panji was a little surprised. But Angreni had also refused him at first, a refusal that had only made him worship her. He lay back down next to Andayaprana, who was still sitting up beside him.

Putting her jewelry back on, Andayaprana said, "I can only imagine how wonderful it will be to make love with you once we know each other better and have closed the distance that still separates us. I can only imagine how elated I will feel when I offer you my honor."

Panji closed his eyes. He heard Andayaprana leave the room.

Outside the room, Andayaprana became aware of how much she loved Raden Kelana. She realized he not only desired her body, but also wanted her love. The fact that he had responded calmly and politely to her refusal was indisputable evidence.

———◆———

By the time Panji's company set up camp south of Blambangan, news of the conquest of the Bali kingdom by a man named Kelana Jayengsari and his army had reached the adipati of Blambangan. The adipati also heard that Kelana Jayengsari intended to conquer other areas near Bali. But because the spies he had planted at the border had not reported any enemy movement, the adipati saw no need to safeguard his region.

Chapter 9

THE CLAMOR OF CONQUERED FLOWERS

Dressed as peasants, Sekartaji and Gunungsari left the Kadiri palace on horseback. They followed the bank of the Brantas River before crossing on a ferry. When they arrived in Janggala, they entrusted their two horses to a stable near the market.

At the market, Sekartaji bought a woven bamboo basket and filled it with spices. She then imitated the way merchants carried their merchandise in the market. As a crown princess accustomed to mingling with commoners, Sekartaji had no trouble acting as a spice peddler. Meanwhile, Gunungsari bought a collection of kitchen utensils used to make herbal medicine. Disguised as a husband-and-wife team who sold spices, they headed — as planned — for Panji's residence.

"Sir! Madam! We have all kinds of spices: ginger, cutcherry, galangal, turmeric — all thinly sliced and dried!" Sekartaji hawked loudly outside the gate of Panji's estate. "We also have all kinds of medicinal herbs!"

"Just go directly to the kitchen," shouted the estate gardener, who was cutting the grass in a deserted front yard.

Sekartaji and Gunungsari thanked the gardener and entered Panji's mansion. A few moments later, they were engaged in a bantering conversation with the handmaids and servants, interspersed with typical jokes amongst village women. Sekartaji and Gunungsari learned that Panji's household was mourning the death of their master. The household staff said that it was believed that Panji had drowned at sea. But, they said, Panji's body was missing along with his wife's corpse.

"His wife's corpse?" Sekartaji asked a handmaid who was sorting through dried slices of ginger. "Are you saying that his wife died before the storm?"

"That's right," the handmaid whispered. "His wife, Angreni, was killed by her husband's brother. Don't tell anyone; it's a secret."

"Killed? What did she do wrong?"

"If you want to know more, you need to go to the prime minister's house. Angreni was Patih Kudanawarsa's daughter." The handmaid looked closely at Sekartaji. "Say, why do you look as beautiful as a princess?"

"Ah, you are flattering me," Sekartaji said, putting away some coins. Even though she had not applied any of the usual salves and powders to enhance her appearance and instead had smeared some charcoal on her cheeks and neck, Sekartaji still looked beautiful.

After thanking their customers, Sekartaji and Gunungsari excused themselves and left, followed by the curious eyes of Panji's servants, who wondered who the handsome couple was.

They were not far from Panji's residence when they heard someone calling out.

"Wait!" The estate gardener caught up with them. Pointing an accusing finger at them, he asked, "Who are you really?"

"We are a husband-and-wife team of peddlers who sell spices and herbal medicine," Gunungsari said guardedly.

"I don't believe you," the man said. "Tell me the truth, or I will tie you up and report you to the authorities."

"Excuse me," Gunungsari replied politely. "We don't like being tied up." He and Sekartaji turned around and resumed walking.

Furious at being rebuffed, the gardener lunged at Gunungsari.

Gunungsari had expected this and easily dodged the attack. But when the gardener tried to attack him again, Gunungsari retaliated and struck the gardener on the back of his neck. The gardener fell to his knees.

Gunungsari gently dragged the gasping man to a shady tree and said, "I don't like to be seen fighting in the middle of the road." Sekartaji picked up the gardener's hat, lying in the road, and joined them.

Brother and sister offered the man a drink from their bamboo canteen. At first, the gardener shook his head, but when he saw Sekartaji and Gunungsari drinking from it, he shyly nodded when they offered it to him a second time.

"Kang, why did you attack us?" Gunungsari asked with a smile.

"We have become very vigilant since the kidnapping of our master's wife," the gardener said. "We thought you were evil spies."

"We are not evil spies, but we're not really peddlers either," Sekartaji confessed.

As the three of them talked beneath the shady tree, Sekartaji and Gunungsari learned that Panji's wife had indeed been killed by Brajanata, just as the handmaid had told them.

"If you want to know exactly what happened, you need to visit the royal physician and see Sumbita there," the gardener said.

"Sumbita?"

"Yes, she is the handmaid who knows exactly what happened during the murder. I can take you to her."

"All right, thank you, Kang," Sekartaji said, rising. "Here are a few coins for you. Please don't tell anyone about our meeting. Trust me, we are not bad people."

Accompanied by Panji's gardener, Sekartaji and Gunungsari continued their journey to the Janggala capital. The gardener led them straight to Usada Hall, where the royal physician lived and worked. Then the gardener bade them farewell.

The hospital was actually a house, though larger and taller than the surrounding houses. At the entrance, two uniformed soldiers checked Sekartaji and Gunungsari before letting them in.

Inside the facility, many soldiers and women dressed like court servants walked around. Usada Hall looked like a hospital managed directly by the palace.

Onengan — Panji's sister and daughter of the Janggala king — mingled among the women. Clearly there was no visible caste barrier between the princess and the servants. No one hesitated to talk to Onengan. Sometimes, they even burst into laughter in her presence, only to then quickly cover their mouths.

Onengan was helping to carry an old, skinny woman on a bamboo stretcher to a room when Sekartaji and Gunungsari politely approached her.

"My Lady, may we visit Sumbita, our relative?" Sekartaji asked.

Surprised, Onengan eyed the two people who had respectfully engaged her.

"Are you Sumbita's relatives?"

"Yes, My Lady," Gunungsari answered. He felt attracted to this unknown girl who looked like a princess.

Onengan set aside the bamboo stretcher. "If you are indeed Sumbita's relatives, then tell me the reason she is being treated by the royal physician at Usada Hall."

"She was wounded while defending her mistress against the murderous attack of a palace representative," Gunungsari whispered.

Onengan nodded before putting a finger to her lips and quietly inviting them to follow her.

Sekartaji glanced meaningfully at Gunungsari. He understood her message: To protect their identities, Sekartaji did not want Onengan to be present during her visit with Sumbita.

"My Lady, may I ask you something?" Gunungsari asked to prevent Onengan from following Sekartaji into Sumbita's room.

"Go ahead," said Onengan, as she stopped and faced Gunungsari, "as long as it is not about the tragedy that recently befell Sumbita."

"That's a pity." Gunungsari casually moved closer to Onengan and held her eyes. "I wanted to ask what you know about the court representative who killed Sumbita's mistress."

"I don't know anything about that." Onengan turned her head. Gunungsari's intense staring embarrassed her. She also wondered why his rudeness did not anger her.

They stood, not speaking.

"What city are you from?" Onengan asked suddenly.

"I come from a village," Gunungsari answered cautiously.

"There are no villagers with clean nails like the two of you," Onengan said sharply.

Gunungsari, impressed by the girl's keen observation, forgot his promise to Sekartaji to keep their identities a secret. He retorted with a cocky smile, "If you like, I'll take you to meet my parents and introduce you to them so that you no longer need to ask what city I come from!"

Gunungsari's flirtatious behavior caused Onengan to turn quickly and leave. She felt uncomfortable in the presence of a man who was dressed like a peasant but who behaved like a wanton, entitled nobleman.

Before Onengan disappeared around the corner, Gunungsari shouted, "I'll come back and look for you, my dear!"

———•—•—

Panji's company had camped overnight at the border of Janggala and Blambangan. The men were preparing their weapons to attack the region's capital.

Only a few kepels remained. Because the weapon was made with gunpowder, a compound imported from China and not widely known in Java, it took time to make more.

Although the idea to attack Blambangan was originally Wiranata's, who believed that Kebotendas was hiding in this eastern coastal area of Java, Prasanta was worried that the Janggala army would come to Blambangan's aid, because Blambangan was a region within the

Janggala Kingdom. Tunggulwulung, on the other hand, believed that Janggala would not support Blambangan because the Janggala court was too preoccupied with the loss of their crown prince and the hundreds of soldiers who had accompanied him. Their loss was so great, they would not pay attention to anything that was happening outside of the capital.

In the end, everyone agreed to attack Blambangan.

———•◦•———

When the two scouts arrived at the capital of Blambangan, they parted ways to find out how prepared Blambangan was for an attack.

One scout mingled among court officials who frequented a popular eatery in the city. The other infiltrated the main market and its merchants at the outskirts of the city. After a few days, the scouts reconvened at an inn.

"The Blambangan authorities already know that we conquered the kingdom of Bali," the first scout said.

"Even the merchants know that we're now ready to attack their capital," the second scout said. "It seems that the merchants have sharper eyes than the authorities."

"The authorities did not seem interested in defending their region if it were attacked. Instead, they plan to save themselves by leaving the city."

"The merchants even sent a representative to persuade the adipati to surrender to the conqueror they know as Kelana."

They ended their conversation and returned immediately to Panji's camp. The scouts proposed that Panji announce his army's arrival by shooting fire arrows and throwing kepel on the road leading to the town center. The people who resided at the adipati's mansion might see the fires or at least hear the explosions. Of course, the perfect time for the attack was right after nightfall so that the commotion would attract people's attention.

Panji's army only had to use this bluffing tactic for one night, because it had an immediate impact on the region's elders. At midnight, the adipati of Blambangan called a meeting of the region's leaders.

When the adipati asked the most respected elder amongst them for his opinion, Tumenggung Dira answered, "We certainly don't want to sacrifice our lives in vain while there are better options."

"And what better options would those be, Tumenggung?" the adipati asked.

"Before I give you the options, let me share some news I heard from an ally of the king of Bali. When Kretabasa, the general of the Bali kingdom's army, found out that Kelana's troops had attacked them, he deployed five hundred soldiers to intercept Kelana's men, and stationed another five hundred to defend the palace. Before doing that, he had sent two hundred soldiers to crush the invaders when they first arrived at the port. And what happened? Those twelve hundred soldiers were nothing against Kelana's elite forces. Kelana's attacking company still advanced and easily took control of the Bali palace.

"The royal officials and the commoners were convinced that Kelana and his company would subjugate the kingdom of Bali, and Kelana would proclaim himself the king. But this was not the case." Tumenggung paused for a moment. "When the king handed over his beautiful daughter, Kelana simply took his leave with the princess."

Tumenggung let his news sink in for a moment. "So instead of fighting the war, I opt to hand over one of your daughters to Kelana as a token of Blambangan's concession. I'm certain that when he sees your daughter, Kelana will take her and leave."

"Now wait a minute, Tumenggung," said the adipati of Blambangan incredulously. "Are you suggesting that I hand over one of my daughters as an 'offering' to be raped by Kelana, or maybe even by his soldiers?"

"Oh, please, forgive me," Tumenggung quickly responded. "I neglected to tell you one more important thing. Kretabasa told his allies that when Kelana is in the presence of a beautiful girl, he acts like a child. He saw for himself how the Balinese crown princess comforted Kelana, who was crying like a spoiled child whining for his mother to carry him. The latest news I heard is that Kelana has made the Balinese crown princess his wife."

Deep silence cloaked the midnight meeting.

The adipati of Blambangan's voice broke into the night, "Tomorrow afternoon, I want you to take my daughter Citrasari to Kelana's camp. I will dress her up well to show that she is not an ordinary girl. Escort her with five hundred fully armed soldiers to show that we are not afraid of war but we prefer peace."

The next afternoon, the beautiful Lady Citrasari, dressed in her finest silk clothes and adorned with pure-gold jewelry, was taken to Panji's camp, escorted by five hundred fully armed soldiers. The procession was so glamorous that everyone at Panji's camp took notice while it was still some distance away.

Tumenggung Dira, as the leader of the parade, was at the front. They stopped a few yards outside the entrance of Panji's camp. Tumenggung, escorted by four horsemen, slowly approached the camp.

Panji's soldiers, who were already prepared to receive the entourage, immediately ran to meet them.

Tumenggung Dira dismounted and said, "I am here to meet your leader."

One of the soldiers bowed slightly. "Please wait here, sir, while I summon Kelana Jayengsari."

Meanwhile, Tunggulwulung and Prasanta closely watched the movements of the Blambangan cavalcade. The arrival of fully armed troops at the camp was enough to put Tunggulwulung on high alert.

Panji, accompanied by Wiranata, walked out to meet Tumenggung Dira. "Welcome. I am Kelana Jayengsari and this is Wiranata, my representative."

"I am the representative of the adipati of Blambangan. My name is Tumenggung Dira."

"What is the intention behind your coming to our camp with fully armed soldiers?" Wiranata asked.

"We are ordered to hand over the daughter of the adipati of Blambangan as a token of peace," Tumenggung replied.

"Does this mean that the adipati is handing over his region to us?"

"Yes, Raden," Tumenggung Dira said. "After the handover of his daughter, the Blambangan region is yours."

"All right," Wiranata said. "We'll wait here for the handover of the adipati's daughter as a token of his capitulation."

Tumenggung summoned Citrasari, the adipati's daughter, and handed her over, along with a cart of supplies and two handmaids.

"If you'd like to visit the capital now, we are ready to escort you, Raden," Tumenggung Dira said.

"Not now, Tumenggung," Panji said calmly. "Let the adipati run everything as usual. We will stay here for now."

Tumenggung looked relieved. "Then, we will excuse ourselves."

"We have one request," said Wiranata, glancing at Panji. "Please bring your guest, an envoy from the king of Janggala, named Kebotendas, to our camp."

"Certainly, Raden," Tumenggung said. "We will bring the guest here as soon as possible."

Inside Panji's camp, Citrasari was taken to Andayaprana. Both women showed respect for the other and were so careful with their words that their conversation was awkward and stiff. Fortunately, their handmaids helped break the ice with their jokes.

With the gold coins they had brought from Bali and the jewelry they were given from Blambangan, Panji's campsite, within the borders of the Janggala kingdom, had quickly turned into a comfortable place to live — they were protected from the elements, at any rate. With help from the locals, they built a tall, spacious house that had big bamboo columns, woven bamboo walls, and a thatched roof. No one at the camp ever went hungry or thirsty. Panji was grateful to Andayaprana for managing the camp kitchen. The Balinese princess was good at using ingredients that were readily available around the camp. She distributed the food fairly so it could be equally enjoyed by all.

The next day, Tumenggung Dira returned with two soldiers. Tumenggung reported that Kebotendas had indeed stayed as a guest in the region for several days, but when the news of a possible attack by Kelana reached the capital, he had quickly left. "We asked several people who knew Kebotendas where he went, but, unfortunately, no one knew. Please be kind enough, Raden, to forgive our inadequacies."

"I'm sure you have done your best," Wiranata said, with Panji standing silently beside him. "We will continue searching for Kebotendas ourselves."

After being treated to a simple meal at the camp, Tumenggung Dira and his two soldiers said goodbye and returned to Blambangan.

Panji did not immediately return to the camp after he watched Tumenggung Dira leave. Instead, he stood for a long time on the grassy field outside the compound. The conversation between Wiranata and Blambangan's representative had confused him. *Who is Kebotendas? Why is he so important?*

Noticing Panji still standing in the field, Prasanta approached him. "Raden, why don't you come with me and rest inside?"

"Prasanta," Panji sighed wearily, "why am I still alive today?"

"You always fought bravely," Prasanta said. "Even now, you're ready to fight again. The matters of life and death are in the hands of the gods."

"Is there another palace or region nearby, Prasanta?" Panji asked.

"The Nusabarong region is not far from here. Of course we will come along if you want to conquer it."

Panji stroked the kris he always carried and said, "Tomorrow morning, we will conquer the Nusabarong region."

Prasanta bowed. "I will tell the soldiers immediately."

After Prasanta, Wiranata, and Tunggulwulung finalized their detailed plans to attack Nusabarong, the three comrades went to discuss their strategies with Panji, who was in the main house with Andayaprana and Citrasari.

"Raden," said Wiranata, "it will be too much trouble to bring all of our belongings with us for the attack. Our camp has grown — especially since Lady Andayaprana and Lady Citrasari have joined us. Let us just leave everything here along with the women and their handmaids."

"Compared to the region of Blambangan and the kingdom of Bali, Nusabarong has a much weaker defense," Tunggulwulung added. "There is no need to bring all of the soldiers, either; half of them will be enough. We will leave the other half to guard our camp."

"Which means," Prasanta concluded, "that we only need to take fifty men to conquer Nusabarong."

Wiranata, curious about Panji's state of mind, asked, "Panji, what do you think?"

Panji glowered at Wiranata. "All I want is to die honorably, in a battle."

The next day, Panji rode in the front line of a cavalry numbering fifty horsemen. Tunggulwulung rode in the rear, while Wiranata and Prasanta, along with the remaining fifty men, stayed at the camp.

According to Panji's scouts, the news of Panji's advancing army had reached the adipati of Nusabarong, most likely via Tumenggung Dira, and the Nusabarong soldiers were standing in formation along the roadside leading to the capital.

Panji signaled his men to halt when a Nusabarong soldier approached him.

The soldier bowed respectfully. "I have a letter from the adipati of Nusabarong for Raden Kelana."

"I am Kelana Jayengsari," Panji said, while observing his surroundings. It would be impossible to hide an ambush unit on this flat, open countryside. Archers could be easily spotted, and Panji's men, with their metal shields, were prepared to ward off any arrows.

Panji opened the bamboo cylinder and took out a palm leaf scroll with Javanese lettering. After reading the letter, he looked around, as if something bothered him.

Tunggulwulung, who suspected that Panji might have trouble comprehending the letter, immediately rode to his side. "May I assist you, Raden?"

"I do not believe the contents of this letter. I'm worried that I'm misunderstanding the message. Here, you read it." Panji handed Tunggulwulung the scroll.

Tunggulwulung read the scroll carefully several times. Each time he read the letter, his eyebrows lifted higher, and the furrows in his forehead deepened.

"Is it true, Tunggulwulung," Panji asked, "that the letter says that the adipati of Nusabarong surrenders and will hand over his daughters as a token of his concession?"

"Yes, that is correct, Raden," Tunggulwulung said. "It says that the princesses are waiting at the pendapa right now."

"Does that mean we are not going to war against Nusabarong?" Panji looked disappointed.

"Yes, that is correct, Raden," Tunggulwulung repeated. "Instead, you have been challenged to fight and defeat the adipati's daughters."

"To fight and defeat *girls*?" Panji asked quizzically.

"Maybe they are female warriors skilled in combat," Tunggulwulung answered, hiding his smile.

But Panji took Tunggulwulung's joke seriously. He turned to the waiting messenger from Nusabarong and said, "I am ready to go there now. Tell the adipati of Nusabarong and his daughters to prepare for my arrival."

The welcoming reception at Nusabarong was more lavish than Panji and his men had expected. Panji entered the pendapa, which was guarded by only ten soldiers. Tunggulwulung remained vigilant, ready to face any potential traps.

The adipati of Nusabarong was older than the king of Bali and the adipati of Blambangan. Dressed in a loose-fitting garment, he pompously greeted Panji, his conqueror.

"We have announced our surrender as stated in the letter we sent, Raden," the adipati of Nusabarong said as he walked closer to Panji.

"Yes, I have read your letter and understand its content."

"I have prepared my twin daughters to be handed over to you as a token of Nusabarong's capitulation."

"I'll gladly accept the token you offer." Panji eyed a row of beautiful girls standing at the edge of the pendapa. "I can see many beautiful girls here. Which ones do you wish to hand over?"

"The twins who are dressed as soldiers, Raden," the adipati said. "I apologize for needing to tell you that my daughters like martial arts, even though they are the most spoiled among my children. If you don't mind, they would like the experience of fighting you, who is well-known for your fighting skills."

"What a coincidence!" Panji said happily. "I am delighted to be gifted two girls who are tough fighters."

It appeared that the adipati had prepared for the fight in advance. As soon as Panji and the twins took their places on the grassy field in front of the pendapa, the gamelan musicians began playing energetically, adding to the lively atmosphere.

The twin daughters of Nusabarong's adipati immediately attacked Panji with quick and well-aimed moves. Panji fought barehanded against the two young girls. He felt as if he were being attacked by two ruthless young men, instead of two beautiful young girls. He had to apply all of his training to effectively block the attacks from the two girls, who fought as if possessed.

If Panji could have listened in on the conversation the adipati had with his two daughters the day before, he would have prepared himself before accepting the challenge from these two female warriors.

But Panji had no way of knowing that after the adipati of Nusabarong received Tumenggung Dira's message warning about Kelana Jayengsari's plans to invade Nusabarong — as well as Tumenggung Dira's suggestion for solving the problem — the adipati had summoned his twin daughters and said, "My daughters, Sariani and Sariana, tomorrow or the day after, we will have a guest."

"From what I've heard, he is not a guest but an enemy, Father," said Sariani, who had heard rumors of possible attacks by phantom warriors.

"The enemy will be our guest if you both are willing to help your father."

"We are ready to defeat the enemy and force him to behave like a guest," Sariana added firmly.

"These are not ordinary warriors, my daughters," the adipati warned. "They are phantom warriors."

The two girls, who were equally beautiful and fierce, were silent for a moment. They had practiced martial arts for many years and were well-known as a pair of goddesses of death. Many men had died at the hands of these two girls. However, they had no other skills besides martial arts, and did not know anything about magic, let alone know how to fight a phantom.

"I will send both of you to Raden Kelana so he becomes our guest, not our enemy." The adipati paused before adding, "Do you understand what I mean?"

Sariani straightened and looked her father in the eye. "You are going to hand us over to the invaders as a token of surrender."

"Raden Kelana is not an ordinary person," the adipati cajoled. "You'll see for yourself; he is very handsome and strong. I will surrender the two of you to him because he's known for treating his women well; but most importantly, I know that you are great fighters and can protect yourselves."

"If we challenge him to a fight and kill him, will you still submit to the dead body of this invader?" Sariana demanded.

"Of course not, my dear." Their father lowered his voice. "If Raden Kelana dies by your hands, I will destroy his leaderless army."

So now, on the grassy field in front of the pendapa, the girls fought Panji for their father's autonomy.

Panji was thoroughly enjoying his fight with the girls. It looked like his wish to die by the hands of his opponent was about to be granted. The girls' aggressiveness enchanted him, and he easily dodged their attacks. He wanted to prolong the fight with the two tigresses, so he never once threw a punch or kick.

The two female warriors never expected Panji to fight like this. They felt belittled when Panji refused to retaliate. Their rage escalated the intensity of their fighting. They had never fought like this before. Typically, their opponents fell after three or four attacks.

But fighting against this enemy leader was completely different; they had attacked him more than a hundred times with all their strength and training, to no avail. They became exhausted from expending so much energy. Against the expectation of everyone watching the fight, both girls suddenly dropped to the ground. Sitting back to back, they panted with frustration, their legs thrashing and their fists pounding the ground.

Panji stood for a moment, looking down at his two distressed opponents. Then he knelt down in front of them, embraced them both, and guided them calmly back into the pendapa.

Thus, the handover ceremony was beyond the expectation of both parties. Four soldiers stayed with Panji at Nusabarong; the others returned to camp.

After three days as a guest of the adipati of Nusabarong, Panji departed, taking Sariani and Sariana to his camp. The twins came with two carts full of household goods, even more than what Citrasari had brought from Blambangan. Panji's departure from Nusabarong with the two conquered girls was celebrated with gamelan and dances that added to the cheerful mood.

Chapter 10

THE SPARKS OF WAR

Exactly one month after Andayaprana left the kingdom of Bali, a messenger arrived at Panji's camp with a letter. The letter was from the king of Bali, asking about his daughter's well-being and requesting that Panji bring Andayaprana to the Bali palace.

Initially, Panji was not interested in going to Bali, but he changed his mind when he got to the end of the letter, which stated that if Panji did not come to Bali, one of Bali's neighbors would attack the Bali kingdom. The attackers apparently knew that the king was still physically ill from his fight against Panji, as well as emotionally ill from losing his beloved daughter.

"We have to visit him, dear Ndaya," Panji said after sharing the letter with Andayaprana.

"I better go there alone, Raden," Andayaprana said quietly. "I only need a few soldiers to accompany me."

"I can take you there, my love," Panji persisted.

"Take me there as a captured princess?"

"No, as my wife, of course."

Panji and Andayaprana said nothing for a long time. Although the dim light hid Andayaprana's expression, Panji could still hear Andayaprana's sigh of relief. He held her and stroked her hair. In between Andayaprana's sighs, Panji, whispering, praised her beauty.

When Panji brought his face closer to Andayaprana's, the girl turned her face away. But when Panji tried to kiss her lips, Andayaprana eagerly welcomed his kiss. Panji folded Andayaprana's willing body in his arms. Gently lying her down on the thick, lacy mat, Panji felt an urgency to continue their lovemaking. Soon, brief, muffled moans and the sound of hurried and passionate breathing spilled into the cold and silent night.

The next day, Panji left for Bali with his entourage: Tunggulwulung; Andayaprana and her younger brother, Kudanatpada; Citrasari, the daughter of the adipati of Blambangan; and the twin daughters from the adipati of Nusabarong, Sariani and Sariana, along with their handmaids.

The two royal carriages and one horse carriage, escorted by fifty horsemen, traveled through the dense forest. The cool, fragrant air and serene atmosphere made the women sleepy.

When the entourage passed a row of angsana trees in full bloom, Panji suddenly ordered the group to stop. He dismounted and strode to one of the blooming angsana trees. Bending over a low, twisted branch covered with the tree's yellow flowers, Panji stroked and kissed the blossoms.

Andayaprana, awakened by the fresh fragrance of flowers, sensed that something was amiss and stepped out of the carriage. When she saw her husband leaning against the tree, she rushed towards him, but before she could reach him, Panji crumpled to the ground. Tears streaming down his cheeks, he shook his head, grappling to support his body.

Andayaprana dropped on her knees and took Panji in her arms. Placing his head in her lap, she held him tightly as she gently caressed him.

The handmaids and other women had woken up. Whispering to each other, they watched Andayaprana and Panji disapprovingly. Public intimacy between a man and a woman — even if they were married — was improper according to Javanese nobility custom.

Citrasari, too, had poked her head out of the carriage window, but she merely watched silently. Finally, Andayaprana managed to help Panji up.

The guard jumped off his horse and ran to help Andayaprana assist Panji to the carriage. Kudanatpada, who was riding beside the guard, hurried to take the reins of Panji's riderless horse.

Back in the carriage, Panji lay helplessly on Andayaprana's lap while she wiped his tears with her scarf. Andayaprana's actions violated the accepted customs in nobility circles and strained the atmosphere. Eventually, Panji fell asleep with his head resting in Andayaprana's lap. He woke up when the carriage rolled across a rocky road.

"Who's taking care of my horse, dear?" Panji asked.

"My brother, Kudanatpada, is taking care of it," Andayaprana soothed. "Just stay here for now and get some rest. When you feel better, you can ride your horse."

———•••———

Back at Panji's camp, Wiranata and Prasanta were on an inspection walk around the property. The grassy field, vast enough to accommodate a hundred grazing buffalo, was now enclosed by a two-meter-high fence. The tents, originally set up simply for shelter from the heat and rain, had been dismantled and replaced by simple bamboo houses with woven palm-leaf roofs. From a distance, the camp looked like a common village, with flocks of chickens busily clucking between the houses. The chickens had been purchased from the nearest market to provide meat and eggs.

"Who are those people, Prasanta?" Wiranata pointed at a group of men.

"They are builders sent by the adipati of Blambangan and the adipati of Nusabarong to remodel the simple houses of our camp into more comfortable villas for their daughters," Prasanta answered.

"Who will pay and feed the builders?" Wiranata asked.

"The adipaties who sent them, of course. The builders brought rice and dried meat, which the handmaids can cook for their meals."

Wiranata and Prasanta silently watched the men at work.

"Do you think Panji has forgotten Angreni?" Wiranata asked suddenly. "After all, he's now accompanied by such beautiful women as Andayaprana, Citrasari, Sariani, and Sariana."

"The battles Raden Panji has fought and the women he obtained as trophies, did fade his memory of Angreni." Prasanta recalled the advice Rara Suci had given him when he visited her in Pucangan two months ago. "But he won't be able to forget her completely until he finds the princess who carries Angreni's reincarnation."

"Of course, no one knows who carries Angreni's reincarnation, right?" Wiranata thought that Prasanta was being too optimistic. Wiranata himself was not interested in the topic of reincarnation.

Prasanta shrugged. "Let's just accompany Raden Panji on his journey. Look at this camp; it has almost turned into a small town. It might become an autonomous region, with a stronghold in its center. This is a sign that Raden Panji's journey will end soon. It means that Angreni's reincarnation is already close to him."

———•◦•———

The sun had almost set when Panji and his entourage entered the palace gate of the Bali kingdom. General Kretabasa, among other royal officials, welcomed them warmly.

Andayaprana and Kudanatpada immediately rushed to their father's chamber. Panji, Tunggulwulung, and Kretabasa followed closely behind.

"I apologize for having caused the king's illness by fighting against him," Panji said to Kretabasa, who sat next to Tunggulwulung. The quick disappearance of daylight at dusk added to the gloomy atmosphere of the meeting.

"Actually, what made him sick was not the fight," Kretabasa said softly, "but rather the shame of being found out by his beloved daughter, Andayaprana, that he used poisonous rings and anklets to fight you." Kretabasa paused. "Now his daughter has become your wife."

"Then there's really nothing to worry about," Panji said, relieved. "We forgave each other before I took Princess Ndaya with me. His Majesty seems to be troubled emotionally, not physically."

Everyone remained silent for a long time. Panji ignored the food on the table; he was preoccupied with finding a pathway to a dignified death. The angsana flowers that had caught his attention on the way to Bali had flooded him again with memories of Angreni. This time, however, the memories came with the understanding that Angreni was dead.

"Who is the king who turned from an ally to an enemy and is now threatening this kingdom?" Panji emphasized the word *threatening*.

"He is not actually a king," Kretabasa clarified. "He's only an adipati who rules over an autonomous region within the Bali kingdom. But his vast territory and strong army have made him king-like."

Panji was amazed. "How could he so easily expand his territory and have such a strong army?"

"It is all because of trade." Kretabasa looked into the distance, then continued, "Our king realized too late that trade is as important as war. Many people have already forgotten the real name of this rich adipati who owns dozens of merchant ships. He is now known as Adipati Burik, the Pocky Adipati, because his face is pockmarked. The region he rules is now known as Kaburikan."

"Take me there, General," Panji said firmly.

Kretabasa gasped and silently bowed his head. Andayaprana had told him that Raden Kelana was mentally disturbed by the death of his first wife. Kelana's eagerness to go to war surprised Kretabasa. *Is going to the battlefield to risk your life the same as betting coins at gambling tables?* Kretabasa concluded that war and death were insignificant to Kelana.

"Can you take me tomorrow to Kaburikan, General?" Panji repeated impatiently.

"Yes, I will," Kretabasa answered. "But right now they are mourning the death of their head priest and are busy conducting the prayer ceremony. People will think badly of you if you attack them while they are in mourning."

"All right, General. Knowing that I will not face any significant resistance has dampened my desire." Panji sighed, disappointed.

"You're welcome to rest here until Kaburikan is out of mourning," Kretabasa persuaded. "Meanwhile, you can enjoy yourself."

———•••———

On the second day Panji was in Bali, he slept late.

Panji's and the king's wives were already in the pendapa. One of them mentioned that Kelana had not awakened yet. The handmaids guessed that he had gone to bed with one of his wives. They tried to guess which one.

"I'm sure he slept with Her Royal Highness Princess Andayaprana," one handmaid said.

"She deserves to sleep with Raden Kelana," another handmaid added.

"No, it couldn't be Lady Andayaprana. I just saw Her Royal Highness alone in her room. She was reading the Kudasrenggara."

"What book?"

"Kudasrenggara."

"How do you know? Can you read?"

"She once told me that she likes to recite from the Kudasrenggara over and over before going to bed."

As usual, the handmaids' conversation soon moved on to another topic.

That afternoon, the palace summoned musicians to entertain Panji and his party. The gamelan accompanied the guests singing happy songs together. There were also fighting competitions and cockfights. The palace was indeed providing Panji with entertainment during his stay there.

In the middle of the festivities, Kusni, the traveler from Perlak, and Tandang, the eldest son of Siwur the gambang-maker, arrived in a carriage from Janggala.

General Kretabasa received the guests in the right wing of the palace.

"We were sent by Her Holiness Rara Suci, the King of Janggala's sister, to retrieve the book of Kudasrenggara," Tandang said after introducing himself and Kusni. Tandang was the spokesperson because he was more fluent in Balinese than Kusni.

"I have heard that the book is in this palace; many priests talk about it," Kretabasa said. "But I can't give it to you because I was not the one who borrowed the book. A court priest, who's currently on a retreat at an unknown location, was the one who borrowed the book."

"May I look at the book for a day or two and read it here?" Kusni, unable to restrain his eagerness to browse through the book, pressured impatiently.

"Before leaving on his retreat, the court priest entrusted the book to the king's daughter, Her Royal Highness Princess Andayaprana, who loves to read. She happens to be here now. Maybe I can ask her to lend this book to…"

"Kusni. My name is Kusni."

———•———

For the next two days, Kretabasa hosted Kusni and Tandang as royal guests. While Kusni intently studied the book of Kudasrenggara, Tandang wandered around town. One of his duties as a spy of the kingdom of Janggala was to make a map of the neighboring kingdoms.

Kusni made notes of the essence of Kudasrenggara. His diligence aroused Kretabasa's curiosity. He went to the room where Kusni studied.

"I am sorry to disturb you," Kretabasa said, bowing slightly, after noticing that Kusni was a little surprised to see him.

"Oh, absolutely not." Kusni pushed away his writing. He invited Kretabasa to sit on the mat with a round table in the middle.

"I am very fascinated by your diligence in reading and writing," Kretabasa said. He rarely saw any Balinese officials read books. More often, he saw them screaming at the cockfighting arena.

"This is a very special book, General."

"About warfare?"

"About a war without arrows and swords."

"I don't understand."

"The battle between good and evil."

"Please, Ki Kusni, enlighten your ignorant host."

"I'm also ignorant, General. That's why I'm reading this book. Let's study together." Kusni slowly turned the lontar leaves. "This book starts at a place from where this entire world is controlled — the place where Mahadewa, the king of the gods, dwells.

"Mahadewa held a meeting with the gods and told them that he intended to create humans. The gods immediately raised their objections. They worried that the humans he created would do more harm than good.

"Mahadewa said that he knew better than any of the gods, and he created a man. He named the man Jaka and introduced him to the gods. Mahadewa ordered the gods to bow in front of Jaka. All of the gods, except for one, obeyed. Umuk refused.

Mahadewa then asked Umuk for the reason of his refusal. Umuk said it was because Mahadewa had created him, Umuk, from a better substance than the human. Mahadewa had created the human from soil, while Umuk had been created from fire.

"Mahadewa was furious when Umuk refused to obey him. He rebuked Umuk and banished him out of his sight.

"Umuk left, but not before he asked Mahadewa's permission to distract and mislead Jaka, to prove that Jaka was indeed inferior."

"Pardon me, Ki Kusni," Kretabasa interrupted, unable to suppress his curiosity. "It seems that the book tells us about the origins of the humans who inhabit this world."

"Let's save our conclusions until we finish the story, General," Kusni answered, smiling. He was pleased that his host was interested.

"Oh, certainly, Ki Kusni. I apologize for interrupting. Please continue."

"Mahadewa gave Umuk permission to distract and mislead Jaka, but Mahadewa did so with a warning: 'As long as Jaka believes in me, performs good deeds, and believes in Judgment Day — the day all lives will end — you will be unable to mislead Jaka.'

"Mahadewa then placed Jaka in a beautiful and comfortable paradise called Svarga Loka. Jaka lived there with everything he could possibly want. Yet despite all of the abundance laid in front of him, he still was not happy. He felt lonely living by himself in Svarga Loka. He wanted another human to be his companion.

"So Mahadewa created another human to be his partner, a woman he named Dara. The two humans, Jaka and Dara, were created differently so they could complement each other.

"Jaka and Dara enjoyed living the life of abundance in Svarga Loka. But although Jaka was no longer lonely, he now had to fulfill Dara's wishes, something he had never experienced before.

"Dara wanted to live forever in Svarga Loka. She felt that she owned this beautiful place and was afraid of losing it. She shared these feelings with Jaka, her mate.

"Umuk, who knew of the couple's worries, immediately approached both of them and confirmed their fears —"

"Pardon me, Ki Kusni. How could a god —"

"Umuk, you mean?"

"Yes, Umuk. How did Umuk know about Jaka and Dara's worries? Did he live among them? Did the three of them live in Svarga Loka?"

"We were told that Umuk was created from fire, right? We cannot hold fire in a cup, but we know it exists; we can feel the heat. Well, in much the same way, Umuk could stay near the husband and wife without being seen."

"Oh, I see. My apologies, I couldn't help but ask."

"There's no problem, General. I am glad that you enjoy this story. Shall I continue?"

"Please, Ki Kusni."

"So Umuk positioned himself inside Dara's ear to affect her hearing, and settled in Jaka's eye to affect his vision.

"Jaka and Dara began to take notice of the plants and animals around them. The plant survived because a young plant replaced the old one; the animal survived because a young one replaced the old one. They began to observe what caused the creation of young plants and young animals. They then tried to imitate the plants and animals around them, hoping that a younger version of themselves would emerge from their actions.

"The desire to stay in Svarga Loka gave them pleasures they had never felt before. The love that developed between them made them worry about losing one another, and that worry made them want to get as close to each other as they possibly could.

"At first, they put their hands together and squeezed them. Then they combined their saliva, uniting their taste buds. Finally, they united the most essential difference they had, their genitals. But the fulfillment of their desires led to resentment and confusion — as well as the loss of their special status as dwellers of Svarga Loka."

"You mean, they lost their privileges?" Kretabasa asked.

"They became equal to the plants and animals, which only decorated paradise temporarily. They were no longer the eternal masters of paradise."

"Oh, I see. Please continue."

"So they became just like plants and animals, which aged and died. Afraid of losing their pleasures, they desired immortality. Immortality meant that when they aged and died, their offspring would be the continuation of their lives. And although they could die and only their bones would remain, their successors would still live and enjoy the pleasures Mahadewa provided in Svarga Loka.

"But Jaka and Dara had degraded themselves. They were now equal to plants and animals. They were no longer Mahadewa's creations that equaled the gods, and more importantly, they had denied the Judgment Day, the day all lives would end. Their rejection had angered Mahadewa.

"The parents of one of Jaka and Dara's great-grandchildren expected their son to become a powerful man. They used all their power, strength, and wealth solely to cultivate the boy's greatness. Their excessive expectations drove the boy to perform better, study harder, and achieve more than a typical child would. As a reward, the parents spoiled him beyond reason. This over-indulgence led the child to evil."

"Wait a moment, Ki Kusni," Kretabasa interrupted. "Did Jaka and Dara's great-grandchildren still live in Svarga Loka?"

"This book doesn't mention anything about their whereabouts. However, if Mahadewa had expelled Umuk from Svarga Loka, it is very possible that they no longer lived there. Like Umuk, Jaka and Dara had angered Mahadewa."

"I see. Please continue."

"Kudasrenggara, the great-grandson of Jaka and Dara, became a strong, smart, and eloquent man. But he loved the world too much and feared losing it.

"Umuk, who liked Kudasrenggara's behavior very much, approached him. Like Umuk, Kudasrenggara considered himself special. Whereas Umuk felt superior to Jaka and Dara — who were created from soil, not fire like him — Kudasrenggara felt superior to other humans because he was a descendant from the highest caste of men, the brahmins. He relished the division of humans into four castes: the *brahmins*, religious leaders and priests; *kshatriyas*, kings and nobilities; *vaishyas*, traders and craftsmen; and *shudras*, peasants and laborers.

"In his opinion, the greatest kind of humans were those closest to Mahadewa. Because the brahmins knew how to please Mahadewa best, they were superior to all others. Kudasrenggara spread his belief that the brahmins were the greatest among human beings to religious leaders throughout the world.

"This belief made religious leaders, the brahmins, approach the most powerful people, the kings. However, in the brahmins' minds, they regarded the kings as only kshatriyas — one level beneath them. Thus, the brahmins did not feel inferior to the kings. Such conviction filled the priests with arrogance.

"Because Kudasrenggara succeeded in spreading his belief, which was Umuk's teaching, among clergy in the world, religion became the cause of more turmoil than any human being."

"Ki Kusni, I know many priests. As far as I know, they conduct themselves properly." General Kretabasa felt uncomfortable that the teachings in the book Ki Kusni was studying humiliated religious leaders.

"So do I, General." Kusni nodded, seemingly concurring with Kretabasa's objection. "I also know many good religious leaders. I think this book only intends to warn us to beware of brahmins who like to be near the people of power."

"Now I am even more curious about the ending of this book. Please continue, Ki."

"Kudasrenggara, who had wanted to live forever, died at the age of forty during a natural disaster. While he and his four wives were vacationing in a mansion at the foot of a hill overlooking the sea, they were hit by a landslide.

"Kudasrenggara had forty-eight children from his four wives. With that many offspring, it seemed that his teachings would never vanish. The youngest child of his fourth wife was the child who suffered the most. Srenggi and his mother were the only survivors of the landslide. They had been buried under furniture and therefore still had air to breathe. Holding Srenggi in her arms, his mother managed to crawl out and solicit help from the locals.

"Srenggi's mother then worked as a household servant and barely earned enough to live on. Even though Srenggi was only ten years old, he felt that he needed to help his mother earn a living. He gathered firewood in the forest and exchanged it for food.

"When Srenggi tried selling the firewood for money instead of exchanging it for food, he was able to earn cash. He asked his mother to quit her job as a household servant to help him sell firewood. People preferred to buy Srenggi's firewood because it lasted longer and lighted easily.

"When the palace's chief of staff entrusted Srenggi with supplying firewood for the royal kitchen, Srenggi became a rich firewood merchant.

"His wealth elevated his status to someone who was close to king. His new social position enabled him to see that the court priests were generally evil because they loved their worldly possessions too much. Srenggi asked the king to be careful with them.

"Because the king felt indebted to Srenggi, whose wood kept the palace kitchen fires burning, he followed the young merchant's advice.

"The change in the king's attitude and behavior upset the priests. They investigated what caused the change and found out that Srenggi was the culprit.

"The priests met Srenggi at his house. They told him ardently that his wealth was nothing compared to Mahadewa's rewards for those who understood how to worship and please him. Only a priest could guarantee people a happy life after death.

"Srenggi responded that Mahadewa would be happy with anything that made his creation happy. Mahadewa did not need his creation to please him. For example, Srenggi was certain to please Mahadewa if the soldiers or house servants ate well because he had provided them with good firewood.

"The priests of the brahmin caste left Srenggi's house, screaming and swearing. They yelled thousands of profanities, as if trying to dirty the walls of the young merchant's house. They gathered people under their influence to attack and burn Srenggi's house.

"But the people who worked for Srenggi and had benefited from the good firewood he supplied defended the firewood merchant. In the end, the evil priests and their followers ran away, frightened.

"The priests, Umuk followers, realized they had to change their tactics. Srenggi, a vaishya, had defeated the brahmins in every way."

Kretabasa straightened his back. The word "vaishya" reminded him of Adipati Burik of Kaburikan, a kshatriya who had a penchant for trade. Before Kretabasa could ask about the importance of the vaishya caste in a kingdom, Kusni said, "The story of Kudasrenggara ends with the re-appearance of Umuk to mislead Jaka and Dara's grandchildren and convince the religious leaders to believe that theirs was the only right way to worship and any other way was wrong. Umuk was happy because all of the priests had followed him even though they practiced various religions in this world. The enemy they feared the most was the group of merchants who believed in the existence of Mahadewa, performed good deeds, and believed in Judgment Day."

"Apart from advice to be wary of religious leaders, this book offers another interesting theory." Kretabasa looked at Kusni, who was stacking the lontar leaves in front of him.

"Hmm, what is that, General?"

"The necessity to cooperate with the merchants."

Kusni paused and scanned Kretabasa's face. "The story in this book is indeed special, General. A good story doesn't instruct its reader to do certain things. The reader is free to interpret it."

After Kretabasa left, Kusni resumed making notes of the essence of the Kudasrenggara to take to the religious leaders in the Perlak kingdom.

———•◦•———

After recuperating for a week at Usada Hall, Sumbita, Angreni's loyal handmaid, was sent home. Now, on the veranda of a simple bamboo house that Sekartaji had rented not far from the hospital, Sekartaji and

Gunungsari, still dressed as spice merchants, met with Sumbita and asked about her plans for her future.

"What are you going to do now, Sumbita?" Sekartaji asked. The story Sumbita had told her about Angreni's death still brought tears to her eyes. She felt guilty without knowing what she had done wrong.

"If I was allowed to leave Usada Hall, it means that I'm well," Sumbita said pensively. "As I told you, I want to follow my dead mistress. There's no point in living. I failed Lady Angreni, who helped me and my family." Sumbita sighed, then added firmly, "But, I am not willing to die before I kill Kebotendas."

Sekartaji and Gunungsari glanced at each other before bowing their heads. They were touched by the handmaid's undeterred loyalty and love for her mistress.

Sumbita had told them how Angreni had helped her and her family. Sumbita's mother was a peddler in the market; her father was a tapper, who collected *nira*, the sap of the coconut tree's blossoms. After her father fell while tapping a coconut tree, Sumbita, as the only child, had to take care of him. When Angreni, one of her mother's customers, heard about the tragedy that had befallen the family, she ordered Sumbita's father to be taken to the prime minister's residence for medical treatment and made Sumbita her handmaid.

"You told me that you don't know Kebotendas's whereabouts," said Sekartaji. "How can you kill him? Just meeting him by chance would be nearly impossible. He must be hiding where it would be very difficult to find him."

The three of them fell into a long, deep silence. The bamboo house that Sekartaji had rented was close enough to the hospital that every so often, they could hear someone screaming in pain or in the agony of death. It reminded Sumbita of Angreni's fight against Kebotendas.

The terrifying memory evaporated when a soldier, who Sumbita seemed to recognize, quickly crossed the small yard and walked up the few steps to the veranda.

"There you are!" The soldier sounded relieved.

"Raden, I'm sorry. I left without telling you first," Sumbita said.

The soldier shook his head and waved, dismissing Sumbita's apology. The well-built man cupped his hands in front of his chest to greet them and introduced himself to Sekartaji and Gunungsari as Banyakwulung, a drill sergeant in the Janggala palace who, with his older brother Tunggulwulung, had trained Kebotendas to become a bodyguard for the king's son.

"I was one of the horsemen who took part in Angreni's kidnapping," Banyakwulung said softly. "I took Sumbita to Usada Hall after she was almost killed." As a soldier and drill sergeant, Banyakwulung was no stranger to the Usada Hall where soldiers were treated for injuries. After taking Sumbita to the hospital on that fateful day, he had visited her often.

Sekartaji and her brother returned the greetings.

"The most important thing is that you have recovered, Sumbita." Banyakwulung looked more closely at Sekartaji and Gunungsari and said, "You two look familiar. Have we met?"

"Ah, you are mistaken, Raden," Sekartaji replied quickly. "Perhaps we just look like someone you know."

"Please call me Banyakwulung; I'm just a lowly soldier," Banyakwulung said. "I have forbidden Sumbita to call me Raden, but she still does."

"We just want to help relieve Sumbita's pain," Sekartaji murmured softly.

"Her pain will only be relieved after she kills Kebotendas," Banyakwulung said. "It looks like only my brother, Tunggulwulung, knows where he is now. But I don't know where my brother or Kebotendas is. I don't even know whether my brother is still alive or if he, along with everyone else, drowned at sea. He was gone by the time I came back with Wiranata."

"Yes, we heard about the disaster that struck Raden Panji and his party while on an outing at sea," Sekartaji said, then suggested, "What if Sumbita stays with us while you to try to find Kebotendas?"

"Where can I find you after I find him? Here?"

"No, go to the Kadiri palace," Sekartaji said. "If you show this small kris to the guard at the gate, he will take you to me."

"You work there?" Banyakwulung asked, looking at Sekartaji's small kris in his hand.

The siblings nodded in unison.

In the early morning of the third day after Panji's arrival at the Bali palace, Citrasari ordered her handmaid to look for angsana flowers and decorated her room with them.

"Citrasari!" Andayaprana shouted in alarm, standing in Citrasari's doorway. "Why are you decorating your room with angsana flowers?"

The servants preparing breakfast stopped working and looked at Andayaprana, who faced Citrasari with her shoulders pulled back and her chin up.

"I'm bored," Citrasari said, showing no fear of Andayaprana. "I want a change."

"Even if you are bored, you do not have to decorate your room with angsana flowers," Andayaprana scolded even louder.

"Oh? Is there a rule that we cannot decorate our room with angsana flowers?" Citrasari challenged.

All the handmaids now sat down and stared at the floor. No one dared to raise their head.

"No, there are no such rules." Andayaprana softened her voice, realizing that as a hostess, she should be more gracious. "Please, just don't use angsana flowers."

"Does this request have anything to do with Raden Kelana?"

"What do you mean?"

"Are you worried that Raden Kelana will visit my room?"

"Raden Kelana can visit any room he desires to frequent."

"That's the way it should be," Citrasari acknowledged, "but Raden Kelana only sleeps in your room. Aren't we equals? We are both war trophies."

"You and I, we are not the same!" Andayaprana raised her voice again. "Raden Kelana fought to the death to possess me, while he obtained you without a fight, not even one drop of blood was spilled."

Citrasari spun around and slammed her door shut.

Panji, standing behind Andayaprana, gently pulled her to her room. After staying for a moment with her, Panji returned to Citrasari's door. He looked at the string of angsana flowers draped around the door frame before knocking gently. It took some time before the door slowly opened.

It was late afternoon when Panji left Citrasari's room. The handmaids noticed how radiant Citrasari looked as she saw him out of her room. Kelana must have made her happy.

The incident between Andayaprana, Citrasari, and Panji ruined Kretabasa's plan to keep Panji in the palace. The next day, Panji was ready to attack Adipati Burik and remove his threat to the Bali kingdom.

Kretabasa's efforts to keep Panji from going to war were futile.

The next day, when the sun was halfway up into the sky, Panji — guided by Kudanatpada, accompanied by Tunggulwulung, and escorted by fifty fully-armed soldiers — marched towards Kaburikan, the rebellious autonomous region in Bali. They marched over grassy roads, cutting through a forest with giant trees and hundreds of noisy monkeys hanging from the tree branches. Kudanatpada had carefully chosen this route to prevent attracting unwanted attention.

"According to Kudanatpada, it is three more miles to reach Kaburikan's pendapa," Tunggulwulung said. "It's time for us to break up. One group will attack from the front, while the other attacks from a different direction."

"We don't need to break up, Tunggulwulung," Panji said. "We can attack this small region from just one direction. Let's advance directly from here."

"It is too dangerous, Raden. We don't know the exact strength of our enemy. A detachment from the main group will help us if something unexpected happens." Tunggulwulung was worried about this war. The preparation time had been very short, and they were engaging with only half the number of men they usually used to attack an enemy.

"Don't worry, I will be at the front line." Panji's words were final. "I'm ready."

Tunggulwulung exhaled. There was nothing else to do but follow Panji's orders. He remembered Prasanta and Wiranata saying that they went to war solely to heal the crown prince.

When the troops were a stone's throw from the region's border, Panji sent two messengers to deliver a letter to Adipati Burik.

When evening fell and the two messengers had not returned, Panji summoned Tunggulwulung and said firmly, "We will attack tomorrow morning."

"Let's attack now, Raden," Tunggulwulung urged. "By tomorrow morning the enemy will be well prepared. I'm sure that as we speak, they're torturing our two soldiers in an effort to extract information about our strength and position."

Panji thought for a moment. "All right, let's go."

It did not take long to assemble the men. Under the cover of darkness, they advanced.

Panji and Tunggulwulung were both shocked when they were met by an army of some one thousand soldiers who guarded Kaburikan. On the other hand, this was to be expected, because Adipati Burik had been preparing to attack Bali. So of course, they had strong army, ready to fight.

Without wasting any more time, Panji's men sounded their battle cry, and the fighting commenced immediately. Both sides skipped the usual preliminary exchange of arrows. Instead, they entered the battlefield with swords in hand.

Panji fought as if possessed by a demon. He goaded his soldiers by jumping around and shouting, while he slashed his sword and stabbed at anyone who tried to block their advance to the adipati's mansion. It was impossible to know how many enemy soldiers Panji killed or wounded. Panji's own wounds did not weaken him. On the contrary, the pain aroused a blind fury inside him. He was certain that he would meet Angreni after this fight.

Panji's soldiers watched their leader fight fiercely and followed his furious example. It was not unusual for one soldier to confront five or six opponents simultaneously.

Only Tunggulwulung still thought with a clear head. Fifty men, regardless of their training and courage, could not possibly defeat a thousand. He galloped over to Kudanatpada, who was fighting fiercely at a formation in the rear.

"I will lead you out of this battle!" Tunggulwulung shouted. "Go back to the palace and ask for reinforcements of fifty of the best Balinese soldiers, then attack from the east. Do you understand?"

Kudanatpada nodded and separated himself from the battle under Tunggulwulung's protection.

Tunggulwulung's fears were realized. Kaburikan's force began to overwhelm Panji's men, like a hungry tiger charging toward a dozen wild bulls ready to attack.

The enemy, seeing one of Panji's soldiers collapse, covered in blood, and realizing that they indeed had slayed one of the phantom warriors, boosted their vigor. Their renewed strength soon brought down another of Panji's soldiers. For the Kaburikan force, the only way to stop the fighting was to annihilate all the invaders.

Tunggulwulung ordered the soldiers to spread out and back away from the battlefield. That way, they could still engage the enemy and keep the battle going until reinforcements arrived.

Spreading out, Panji's men brought the battle to the streets and alleys of Kaburikan's residential areas. Women and children screamed and cried as the fighting entered the yards of people's homes. Panji's soldiers only fought when they were forced to. The darkness of night helped keep them safe.

Tunggulwulung could only protect Panji from a distance. Twice, he had used his knife-throwing skills to save Panji when several enemy soldiers cornered him.

Nevertheless, Panji's courage and recklessness had discouraged his opponents. Only those with good close-combat skills and experience dared to approach him. When Panji finally stood at the gate of Adipati Burik's estate, he shouted, "Adipati Burik, come out! Face me!" After the fourth time he challenged Adipati Burik, the adipati appeared in full armor, holding a sword.

"So that's what the feared Kelana looks like!" Adipati Burik bellowed, silencing the war cries. "It turns out that your strength only resides in your recklessness. The fighting skills many people laud are merely trickery." Stepping out and swinging his sword, he shouted, "All of you, step aside! Let me cut off Kelana's head!"

The Kaburikan soldiers were reassured by the appearance of the adipati. Exhausted, they sheathed their swords and surrounded the area to watch the fight. This also gave Panji's men time to regroup and rest.

Tunggulwulung was quite relieved that Panji would now only be engaged in a one-on-one battle with Adipati Burik and would no longer be under the attack of a crowd. Tunggulwulung left to go keep the remaining enemy soldiers at bay.

The fight between Panji and Adipati Burik was not even. Panji, who had already lost a lot of blood, was exhausted. During his fight with Adipati Burik, he jumped backwards more often than he lunged forward with his sword. Despite falling several times while evading Adipati Burik's merciless sword, Panji was still able to resist his opponent and managed to graze Adipati Burik's neck and brow with his sword.

Finally, Panji fell on his face. His sword flew out of his hand and stuck into the ground. Adipati Burik kicked Panji onto his back, then kicked him in his open chest wound. The Kaburikan soldiers burst into cheers.

With Panji lying helplessly on the ground, Adipati Burik motioned to his soldiers to hand him a spear. "I'll kill you like I would kill a boar," Adipati Burik snorted.

"I'm ready, spear my chest," Panji smiled.

Panji's smile caught Adipati Burik by surprise.

All the soldiers witnessing this final moment of the fight held their breath while waiting for the spear to pierce Panji's chest. Then, out of nowhere, an arrow whizzed through the air and penetrated the shoulder of Adipati Burik, who fell to the ground.

All eyes turned in the direction the arrow came from. Everyone stared wide-eyed at the two beautiful women who, dressed as soldiers and looking alike, were holding bows.

The soldiers who had previously circled the area to watch the fight now scattered to surround Sariana and Sariani, who calmly faced their opponents. The twins threw down their bows and grabbed the swords sheathed at their waists. Standing back to back, the female warriors faced the soldiers who furiously retaliated against them for wounding the adipati.

Panji rose, picked up his sword, and approached Adipati Burik, who lay moaning on the ground, gripping his shoulder. Seeing Panji, ten of the adipati's men immediately surrounded the fallen leader to protect him.

Panji had a decision to make: fight Adipati Burik's protectors or help Sariana and Sariani, who were being overpowered by their attackers. He chose to help the twins who had saved his life from the duke's spear.

The uneven battle that had taken the lives of two of Panji's men and dozens of Kaburikan's soldiers became even when Kudanatpada arrived with reinforcements from the Balinese palace. Enveloped in a thick cloud of dust, the fifty Balinese cavalry and their fierce horses thundered across the roads and immediately attacked the Kaburikan defense force.

Panji's men who were resting in nearby houses now rejoined the rest of their company. After Panji and the Nusabarong twins subdued their attackers, they proceeded to the adipati's mansion.

Dozens of soldiers guarded the room where Adipati Burik had been taken to treat his shoulder wound.

Panji and his exhausted soldiers wanted to avoid fighting the guards, who were still fresh. Panji told Sariani and Sariana to divert the guards' attention by using arrows without injuring them. Some of the guards raced after the two archers, who escaped, guarded by Panji's soldiers.

During the commotion, Panji and five of his men broke into Adipati Burik's room.

The middle-aged man still looked strong and fierce. His medicine man had removed the arrow from his shoulder and was now treating the wound.

Panji's group was blocked by five guards inside the room. The close combat that followed was fierce. In the cramped space, swords were of little use. Hand-to-hand combat was more effective. Adipati Burik's guards died with blood gushing out of their noses and ears.

Panji stood towering over Adipati Burik and said, "You're surrounded, and I can cut open your belly as easily as I can cut open a ripe papaya, unless you order all your soldiers to surrender."

Huddled in a corner of the room, the shivering adipati asked, "Will you occupy Kaburikan after I surrender?" The adipati was afraid to die, but he was also afraid of losing his property.

Panji was still breathing heavily. He had just broken the neck of one guard and cracked the head of another, and his hand still trembled. "I, Kelana Jayengsari, have never occupied any land I've conquered," he snorted. "I only want you to surrender."

"All right, I admit defeat. But please treat me according to my stature. I will hand you my only daughter who is still unmarried."

"Of course, Adipati," Panji's voice softened. He now regarded the older man shaking quietly in the corner of the room as part of his extended family. "I always respect courageous people who fight like you. I accept your daughter as a token of your surrender."

Then Panji gently lay Adipati Burik on his bed, and covered the adipati's feet with a blanket before leaving the room to look for Tunggulwulung.

The next day, accompanied by Panji on his right and Tunggulwulung on his left, Adipati Burik ordered his entire army to surrender. When the sun was halfway up into the sky, they held a ceremony to hand over Adipati Burik's daughter as a token of capitulation.

Tunggulwulung felt that it was right to take some valuables to their fallen warriors' heirs. Therefore, Panji and his troops departed Kaburikan not only with Sundari, the adipati's daughter, but also treasures of gold and jewels.

After Panji's group arrived back at the Bali palace, Panji made sure that his wounded men were cared for, then rested in a room overlooking the garden. He heard voices from outside and saw two men cross the garden. Panji recognized Kusni and Tandang. For a brief moment, he was tempted to greet them, but he then remembered that doing so would expose his identity. So, he rolled down the bamboo shade in front of his window instead.

Tandang and Kusni took a seat on a bench in the shade of a nearby tamarind tree to wait for the carriage that would take them back to Janggala.

Through the open window, Panji could hear their conversation.

"Are all religious leaders evil?" Tandang asked.

"Religious leaders who are followers of Umuk are dangerous," Kusni answered. "They think that their religion is the only legitimate one and that all the others are wrong. In other words, they are as arrogant as Umuk."

"How do you identify such religious leaders?"

"They usually like to mingle with people of power."

Panji heard carriage wheels crunching the gravel on the road. Peering through the blinds, he watched Kusni and Tandang get into a carriage with the emblem of the Janggala kingdom.

Panji could still hear Kusni's last words before the carriage departed: "The Kudasrenggara confirms my theory that all religions — Buddha, Shiva, Vishnu, and others — come from the same source…"

On the seventh day that Panji and his entourage were in Bali, the king of Bali died. Immediately after the king's funeral ceremony, Kudanatpada was crowned, with the blessing of Andayaprana as the eldest daughter.

The coronation celebration did not appeal to Panji. On the next day, Panji said goodbye. As befitted a conqueror, Panji's departure was accompanied with great fanfare; he was provided with enough provisions for every soldier, including those guarding their camp.

———•◦•———

Panji's encampment caught the attention of those who lived nearby. Feeling safe in the company of the men who fiercely confronted their enemies but were generous to their friends and neighbors, many locals moved closer. The settlement became a small village, with the big house where Panji lived at the center.

Skilled masons and carpenters continued replacing the tents with huts built of wood, bamboo, and stone. The new structures looked beautiful and elegant.

Panji, following the advice of his close companions, ordered the soldiers to start farming and raising livestock. These activities brought them closer to the residents of the Blambangan region. Some of the soldiers married the daughters of neighboring local residents.

Panji's memories of Angreni did not torment him anymore. He no longer suffered from nightmares of Angreni's death. Panji's desire to go to war to meet death had greatly diminished.

The roles that Andayaprana and Citrasari played in Panji's emotional healing were very important. The incident of Andayaprana and Citrasari's argument in Bali had been the beginning of Panji's release from his trauma-induced insanity.

Panji remembered when Andayaprana suggested that he sleep with Citrasari. Up to that point, Panji had only slept with Andayaprana. But being a woman, Andayaprana understood that Citrasari was jealous. Panji also remembered the physical and mental struggle that had occurred inside Citrasari's room.

"Your room is so beautiful, Citrasari," Panji had said upon entering the room.

Sitting on the edge of her bed, Citrasari asked, "Do you mean that, Raden?" She tried to find Panji's eyes. "I see your lips trembling."

Panji sat down on the bed next to Citrasari and took a deep breath. He picked up one of the flowers decorating the bed and whispered, "This flower reminds me of something I can never forget."

"If you don't mind, please tell me what happened," Citrasari probed.

"My wife was murdered," Panji said. "The mound of angsana flowers that covered her body when I found her continues to give me nightmares."

"Please face the door and close your eyes," Citrasari beseeched. "Don't turn around until I ask you to."

Panji nodded and rose. Facing the door with his eyes closed, Panji heard rustling. *Citrasari seems to be preparing her bed. It won't take long.* He was eager to see what Citrasari was doing, but he kept to his promise not to look until asked to.

Finally, Citrasari called softly, "Kanda, please turn now." Panji opened his eyes and whirled around. What he saw made him stagger, then fall to his knees, hitting the floor with a thud.

"What's the matter? Is this the way it is in your nightmares?" Citrasari's voice floated in the air. She had buried herself under a mound of angsana flowers. "But now, this is not a dream. This is real."

Panji, still on the floor, looked around the room.

"Come here and do everything you did in your dream," Citrasari coached gently. "Come. Come here. Let's turn your nightmare into a beautiful reality — a truly beautiful reality, my dear."

Slowly, Panji rose to his feet, then eased toward the mound of angsana flowers on the bed in front of him. Like he did in his dream, he gently dug into the heap of flowers. But whereas in his nightmares he would find Angreni's pale, blood-stained corpse, he now found Citrasari's vibrant, invitingly naked body.

Panji stood staring at her. Then he took off his clothes and joined Citrasari amongst the remaining flowers. For a long time, they silently caressed each other.

Citrasari did not want to surrender herself to Panji without being pursued. To entice him, she closed her thighs tightly. Panji had no other choice than to lovingly pursue her until she finally allowed him to capture the flower of his real-life desire.

Citrasari let out a muffled scream of mixed pain and delight when Panji broke through the veil of her virginity. Afterward, as they lay side by side, Citrasari whispered, "Now, there will be no more nightmares, my love. All that remains is a beautiful reality."

Panji rose and sat on the edge of the bed for a while. His nightmare intertwined with reality, and the two were now merged into one.

———•••———

The name Raden Kelana Jayengsari became widely known in eastern Java and Bali. People said that he was a warrior who led a phantom army. But this warrior was not a cruel conqueror and plunderer, but rather a kind-hearted and generous fighter.

Unlike other conquerors, Panji dressed very simply. His appearance closely resembled that of a brahmin; he tied his long hair in a bun and wore a mustache and beard. But his simple appearance could not hide his good looks and well-built body. All the women he had acquired as war trophies had become his wives of equal standing. Panji's desire to die on the battlefield had greatly diminished, while his desire to make those around him happy had intensified. He often spent time thinking about the welfare of not only his soldiers, but also of the people who lived around his settlement.

———•••———

Panji was enjoying the company of Tunggulwulung, Wiranata, and Prasanta in their settlement when a guard announced a messenger from the Kadiri kingdom. King Amerdadu of Kadiri had written to request help. King Amerdadu was expecting an attack on his Kadiri kingdom by King Metaun. If Panji's forces helped Kadiri defeat King Metaun, Panji would be given the crown princess of Kadiri as a trophy.

Panji smiled dryly. *Poor Sekartaji, all you seem to be good for is to become a reward for the man who can help your father win a war.*

"Raden, His Majesty is eager to meet you," the messenger said. When he saw Panji smile, he added, "We have prepared accommodations for you and your party in Tambakbaya, our guest village built specifically to honor royal visitors."

"It is only right to help each other," Panji answered. "But I can't see the king right now. I need some time to prepare."

"Would it be possible to give me your reply in writing?" the messenger asked. "That would make it easier for me to relay your message to the king of Kadiri."

"Yes, I will give you my response to this letter in writing," Panji said. "I respect His Majesty and will try to make him happy. Give me a minute."

Handing his response to the messenger, Panji asked, "Do you know why King Metaun wants to attack the Kadiri kingdom?"

"King Metaun proposed to the crown princess of Kadiri, Her Royal Highness Princess Sekartaji," the messenger explained. "After conferring with the court officials and the crown princess, the King of Kadiri decided not to accept the proposal. King Metaun then threatened Kadiri with an attack."

After enjoying a simple meal, the messenger asked permission to leave and spurred his horse back to Kadiri.

Panji held a meeting with his closest companions: Tunggulwulung, Wiranata, and Prasanta. Panji told them that in his response, he had neither granted nor rejected the king's request, and Panji asked for their opinions. Later, he also consulted Andayaprana, Citrasari, Sariana, Sariani, and Sundari.

Andayaprana was the one who came up with a clear plan. She suggested that Panji immediately order the soldiers to prepare everything to defend the king of Kadiri.

Panji praised her courage. It was understandable if his closest companions suggested defending Kadiri, because they knew that King Amerdadu of Kadiri was the brother of King Amiluhur of Janggala, who was Panji's father. But it was quite surprising when Andayaprana suggested defending Kadiri, because the Balinese princess didn't know anything about Panji's kinship with the king of Kadiri.

After the meeting, the women rose to return to their rooms. Panji stopped Andayaprana and asked her to join him for a bath in the pond. While they soaked in the tepid water, Panji sang the *Kenyakadiri* song for Andayaprana. The love song told a story about a young man of Kadiri nobility who succeeded in capturing many kinds of wild animals on the slopes of Mount Semeru but failed in capturing the heart of an ordinary village girl. He failed because he did not distinguish the difference between capturing wild beasts and capturing a common village girl's heart.

Andayaprana was Panji's favorite wife when he wanted to talk. She never questioned, let alone become angry, when he mistakenly called her Angreni; the others would suddenly burst into tears or just run away.

The night had come, and the moon had risen. The women played cards and checkers under the moonlight. Some of them busied themselves with domestic tasks, such as arranging flowers, making body scrubs, and the like. Others prepared meals and snacks for their travel to Kadiri the next morning.

Panji's wives gathered together before dawn broke. They talked about Panji, especially about the wars he had fought. The conversation was engaging and evoked great admiration in the women. As the women dispersed for their own activities, Sundari, the daughter of Adipati Burik, approached Andayaprana and asked, "Will Raden Kelana help the king of Kadiri fight King Metaun?"

"Yes, I suggested to help this troubled king," Andayaprana explained. "He reminds me of my father, when he needed Raden Kelana's help. As far as I know, Kadiri has two kings: King Jayabaya, the emeritus king who is the symbol of the kingdom, and King Amerdadu, the young king currently ruling Kadiri."

"You're the closest to Raden Kelana. In your opinion, in which war was he wounded the most?"

"Your father and his army probably inflicted the most wounds on him," Andayaprana answered. "But this didn't happen because of the greatness of your father's army. It happened because Raden Kelana had left to fight with almost no preparation and took far too few soldiers along."

"I never think about the might of my father's army," Sundari said. "I only want to say that my father is one of King Metaun's trusted confidants."

"Oh! Please tell me everything you know about King Metaun. Who knows, maybe your information can help Raden Kelana."

"After defeating my father, King Metaun's force was reduced considerably." Sundari paused. "But there is still another force that must be considered."

"Who would that be?"

"The army led by the older brother of Patih Kudanawarsa from Janggala."

"Do you have anything else to tell me?"

"No, that would be all." Sundari hesitated, then added, "Oh, and Raden Kelana has never spent a night in my room."

"You are still too young," Andayaprana said. "You're not even seventeen years old, are you?"

The girl nodded before she bowed and went to her room.

Later that evening, Andayaprana told Panji everything Sundari had told her. For a long time, Panji contemplated the information. He tried to make the connection between King Metaun, Adipati Burik, and the older brother of Janggala's prime minister. He concluded that the sooner they arrived in Kadiri, the better they would be able to prepare to fight. King Metaun and his followers could attack Kadiri at any time.

The next morning before dawn, all the women were ready. Panji's closest companions were also present. The carriages were ready to roll. The people who lived around Panji's settlement came to send them off. They promised to help the five soldiers remaining behind to safeguard the settlement. As soon as the first light broke through the eastern horizon, Panji's party departed for Kadiri.

At the front line, horsemen rode side by side. Panji, Wiranata, and Prasanta were among them. Behind the cavalry, Tunggulwulung, seated proudly on an elephant, watched the horsemen in front of him. Behind him, the horse carts carrying supplies and weapons followed. Four horsemen covered the rear of the procession. More than a hundred people traveled in the convoy, which, from a distance, looked like a giant snake slithering forward to catch its prey.

Chapter 11

BETWEEN LOVE, GODS, AND DANGER

The grounds of the Kadiri palace looked deserted. Occasionally, soldiers passed by. Inside the palace, King Amerdadu was meeting with court officials. They discussed the threat of an enemy attack.

The same messenger who had delivered their letter to Panji had just told them that Raden Kelana Jayengsari had arrived at Kadiri's border and would wait there for the king's approval to enter the capital.

"It appears that Raden Kelana Jayengsari, famous for his ferociousness on the battlefield, still exercises courtesy," the king said. "He could have just entered the city with his convoy."

"That's right, Your Majesty." The messenger bowed. "Instead, he is willing to wait at the border, waiting for your approval to enter the city."

The king turned to his son. "Gunungsari, please ride out to meet Raden Kelana Jayengsari. Escort him and his convoy into the city."

Gunungsari bowed and asked permission to leave.

The king ordered his prime minister to prepare a welcome for their guests.

The news of King Metaun's threat to invade Kadiri had spread not only among the court officials, but also among the kingdom's commoners. It was general knowledge that Kadiri's army was weak because it had depended too much on Janggala's army. It was also known that Janggala's army at this time could not send reinforcements — they had just lost many of their best soldiers to a disaster at sea. Kadiri was obviously unable to defend itself against an attack from King Metaun. But that worrisome knowledge was now counterbalanced by the reassuring news that the Kadiri king had succeeded in soliciting the help of Kelana Jayengsari, a powerful warrior. The arrival of Kelana and his convoy brought relief to many of the townspeople.

The very first time Gunungsari and Panji had met was more than ten years ago, when Gunungsari was just a toddler and Panji was a teenager. Now, after being separated for more than a decade, they did not recognize each other.

Gunungsari was amazed by Panji's appearance. He had expected Kelana Jayengsari to be an armor-wearing giant who spoke with a thunderous voice and had a beard and sideburns. Instead, Gunungsari found himself facing a kshatriya dressed like a brahmin.

"Raden, I am Gunungsari. The king has sent me to take you to Tambakbaya, our guest village, before meeting him in the palace."

"As you can see, in addition to my closest companions, I brought many soldiers with me," Panji answered. "May they join me to rest at that village?"

"Of course, Raden. We have prepared to receive your entire party. Tambakbaya is not more than three miles from the palace."

Gunungsari and several Kadiri soldiers escorted Panji and his convoy to the capital's guest village. When the convoy entered the city, many people watched from the roadside. Mesmerized, they looked at the gallant horses and their elegant riders. The shiny carriages with beautiful princesses inside charmed the people, who craned their necks to get a closer look.

Tambakbaya had been built specifically to honor and house royal guests who visited from other kingdoms. The guest village consisted of a large house surrounded by smaller pavilions. The main house with a large yard was for Panji and his wives, as well as for him to receive guests. After getting out of the carriage, the princesses were immediately escorted into the wooden house with a roof of woven palm leaves. The house consisted of one large room and smaller rooms on the right and left. The soldiers were stationed in the smaller, surrounding pavilions.

While his guests were getting settled and rested in Tambakbaya, the king of Kadiri sat on his throne surrounded by the court officials and his closest aides. Gunungsari was among them.

"During this past week I often heard about this Raden Kelana Jayengsari," the king said to his prime minister Gunabadra, who sat cross-legged in front of him. "My trusted aides confirmed that this person succeeded in conquering the kingdom of Bali and the regions of Blambangan, Nusabarong, and Kaburikan."

Patih Gunabadra nodded. "Your Majesty is correct, and what surprises me is that Raden Kelana Jayengsari never occupied the kingdom of Bali nor the regions; he just wanted to be acknowledged as the conqueror. After their concession, he simply left. There never was any looting, rape, or persecution as is often conducted by the victors."

"His soldiers are no less special," the king added. "There aren't many of them, but I'm told that one soldier can kill ten opponents with just three or four moves. They are also equipped with weapons that some said were taken from the core of a volcano." The king paused. "I truly want to meet this strange, extraordinary man, soon."

"The fact that he is already at Tambakbaya means that he is willing to defend this kingdom against King Metaun's attack," Patih Gunabadra concluded.

"I want to talk to him tomorrow, face to face," the king ordered. "Gunungsari, you will take my invitation to him."

Gunungsari bowed then left on horseback to deliver his father's invitation to the mysterious Raden Kelana at Tambakbaya. He arrived at Tambakbaya in the early evening. From afar, he saw oil lamps flickering in the windows. At first, he saw no one outside. But then, when he looked more closely, he saw soldiers in dark clothing guarding each corner. As Gunungsari neared the outskirts of the settlement, several of the dark figures moved quickly and silently toward him. He said, "I am Gunungsari, the son of King Amerdadu. I have a message from the king for Raden Kelana Jayengsari."

"I will escort you to him," one of the soldiers said with quiet authority.

Surrounded by all of Panji's wives, Panji, Wiranata, Prasanta, and Tunggulwulung sat cross-legged on the Indian rosewood floor of the veranda. When Gunungsari entered, Panji was talking to Sundari about King Metaun.

"My father never set foot in King Metaun's palace," Sundari was saying. "And when I asked him about the location of King Metaun's kingdom, he only shook his head. He told me that only a few of his allies ever met face-to-face with King Metaun."

Panji looked up when he heard the soldier approach. "Hello, Gunungsari, please join us," Panji said in welcome. "I'm glad you came. Please, have a seat. I have a few questions for you."

Gunungsari took a seat in the circle next to Wiranata and said, "I am happy to answer your questions, Raden Kelana."

Andayaprana gestured to a handmaid to bring refreshments for the guest.

"Do you know who this King Metaun is, who threatens your kingdom?" Panji asked.

"The threat letter was delivered by two border guards who were ambushed during their patrol," Gunungsari answered. "The guards were bleeding when they arrived at the palace. One of them carried a bamboo cylinder around his neck containing the letter."

"What did the guards report, Raden?" Panji probed.

"One of the guards said that they were ambushed and attacked by a group of masked men who claimed to be King Metaun's men. But before he could finish his report, the guard collapsed and died in front of the king."

"You said there were two guards?" Panji asked.

"The other guard died sitting in front of the king, even before his comrade began his report," Gunungsari answered.

"Who do you think King Metaun is?" Panji asked.

"No one is certain about his identity," Gunungsari said.

Perturbed by the information Sundari and Gunungsari had shared, everyone turned silent.

After a while, Gunungsari handed Panji the king's invitation and asked for permission to return to the Kadiri palace.

———•◆•———

The next day, Panji went to see King Amerdadu. Dressed as a brahmin, Panji was escorted by ten unarmed soldiers. But unlike a brahmin, Panji had a kris fastened to his belt. On closer inspection, Panji was too muscular and sharp-eyed to be a priest.

"Welcome to the Kadiri palace, Raden," Amerdadu said kindly, holding Panji in a steadfast gaze.

"I'm honored to meet Your Majesty." Panji bowed before the king.

"It is an honor for us to have a famous warrior as our guest," Amerdadu said sincerely. He was surprised at Panji's politeness. He had expected the warrior to speak loudly and haughtily, and he would have excused the warrior's impoliteness because the king really needed this conqueror's assistance. But apparently, Kelana Jayengsari was well-mannered and even a bit humble.

"We have decided to ask for your protection when King Metaun attacks." The king paused. "They have already killed two of our border guards."

"We cannot guarantee your kingdom's protection, but we guarantee to do our best if we were to assist Kadiri's army against the ruthless King Metaun," Panji said modestly. "With the blessing of Mahadewa, we will defeat evil."

"You are being too modest, Raden," Amerdadu said, admiring his guest even more.

"I believe you are defending your kingdom against an evil force," Panji said. "All I can do is pledge my life to Your Majesty."

Not only did Amerdadu respect this modest warrior, but everyone in the king's audience praised him as well. The meeting was followed by a royal banquet so spectacular, that even the court officials were impressed. The king silently applauded Panji and his guards when they only nibbled their food, as if they ate only to keep from disappointing their host. Unbeknownst to Amerdadu, the ten soldiers who accompanied Panji were the sons of King Amiluhur of Janggala, and his concubines, and such lavish meals were not anything special for them. After dining, King Amerdadu invited his guests to relax and enjoy the dances accompanied by gamelan.

The evening ended when Amerdadu withdrew to the inner palace, and the guests and royal officials left as well.

———•◦•———

While riding his horse back to Tambakbaya, Panji admired the beautiful buildings on either side of the road. He remembered his conversation with Prasanta the previous night. According to Prasanta, the kingdom of Janggala came into existence only after King Erlangga divided the Medhang kingdom into two — one for each of his two eldest sons. Thus, it was not surprising that the buildings around the Kadiri palace were older and statelier than those around the younger Janggala palace.

As soon as Panji arrived at Tambakbaya, Prasanta met him with a question. "Did you meet the crown princess of Kadiri at the palace?"

"No! I didn't even remember that I was once betrothed to Sekartaji," Panji said. "But my forgetfulness had its advantages; my disguise was flawless. If I had asked about Sekartaji, everyone would have wondered about my identity."

"I heard from the Kadiri court officials and merchants that Sekartaji is very beautiful," Prasanta continued. "Very beautiful indeed."

"No one is prettier than my wife Angreni, Prasanta," Panji retorted sadly. Prasanta's words had unintentionally reminded Panji of the woman he still loved. He brusquely walked away to the backyard of the main house. Tears streaming down his cheeks, he leaned against the trunk of an orange jasmine tree and muttered, "Under this sky, there is no woman as beautiful as my wife Angreni."

Suddenly, a vision of the god Narada appeared to Panji, as if the god were sitting in front of him. Panji bowed respectfully to one of the important gods he'd read about in a Javanese religious book.

Narada smiled and said comfortingly, "Panji, you need to know that men must behave like roosters. A rooster should not pay attention to a particular hen. That way, he will not suffer if the hen leaves. You, too, should not pay attention to a particular hen because you have more than one hen. You now have five beautiful wives. You are doing the right thing. Love them all."

"You are correct, Lord Narada, I have Andayaprana, Citrasari, Sariana, Sariani, and Sundari," Panji said, solemnly, "and I love them all."

"I'm glad to hear that you can love them all," Narada said, pleased. "This means your mental wounds from losing Angreni are healed. Do you want me to teach you how to keep loving all of your wives?"

"Of course," Panji said. "Please, teach me."

"To love and to be loved are matters of the spiritual world, not of the physical world. Look at this orange jasmine tree; watch the way its branches and twigs sway. The beauty and elegance of their movement are created by the wind. The tree does not move by itself; the wind moves it. The wind represents the spiritual world that is invisible, but present and powerful.

"Imagine your wives from the moment of their birth until you married them. When their mothers gave birth to them, they walked the thin line between life and death. Take note of how much these mothers loved their daughters. They wouldn't even allow mosquitoes to go near their child, let alone suck their blood.

"Also take note of how your wives took meticulous care of their bodies when they reached adulthood. Take note of how carefully they took care of their skin so it appeared radiant. Who is their beauty for? It is all for their husband, a man they expect to truly love them.

"How painful would it be if the husband ignored everything they experienced from their birth until they became his wife? This is the reason you should love your wives with all your heart. Make them happy by fulfilling not only their physical needs, but their spiritual ones as well. I don't have to tell you how to fulfill their physical needs; you already know how to do that. When you make love to one of your wives, imagine all that her mother did to comfort her from the day she was born until she became your companion. That way, you won't rush. Take pleasure in your wife's pleasure, and let the moment she reaches the culmination of her enjoyment be the culmination of your pleasure also. Don't make the moment that you plant your seed be the pinnacle of your pleasure.

"If you make love just to plant your seed, you are not different from an animal. But if you make love to please your wife, to give her pleasure, you become a man who honors all the mothers of mankind. Your only duty is to make your wife reach the climax of physical fulfillment. When she has reached it, allow her to luxuriate in her satisfaction. Withdraw yourself, cool down, and get ready to perform your next duty as a man. Remember Panji, to perform as a real man, not as an animal. Don't forget, you may have to satisfy all your wives in one day.

"What I'm teaching you now is a lesson I withhold from many kings and future kings. It is the art of making love as written in the *Asmaragama, Anala, Ajuwita,* and *Atantra,* a series of handbooks on making love. Before I end my teaching, I order you to pleasure your wives as much as possible. But plant your seed as little as possible. Remember, a great kingdom becomes weak and unstable if the queen and concubines give birth to too many offspring. It is even worse if the offspring have no special qualities."

Before Panji could bow and thank Narada, the spiritual being vanished, and a sweet fragrance filled Panji's nostrils.

From a distance, Prasanta could see that Panji was having a conversation with someone. Prasanta felt bad about accidentally bringing up Angreni's name. Worried, Prasanta hurried over to the orange jasmine tree where his master stood, bowed. But when Prasanta reached him, Panji was alone.

"Raden, who were you talking to?"

"No one," Panji said. "I was just listening to the god Narada."

When Prasanta asked him what the god had said, Panji told him everything. "Narada is correct, Prasanta," Panji concluded. "I can't spend too much time thinking about Angreni. She is already in heaven."

Prasanta smiled, relieved.

Panji entered the large room of the main house in Tambakbaya, where he found Andayaprana reading.

"Aren't you tired of reading that book, dear?" Panji rested his eyes on the wooden box he had seen for the first time in the king of Bali's chamber.

"This is the most interesting book I've read so far." Andayaprana placed the lontar leaves on top of the closed box.

"Did your father give it to you?" Panji asked.

"No. According to my father, this book belongs to a holy woman in Janggala. Her name is Her Holiness Rara Suci."

Panji barely caught himself from blurting out, "That book belongs to my aunt!" But he realized that now was not the time to reveal that. Instead, he promised himself to return the book to his aunt after he had taken care of everything else he was faced with.

"Feel free to read it if you are interested." Andayaprana smiled.

"Why don't you just tell me what the book is about?"

"Fine, but don't you dare fall asleep," Andayaprana teased. "Or I will splash cold water on you!"

"Ndaya, I've never fallen asleep when you tell me stories."

"Yes, yes, yes, I believe you. Now, listen to me."

"Just tell me the part you find most interesting."

"All right, then. To me, the most interesting part is the section about a group of people like Her Holiness Rara Suci, who is the sister of the

Janggala King Amiluhur. Umuk, the only god who dared to disobey Mahadewa, the king of gods, used people like her to disrupt the world. You see, Umuk mainly targeted the priests to carry out his disruptive plans. He continually whispered to them that they, the priests, were the greatest kind of human being, the most honorable kind. According to Umuk, the priests were the group of people who knew best how to praise Mahadewa, so that whatever the priests wanted would be done. When properly praised, Mahadewa would fulfill all their wishes. That's what Umuk taught the priests."

Andayaprana paused to let that sink in before continuing enthusiastically, "Her Holiness Rara Suci is one of the few religious leaders who realizes the danger of Umuk's teaching. Unfortunately, there are not many people like her. There are more religious leaders who feel that they are what Umuk taught: that they are the greatest, most honorable kind of human being because they know best how to praise Mahadewa and follow the truest religion in the world. These religious leaders are always seen around kings or people in power.

"Her Holiness Rara Suci behaves the other way around. If she chose to, she could be very close to the center of power. She could even become the ruler of Janggala herself if she wanted to. But she deliberately distances herself from the palace and lives a secluded life to teach wisdom to people who want to attain enlightenment."

"Sorry for interrupting," Panji broke in. "You seem to know a lot about Her Holiness Rara Suci. Who told you about her?"

"The court priest in the Bali palace."

"Is that court priest the kind of religious leader who follows Umuk's teaching?"

"Maybe he did, at first. But then he realized his mistake. He has left the palace, and I don't know whether he will return or not. He said he needed some solace."

"All right, continue your story, love."

"Where did I leave off?"

"How can a storyteller be forgetful?"

They both giggled.

"Did you meet the crown princess of Kadiri?" Andayaprana asked, suddenly remembering that the king of Kadiri had invited Panji to the palace.

"No, dear. Most of the attendees were court officials." Panji didn't mention that he had already met — and became engaged to — the crown princess when he was a young teen.

"The beauty of the crown princess is the topic of conversation throughout the country," Andayaprana said, trying but failing to keep a hint of jealousy out of her voice. "When I went to the market to buy some textiles, everyone was talking about the beautiful princess."

"The crown princess is the talk of the town not only because of her beauty, but also because she is the cause of King Metaun's threat to attack Kadiri," Panji explained.

"What's the connection between the crown princess and King Metaun?"

"King Metaun proposed to the crown princess, but the king of Kadiri did not accept his proposal because the crown princess was already engaged. Now, King Metaun is stirring up unrest. He probably thinks that by doing this, the king of Kadiri will change his mind about refusing his proposal for fear of being attacked. It won't be long before King Metaun attacks Kadiri."

"So, why don't you propose to her?" Andayaprana smiled enviously.

"Because I would suffer the same fate as King Metaun; King Amerdadu would reject my proposal." Panji produced the flower he held hidden behind his back. He took Andayaprana's hand and pressed the flower into it. The princess was delighted. Soon, there were sounds of a creaking bed and muffled moans between rapid breaths.

Sometime later, Panji left Andayaprana's room and headed to Citrasari's room. But he stopped when he heard giggling coming from the direction of the large lotus pond, and he walked to the back of the house instead.

He saw Citrasari, Sundari, and the twins, Sariana and Sariani, joking and laughing at the edge of the pond, while feeding the lively fish swimming around.

Not wanting to disturb them, Panji turned away from the young women to look for Prasanta. He found his aide chatting with some handmaids. "Prasanta," he said, "where are Wiranata and Tunggulwulung?"

"Wiranata left to visit a Kadiri border guard who survived the initial ambush of Metaun's men," Prasanta answered. "And Tunggulwulung is discussing war strategy with the soldiers. As soon as he knows the location of Metaun's camp, he wants to strike the hideout first."

"I am not in the mood to talk about state matters," Panji said. "Tell my wives that I want to see them in my quarters."

When Citrasari, Sundari, and the twins joined Panji in his quarters, he said, "I hope all of you are enjoying your stay at Tambakbaya. And though we're not here to have fun, we might as well enjoy the comforts our host has provided."

The young women smiled shyly. Citrasari said, "Raden, we've been outside all day. The fresh air and sun have tired us. May we be excused to rest in our own rooms?" Citrasari glanced meaningfully at the other three, who returned her look with smiles.

Panji nodded and said, "But don't be surprised when I knock on your door to give you something special."

The girls bowed, hiding their excitement.

———•———

In preparation to satisfy his wife or queen in bed, a prince was expected to be experienced in lovemaking. It was common practice that a crown prince had women to teach him how to make love. Sexual satisfaction of the queen was closely related to the well-being of the sons or daughters born from the queen. To know how to pleasure women, a prince was expected to learn not only from the lovemaking manual written on the palm leaf manuscripts, but also through direct experiences, by making love to women.

Panji always remembered the lessons his father's concubine taught him from the Asmaragama, the ancient manual for lovemaking. He was not even eighteen years old at the time and had not yet met Angreni. The middle-aged concubine, whose trace of beauty was still visible, introduced him to the meaning of a man and woman's union in bed. The Asmaragama went into great detail about this topic. Panji read a dialogue between the god Narada and a future king. The conversation was really about how the future king could make his wives happy.

For a king, the skill of how to make love to four or more wives in a day was as important as the skill of how to fight barehanded or with weapons on the battlefield. Therefore, after giving pleasure to Andayaprana, Panji was required to also give pleasure to his other four wives.

"Sundari? Panji gently knocked on the door. "Are you asleep yet?"

"Please, come in," Sundari answered as she opened the squeaking door.

For a moment, Panji and his youngest wife stood in the doorway, facing each other. Sundari lowered her gaze when Panji placed his hands her shoulders and said, "You have become even more beautiful, dear."

"There are many women prettier than I am," Sundari murmured, still looking down.

Panji gently put his hand under her chin and lifted her face. For a moment, their eyes locked. Then, Sundari turned around and walked slowly towards the bed. Panji followed. It was the first time he had entered Sundari's room.

Noticing a number of dolls propped up on Sundari's pillows, Panji realized that even though her body did not differ much from his other four wives, Sundari was still a child.

"I am sorry; let me tidy up my bed first." Sundari hurried to move her dolls aside.

"You don't have to. I can sit here." Panji picked up some of the seed necklaces that filled the only chair in the room.

"I brought some of the dolls from my home in Kaburikan, and I made the necklaces here," Sundari said shyly.

"How old are you, dear? It seems that you still like to play."

"I am over sixteen years old," Sundari said proudly. "I am ready to be a good wife." She finished tidying her bed.

"Sixteen is too young to be a wife, *Dinda*, dear," Panji said. "A sixteen-year-old girl in a farmer's family is considered an adult. But a sixteen-year-old daughter of an adipati is still a child."

"You don't believe that I'm old enough to become your wife?" Sundari began to take off her clothes, one by one. It appeared that she had asked for advice from the other wives on how to be a good wife. Moments later, Panji's youngest wife lay naked on the bed, waiting for Panji.

Surprised by Sundari's behavior, Panji was uncertain what to do. He didn't want to hurt Sundari by making love to her when he thought she was too young, even though she considered herself an adult. On the other hand, he didn't want to hurt Sundari's feelings.

In the end, Panji decided to make love to Sundari. He took off his clothes and for a brief moment sat on the edge of the bed before laying down beside her. He turned on his side to face Sundari who then also turned to face him. They looked at each other in silence. When Panji moved closer, they put their arms around each other and held one another. Panji did not make love to Sundari as a husband traditionally would, he instead caressed her as if she were his younger sister, full of love, until they finally fell asleep.

After satisfying all of his wives, Panji felt like a wholesome human being, not just like an animal that is driven by instinct.

He promised himself not to spill his seed carelessly.

The change in Panji's mood and behavior did not escape Prasanta's observations. Prasanta became more and more convinced that fighting wars and making love would gradually heal Panji's mental wound.

┣━━◦•◦━━┫

A few days after the king of Kadiri gave a welcome reception for Panji, the court priest found Gunungsari sitting cross-legged on the floor of

204

the palace hall. This was unusual, as Gunungsari was known for not wanting to stay at the palace for any length of time.

The court priest approached Gunungsari and said, "It looks as if something is bothering you."

"I'm fine, Your Eminence." Gunungsari bowed his head.

Seeing Gunungsari's cheeks redden made the priest more curious. He took a seat on the floor next to Gunungsari. "Are you disturbed because Raden Kelana Jayengsari was asked to help defend Kadiri against King Metaun?"

"No, Your Eminence."

"So whatever is bothering you has nothing to do with Raden Kelana Jayengsari?"

"That is correct, Your Eminence." Gunungsari sighed.

The long sigh puzzled the priest even more. He moved closer to Gunungsari and probed, "Perhaps you are a bit jealous of the mighty Kelana Jayengsari?"

"Yes, Your Eminence."

"And perhaps you want to be as famous as Kelana Jayengsari?"

"Yes, Your Eminence."

"Do you dream of having numerous wives as beautiful as his?"

"No, Your Eminence." Gunungsari lowered his head deeper.

The experienced court priest now knew exactly what was bothering the prince. He rose and said, "Ah, I know now. I will accompany you to see the parents of the girl you love."

"No, Your Eminence."

"Come, let's go now."

"No, Your Eminence." Gunungsari shook his head but still rose to his feet and followed the court priest to the palace courtyard, where he told a stableman to prepare horses.

Soon, the young Gunungsari and the old court priest rode their horses in an easy trot off the palace grounds. From the conversation that ensued, the priest confirmed that Gunungsari was in love with Onengan, the daughter of the king of Janggala, who volunteered at the court's hospital. Hence, the priest and Gunungsari headed for

Usada Hall, where the Janggala court physician confirmed the priest's assumption.

The priest, who was well-known among Janggala officials, escorted Gunungsari to meet Onengan in a private location.

"I want to take you to meet my parents," Gunungsari said.

"Why don't you meet my parents first?" Onengan asked.

"I heard that the king is still in mourning in Pucangan. I don't want to disturb him."

"Yes, all of us are grieving right now."

"Because the crown prince died at sea?"

"We're hoping that my brother Panji is still alive."

They were silent for a few moments, both buried in their own thoughts. Gunungsari watched the white clouds drifting across a clear sky; Onengan rested her eyes on the scattered gray boulders in the green courtyard.

Gunungsari suddenly slapped his forehead. "Onengan, I just remembered! Right now, we have a guest of honor in the Kadiri palace, Kelana Jayengsari. When the king invited him to the palace, my sister, Sekartaji, out of curiosity, sneaked a peek at him from behind a window. You'll never guess what my sister said about this now famous man in Kadiri."

"That he's very rich? Very handsome? Very smart?" Onengan guessed.

"No," Gunungsari said, "she said the guest reminded her of her fiancé, Raden Panji, the crown prince of Janggala!"

"Is that so?" Onengan said with interest. "Then let me accompany you to Kadiri to meet Sekartaji."

Soon, Gunungsari, Onengan, and the court priest were riding to the Kadiri keputren.

"Sekartaji, do you remember me?" Onengan asked when she met Sekartaji in the keputren.

"Of course, Onengan," Sekartaji responded kindly. "Come, please sit down."

"It's been a long time since we last saw each other." Onengan looked at Sekartaji closely. She was startled by Sekartaji's resemblance to Angreni.

"Yes, Onengan," Sekartaji said, recalling the event she could not possibly forget. "At the time, King Amiluhur of Janggala and his family visited to arrange the future marriage of Panji and me, you were still in the arms of your nursemaid. I was sorry to hear about the disaster at sea that befell your brother and his party."

"Thank you, Sekartaji. By the way, my brother is why I came here to talk with you. Gunungsari told me that Kadiri's current guest of honor reminds you of my brother Panji. Is that true?"

Sekartaji did not answer immediately. She glanced at Gunungsari, who stood some distance behind Onengan. Bowing her head, she whispered, "Yes, somehow the guest reminds me of your brother."

A sudden silence filled the room.

"Onengan, don't let your tea get cold." Gunungsari broke the silence.

"Yes, please, drink your tea, Onengan." Sekartaji awoke from her daydream.

The remainder of the evening passed with small talk, which became more lively whenever Gunungsari joined in.

Later, Onengan asked Gunungsari to accompany her to meet Raden Kelana Jayengsari, the guest who had reminded Sekartaji of Panji — Janggala's crown prince, Onengan's brother, and Sekartaji's fiancé.

———•◦•———

As usual, the guards of Tambakbaya were quietly observing visitors and people passing by. Tunggulwulung had warned them that the enemy, King Metaun and his thugs, had probably discovered their location. Hence, when the guards saw two horsemen approach the gate, one of them quickly met the riders.

"Raden Gunungsari?" The burly guard recognized one guest then looked intently at the young woman riding behind him.

"Yes," Gunungsari answered. "My friend and I ask permission to see Raden Kelana."

The observant guard suddenly recognized the daughter of the Janggala king. *She could easily expose Panji's disguise,* he thought and quickly acted accordingly. "Please, come in, Raden," he said. Helping Gunungsari dismount, he added, "My comrade will take you to meet Raden Kelana."

He motioned to another guard to come escort Gunungsari. As soon as the two entered the house, the guard immediately rushed to Onengan, who had dismounted. "Your Highness Onengan?" he whispered breathlessly while bowing deeply.

"You know me?" Onengan asked, surprised that someone knew her in this unfamiliar place.

"Of course I know you, Your Highness." The guard decided it was best to immediately take Panji's younger sister to him.

Inside the house, Panji had been told that a guest from Kadiri was waiting for him on the veranda. He was just about ready to leave his room, when there was a knock on his door. A voice said, "Raden, your guest is here."

Panji opened the door slowly. He instantly recognized the woman he knew as well as the back of his own hand. "Thank you, guard. You can go now."

Standing inside the dimly lit room, Panji looked at Onengan, who still stood in the doorway, obviously having difficulty recognizing him.

"Don't you remember me?" Panji stepped closer to Onengan.

Onengan blinked her eyes in disbelief, then gasped, "Panji?"

The two of them fell into each other's arms and held one another in a tight embrace. Onengan started to sob. It took Panji some time to calm his younger sister, who clung to him so tight, it was as if she would not allow to be separated from him for even a hair's breadth.

Panji took Onengan's hand, closed the door and sat with her on the edge of the bed.

"Please tell me how you found me here," Panji said.

Onengan, while holding back her emotions and joy, recounted everything that had happened, from the time that the court physician at Usada Hall had asked her to take care of a seriously injured handmaid until the court priest suggested she meet Gunungsari.

"In that case, I must ask you to pretend that you don't know me," Panji said. "Here, I am known as Raden Kelana Jayengsari. King Amerdadu of Kadiri requested my assistance in helping him defend his kingdom against King Metaun's imminent attack. Please, will you tell Gunungsari that Raden Kelana turned out not to be Raden Panji, who must have been lost in the storm."

"I will," Onengan promised.

"Now, let's go meet Gunungsari," Panji said, rising. "You go ahead; a handmaid will accompany you. And remember, we must act as if we don't know each other."

"Allow me to accompany Onengan, Raden." Wiranata suddenly appeared in the doorway.

Panji nodded. "I will follow you."

Because Wiranata was the son of one of King Amiluhur of Janggala's many concubines, Onengan didn't know him.

"Onengan," Wiranata greeted her warmly.

"Sir," Onengan blushed, embarrassed for not knowing the name of someone who apparently knew her well.

"My name is Wiranata," Wiranata said, sensing her confusion.

"Wiranata," Onengan whispered. She noticed how close Wiranata and Panji were.

Wiranata walked with Onengan to a nearby orange jasmine tree. Leaning against the trunk, he said, "I need to tell you something about Panji, Onengan."

"Yes?"

Wiranata hesitated before continuing. "Panji has changed; he is not the same Panji we knew in Janggala — mentally. After the death of his wife, he lost his mind, although he's much better now."

"Sumbita told me a lot."

"Sumbita?"

"She was Angreni's handmaid who witnessed the murder."

Onengan and Wiranata looked at each other before bowing their heads. Suddenly, Onengan looked up and said, "Brajanata told me where Kebotendas is now."

"Kebotendas? Brajanata's bodyguard? Who told him where Kebotendas is?" Wiranata had not seen Brajanata's bodyguard since they kidnapped Angreni. Kebotendas was already gone when Brajanata ordered him to drive Sumbita to the court physician in his horse carriage. "Kertala, the gardener, told him," Onengan explained. "I can tell Panji where he is."

"Why? Panji does not know anything about Kebotendas's involvement."

Onengan remained silent, then nodded.

Wiranata and Onengan went to join Gunungsari and Panji. During the conversation, Onengan mentioned that Sekartaji had been mistaken when she sneaked a peek at him in the Kadiri palace. Unfortunately, Onengan's brother Panji was still missing, and no one knew whether he was dead or alive. After the visit, Gunungsari and Onengan returned to the Kadiri palace, where Onengan stayed at the keputren with Sekartaji. The crown princess of Kadiri introduced Onengan to the other women as a close friend of Gunungsari.

———••———

The news Sumbita had been waiting for finally arrived.

The Kadiri palace guard immediately recognized the kris Sekartaji had given to Banyakwulung when he visited Sumbita, soon after her release from the hospital, at the small house Sekartaji and Gunungsari had rented near the Usada Hall. The guard quickly led Banyakwulung to the keputren.

After they exchanged greetings, Sumbita, holding back the question she most wanted to ask, inquired, "Were you surprised that the two peddlers turned out to be a prince and princess?"

"Not really," Banyakwulung smiled. "I already guessed that they were not ordinary peddlers."

Sumbita could no longer hold back her curiosity and blurted out, "Who gave you the information about Kebotendas's whereabouts?"

"Kertala told me. He met Kebotendas at an inn in Bali, the day before the palace was attacked by Kelana Jayengsari."

"And after he heard that Raden Kelana had attacked the Bali palace, Kebotendas ran away, right?" Sumbita prodded impatiently. "Where did he go?"

"According to Kertala, Kebotendas apparently succeeded in captivating the king with his talent in singing and playing the gambang, and the king said he could stay in Bali as long as he wanted. The king also introduced him to an artisan who lives in a village in Blambangan. Kertala believes that Kebotendas now lives there."

"I'll go there to find him," Sumbita said fiercely.

"You better not go there alone. Let me accompany you."

"I've troubled you enough already, Raden," Sumbita murmured, looking down.

"I'm happy to be of some help to you." Banyakwulung paused, then added, "Please, don't call me Raden. I'm just an ordinary person who happens to be a soldier."

———•—•———

Arriving in Blambangan, Sekartaji, Sumbita, and Banyakwulung spent most of their time wandering outside the palace. After leaving their horses at a nearby stable, they disguised themselves as peasant peddlers hoping to find Kebotendas's whereabouts.

In the village where Kebotendas reportedly stayed, Banyakwulung only needed to ask the local residents twice to find out where he lived. Known as an artisan and a friend of Bali's king, Kebotendas was quite famous in Blambangan.

"If Kebotendas hears that we are looking for him, he will definitely run away," Banyakwulung said, thinking through the plan. "But in order to make sure that this man really is Kebotendas, we have to meet this artisan who people call *empu*, master."

"Kebotendas will recognize you as the soldier who trained him," Sekartaji said. "Let me go see him. If this man turns out to be Kebotendas, it's up to you what to do with him later."

When they arrived at the craftsman's residence where they believed Kebotendas was hiding, only Sekartaji went in.

Announcing herself, she called, "Empu, I am sent to buy a gambang. Can I take a look at what you have here?"

The young artisan gave his guest a quick once-over before answering, "Please, help yourself, miss."

Sekartaji rummaged through the gambangs on display in the front room. Occasionally, she shot a glance at the empu, who was busy tuning a gambang. Finally she walked over to him and said casually, "I heard that you used to work at the Bali palace."

"Yes, that's right." The gambang master rested his eyes on Sekartaji and continued, "I was a gambang player at the Bali palace."

Standing quite close to him, Sekartaji could see the mole under the empu's right eye. She now was certain that the young man with thick eyebrows was Kebotendas. She said, "This time, I just wanted take a look. I'll be back very soon to buy the gambang you have there, on the top." Sekartaji pointed at a gambang on the top shelf.

"To prevent someone else from buying it, you might want to consider leaving a deposit."

"Good idea! Here, let me give you some money." Sekartaji placed some coins on the counter. "Tomorrow or the day after, a messenger from the Kadiri palace will pay the balance and pick up the gambang."

After saying goodbye to the empu — who had indeed turned out to be Kebotendas — Sekartaji rushed to meet Sumbita and Banyakwulung, who were waiting near Kebotendas's shop. *Sumbita will be very happy with this information*, thought Sekartaji.

⊢—•◆•—⊣

While Sekartaji, Sumbita, and Banyakwulung were tracking down Kebotendas, Panji was having a conversation with Wiranata at Tambakbaya.

Wiranata had decided to test the progress of Panji's mental recovery. "Our uncle, King Lembu Amerdadu of the Kadiri kingdom, does not believe that all the descendants of Janggala's former ruler, King Garasakan, have been killed by King Jayabaya, our grandfather. The descendants of King Garasakan who escaped the massacre are currently building up forces to avenge their grandfather and retake the throne of Kadiri.

"King Garasakan's descendants chose to seize the throne of Kadiri, not Janggala, because Kadiri's defense force has continued to weaken while, on the other hand, Janggala has continued to strengthen its army. As we well know, Uncle Amerdadu believes that trade is the most important facet in managing a kingdom, whereas our father believes that creating a mighty army is the most important element when guiding a kingdom to prosperity. Our uncle doesn't seem to know about the disaster that befell the crown prince of Janggala and his soldiers."

Panji tried desperately to digest the meaning of Wiranata's words. Embarrassed to admit that he didn't really understand the situation, he remained silent and just listened to his younger brother, who was well-known for his intelligence.

Wiranata wanted to continue talking about the information he had received from Onengan. He would have liked to say, "Right now, I suspect that King Garasakan's descendants are approaching Patih Kudanawarsa, the prime minister of Janggala whose daughter was killed by the order of the king. I'm sure the prime minister must hold a grudge." But Wiranata did not have the heart to speak these words to Panji.

Chapter 12

BETWEEN *A* GIFT AND *A* PARCEL

Armed conflicts at Kadiri's borders became more frequent. Dozens of soldiers died under sudden attacks by King Metaun's soldiers. Due to the increasing tension, King Amerdadu asked Panji and his party to visit the palace frequently. The king hoped that the sight of Panji's convoy would calm those who lived in the palace and surrounding areas. Whenever Panji visited the palace, he left only a few soldiers to guard Tambakbaya. Unlike the procession of carriages carrying Panji's wives that headed straight for the palace, Panji's cavalry first rode around the city and briefly stopped at the town square, where they demonstrated the soldiers' skill in horseback archery and spear throwing.

One morning when Panji went to visit the palace, his convoy consisted of not only his soldiers and closest companions, but also included his five wives. The princesses were immediately ushered into the audience hall, where King Amerdadu graciously received them.

"Raden Kelana, your wives are very beautiful indeed. Where do they come from?" Amerdadu asked. He was still trying to collect more information about this famous man whose identity remained a secret.

"Andayaprana is the daughter of the king of Bali; Citrasari is the daughter of the adipati of Blambangan; Sariana and Sariani are the daughters of the adipati of Nusabarong; and Sundari is the daughter of the adipati of Kaburikan." As Panji introduced them one by one, each bowed before the king.

"My dear ladies, please, take a rest," the king said. Then he turned to a handmaid kneeling in the back of the room and said, "Emban, please take care of our guests." Amerdadu wanted to say something that he didn't want Panji's wives to hear.

"Raden Kelana, which one of your wives will be the queen?" Amerdadu asked after a moment's silence.

"I am not a king, Your Majesty," Panji replied. "It is not proper for me to have a queen."

"If you succeed in defeating King Metaun and his allies, and the Kadiri kingdom is safe again, I would like you to stay here to keep this kingdom safe, Raden." Amerdadu paused, then asked, "Will you do that, Raden?"

"It is an honor to have so much trust from Your Majesty," Panji responded respectfully.

"It would be even better if you became my son-in-law," Amerdadu continued.

Panji did not answer. He simply bowed before the king.

"I will give you Sekartaji to be your queen, Raden," Amerdadu continued. "Do you accept?"

"It is a great honor to have your trust, Your Majesty," Panji again bowed deeply.

"I'm glad to hear that, Raden." Amerdadu rose and said, "Let's go for a walk in the palace garden to celebrate this occasion."

The king took this opportunity to unload his mind on Panji. He started the conversation by discussing their current situation. "If only Janggala had not lost the crown prince and a thousand soldiers accompanying him, King Metaun's threat would not impact Kadiri so much." Amerdadu sighed, then continued, "While the king of Janggala believes that a strong army guarantees its people's prosperity, we in Kadiri rely more on the power of commerce as a guarantee to prosperity."

Amerdadu, relieved to impart his thoughts, continued, "And while Janggala believes that a peace-loving kingdom must always also be prepared to fight, Kadiri believes that a kingdom desiring peace should be ready to cooperate in trade with others."

Panji listened, nodding in agreement every now and then.

As the two men walked in the garden, Panji's wives enjoyed a light meal before the queen took them to the keputren to introduce them to Sekartaji. At first glance, the keputren was similar to any other courtyard surrounded by small cottages. But upon closer observation, the cottages here were different. Not only did every window of each cottage face the garden, but each cottage also had windows that faced west and windows that faced east. The many windows enabled the residents to enjoy the sunrise as well as the sunset.

Sekartaji was sitting under a tree with Bayan, her beloved handmaid. "Your Highness, have you met Raden Kelana Jayengsari?" Bayan asked while massaging Sekartaji's calves and ankles.

"No." Sekartaji was too embarrassed to admit that she had peeked at the conqueror when he came to see her father a few days ago.

"Even though his mustache and beard are left unshaven, and his hair has been left to grow long, I'm sure he is really handsome and gallant." Bayan glanced at Sekartaji.

"You are old," Sekartaji joked with her handmaid. "Why do you still pay attention to a young man?"

"He looks like my previous boyfriend, Your Highness," Bayan said, pretending to be shy.

"Your previous boyfriend who is now your husband, right?"

"No, another one, Your Highness. My lover who looked like Raden Kelana died before proposing to me."

"Died? Was he sick?"

"It was nothing, actually. A small nail fell on him."

"A small nail? Poor man, your handsome lover must have been very weak if a small nail could kill him."

"But the nail was holding up a roof beam as thick as my thigh, Your Highness."

"You, naughty one!" Sekartaji laughed. "Why didn't you just say that your lover died because a beam fell on him?"

Their conversation ended abruptly when they saw the queen walking towards them with five beautiful young women.

"Welcome to the Kadiri Palace, my ladies," Sekartaji said and invited everyone to take a seat. With Sekartaji's hospitality, Panji's wives immediately felt at home around her.

Andayaprana thought, *How beautiful the crown princess of Kadiri is. It is only understandable that she could be the cause of war between two kingdoms.*

"Your Highness," Andayaprana said after a friendly exchange of courtesies, "Raden Kelana Jayengsari asked us to present this gift to you." She handed Sekartaji a beautifully carved wooden box, the size of a brick. "It is just a token of gratitude for being so well received here."

"Oh, that is not necessary! We are the ones who should be grateful because Raden Kelana and his army are willing to protect us." Sekartaji bowed slightly, holding the box in both hands.

"Raden Kelana told us that we are very fortunate to meet great people who are famous even in my country," Andayaprana said.

"Ah, he is exaggerating. We were told that you beautiful princesses are from Bali, Kaburikan, Blambangan, and Nusabarong. "May I ask where Raden Kelana comes from?"

"Even we don't know where he comes from, Your Highness." Andayaprana hesitated, then feeling a need to explain why she did not know much about her husband's origins, she continued, "When we asked him, Raden Kelana became very sad and wouldn't say anything for a long time. We regretted our question and never asked him again."

"It doesn't matter." Disappointed, Sekartaji sighed, then said, "The important thing is that Raden Kelana is kind enough to help us protect the Kadiri kingdom."

After Panji and his wives returned to Tambakbaya, Sekartaji decided to open the gift Andayaprana had handed her. She slowly opened the wooden box. Catching her breath, she looked at the glittering necklace, earrings, and bracelet. The set of jewelry was nestled on a piece of white silk. Sekartaji took out the pieces one by one and studied them. After a while, she brusquely rose and walked quickly to the cabinet in the corner of her room. She took out a cloth pouch and emptied it next to the open box on the table. Then she arranged the pieces side by side on the tabletop and carefully compared them. Without a doubt, the pieces were an exact match of each other. Raden Panji had given her the first set when he proposed to her, and now Raden Kelana had given her the second set as he helped her father protect the kingdom.

Sekartaji looked at the two sets of jewelry for a long time. They had to have come from the same jeweler and might very well have been made at the request of the same buyer. Sekartaji brought a hand to her pounding chest and swallowed several times. *Maybe Kelana Jayengsari was Panji in disguise. Moreover, his origin was unknown — even his wives did not know.*

Excitement rushed through Sekartaji, but she promised herself to keep her suspicion a secret. If she turned out to be wrong, she would be very embarrassed; but if she were correct, she would reveal Panji's disguise.

⊢—•◆•—⊣

Panji was waiting for Onengan and Citrasari on the veranda at Tambakbaya. He had asked Citrasari to approach Bayan, Sekartaji's favorite handmaid, to ask a few questions.

Citrasari immediately began her report, "After I asked her to teach me to cook a special Kadiri dish, I asked her about what Sekartaji thought of your gift."

"Yes, yes, that's what is important," Panji interrupted impatiently. "You can tell Andayaprana about your cooking lesson later."

"According to Bayan, your gift has made a great impact on the princess's mood." Citrasari said.

"What do you mean?" Panji leaned eagerly toward Citrasari. "How did it affect her?"

"Bayan said that Sekartaji now daydreams often and startles when she is spoken to — as if she were just awakened from a deep sleep." Citrasari paused before ending with great aplomb, "Bayan also told me that when she asks Sekartaji what she is thinking about, the princess says she is thinking about the gift from Raden Kelana."

Panji beamed. "Thank you, Citrasari, you've done well. I'm contemplating what to do if the war breaks out tomorrow. Should I ask Sekartaji to join in the fight or should I hide her somewhere to keep her safe?" Panji stroked Citrasari's long, curly hair, then said, "You can go rest now."

Panji stayed on the veranda waiting for Onengan. It was getting late. Almost certain that his sister would not come to see him that day, Panji rose to head for his room. He halted when he suddenly heard the pounding of hooves and a horse neighing. In the front yard, Onengan dismounted as a guard quickly approached. After handing him the reins, she bounded up the veranda steps.

"You've spent a few days at the Kadiri keputren," Panji said, once his younger sister was seated. "I'm sure you have a lot to tell me."

"I can tell you about Sekartaji," Onengan said mischievously. "Are you interested?"

"How did you guess! Yes, tell me about her." Panji looked away.

"Sekartaji looks so much like Angreni," Onengan raved. "I hope you're pleased."

At the mention of Angreni, a shadow slid across Panji's face. But unlike before, the memory of Angreni no longer made him want to end his life. He knew that his loved ones needed him, and Sekartaji was among those who made his life meaningful.

Onengan, who didn't notice her brother's clouded face, continued. "I was shocked when I met her. I thought I was seeing Angreni, that's how much they look alike." Onengan looked at Panji, and her voice trailed off. "It is as if Angreni is alive again."

"Enough about Sekartaji," Panji interrupted brusquely. "Now tell me about the people you've met so far in the keputren."

"Well, the young women are taught to play the gambang and sing. But when they're old enough to start their own family, they adhere to a different custom."

"How so?"

"The queen uses their love of singing to observe the kingdom from the outside looking in," Onengan said.

"I still don't understand."

"Imagine Kadiri to be a house. When we look at it from the inside, all we see are the people and items that are inside the house. But when we look at Kadiri from the neighbor's lawn, we will also see the roof and the garden and detect robbers trying to get into the house, while at the same time staying safe.

"Her Majesty the Queen, who masters the Pallava script, translates and records her findings in songs. From reading the Indian manuscript, Her Majesty realizes that she must not only pay attention to home security and the neighboring kingdoms, but she also needs to observe distant kingdoms, which bring changes to human civilization.

"In her leisure time, Her Majesty studies distant kingdoms such as China, India, and Arabia by reading the manuscripts of their grand masters. Don't forget that the Pallava manuscripts also contain the great stories of Ramayana and Mahabharata from India, while the Arabic manuscripts brought new religion to the religions we already have today: Buddhism, Shiva, and Vishnu. According to Her Majesty, Javanese people don't like to shut themselves in their own homes. Instead, they like to open the doors and windows wide."

"I don't want to think like Her Majesty." Panji preferred to concern himself with issues that needed immediate attention. "How does your lover plan to fight King Metaun, who I will face sooner or later?"

"My lover? Who would that be?"

"Gunungsari, of course."

"Who said that?"

"I said that."

Onengan pinched him and Panji groaned playfully. "Gunungsari looks at Kadiri as someone looks at a house from a neighbor's lawn," she said. "He doesn't see any thieves sneaking in or robbers eyeing the house of Kadiri."

"What *does* he see?"

"He sees servants and guards sneaking out the back door only to re-enter the front door wearing masks. King Metaun's followers are the people who know the king of Kadiri — or more precisely, know Jayabaya, Kadiri's King Emeritus. These treacherous servants have been hiding behind King Metaun."

"If that's the case," Panji said, "you'd better stay here with my wives."

"All right," Onengan said. "I want to talk with Sundari about her father, Adipati Burik of Kaburikan, and his relationship with King Metaun's allies."

After having a heart-to-heart chat with Sundari, Onengan's preliminary conclusion was that Sundari's father had no ties with King Garasakan, who was killed by King Jayabaya. Thus, King Metaun was not recruiting his allies from just his own relatives but also from their friends.

During Onengan's stay at Tambakbaya, she heard about the war from the princesses and their handmaids. She also heard about their personal affairs, including Panji's relationship with his five wives.

"It turns out that Raden Kelana is not only great on the battlefield, but he is great in bed too," one of the older handmaids whispered to her friends.

"Your mistress must have told you about that," another handmaid responded.

"No, I asked her."

"Why is someone as old as you are meddling in young people's affairs?"

"Hey! What is wrong with that? I was once young too, you know."

"Your question must have made your mistress uncomfortable."

"No, you're wrong. My mistress was proud to tell me that almost every day, Raden Kelana satisfies her in bed. Imagine, having five wives, how many times Raden Kelana makes love every day. I'm sure ordinary people are incapable of performing such a feat. My husband, who left me, only slept with me once a week, and even then, he rarely satisfied me."

"Do you know why your husband only visited your bed once a week?"

"Yes, because he's not as great as Raden Kelana."

"You're wrong! You smell like sweat and your words made your husband lose his desire for you."

"Whoa! Don't you say that. It is not like that. He left because he had fallen for a witch doctor."

"I don't believe you."

Onengan overheard such conversations often. She was glad to hear that Panji's wives loved him; that way, he didn't have to worry about betrayal.

But there was one subject that no one would ever talk about when Onengan was around. The subject was Gunungsari, a married man, who often came to Tambakbaya to visit Onengan.

Prasanta, when he overheard gossip about Gunungsari, only told Onengan the important parts. One day, he overheard two handmaids bantering.

"Yesterday, Her Highness Andayaprana was angry with Raden Gunungsari," said a handmaid, who had a bad habit of spitting her chewed betel on the floor. The dirty red saliva often caused arguments among the handmaids. Not only did her dirtying the floor incite quarrels, but her habit of mimicking court officials also annoyed her peers.

"Why was she angry?"

"It appears that Raden Gunungsari has a crush on Her Highness Onengan and wants to marry her."

"So? It's normal for two young people who are attracted to each other to want to marry."

"Did you say *normal*? You obviously don't know anything. Raden Gunungsari already has a wife, Sarag. Strange name, isn't it? She is not Javanese; some say she is of Arabian descent. Do you know where Arabia is?"

"Of course, I know where Arabia is. It is near Tumapel on the slopes of Mount Semeru, right?"

"Near Tumapel? Why don't you just say you don't know?"

"By the way, I've heard that Sarag looks like a pig. I think Raden Gunungsari should leave her and replace her with Her Highness Onengan, who is as beautiful as an angel."

"In addition to your ignorance, you seem to lack virtue. Do you know why Raden Gunungsari was willing to marry Sarag? Because she is the only child of the richest merchant in Kadiri. Her father looks like Bagong, that ugly, royal servant in a wayang story, and Sarag takes after him. Now do you still think it is right for him to behave like that? Her Highness Andayaprana was right when she scolded him."

"What would you want to do if Raden Gunungsari really wants to divorce his wife and marry Her Highness Onengan? Would you want to forbid him?"

"Of course, I can't do anything."

Of this entire conversation, Prasanta only told Onengan that Gunungsari was already married, and she had to be careful.

——•◆•——

To prevent boredom while waiting amidst uncertainty, Panji often held events to entertain his wives and soldiers. The entertainment for the princesses was having them take turns singing and playing the gambang, while the entertainment for the soldiers were wrestling matches and cockfights. Of course, the two groups were entertained in separate locations.

Panji also always invited the court officials he had become acquainted with. Gunungsari was among the most frequent attendees.

Bayan, Sekartaji's favorite handmaid, also came frequently. She was a good source of information about the people close to King Lembu Amerdadu. Panji felt a great need to know as much as he could about the "inner circle" of the kingdom that had asked for his help. Panji did not want to be stabbed in the back.

As for his men, Panji believed in their loyalty. They had all known each other since they were teenagers and had trained together at the Janggala royal training camp. Panji had known his closest friends, Prasanta, Wiranata, and Tunggulwulung, since childhood. The only people he was worried about were the people from the Kadiri palace. Apart from King Amerdadu, he was not really close to any of the court officials.

Bayan had given Panji a fairly complete description of Gunungsari, who appeared to have fallen in love with Onengan and intended to marry her. The latest news was that Gunungsari had divorced Sarag — perhaps because Andayaprana had scolded him for his unfaithfulness.

Bayan had told Panji that Gunungsari had married Sarag at the suggestion of the court priest and Patih Gunabadra, the prime minister of Kadiri. But, it was also the court priest who had escorted Gunungsari to meet Onengan in Janggala. Panji concluded that both the priest and the prime minister were among the court officials to keep an eye on.

When Panji shared Bayan's information and his thoughts about it with Prasanta, his loyal aide whistled. *If Panji was able to figure out complicated matters like this, it meant he had recovered from his mental trauma.*

Bagong, the rich merchant, was another individual Panji needed to watch. Sarag's father was very likely offended when Gunungsari divorced his daughter, and thus he could become a threat to the king. It was undeniable that this merchant had enriched many people close to the king.

Chapter 13

SONGS OF THE GODS AT THE KEPUTREN

It was still early morning when Sekartaji came out of her room and stepped into the garden. She took a seat on the bench under a blooming magnolia tree and enjoyed the fragrance. A horse whinnied, and Sekartaji saw Gunungsari dismount.

"My head is about to explode," Gunungsari blurted as soon as he reached his sister.

"What's wrong? Sit down," Sekartaji soothed, then joked, "As long as it hasn't happened, you have nothing to worry about."

"I'm not joking," Gunungsari grumbled and sighed. "I don't feel like seeing tomorrow again."

"Let me guess. This is all because of your divorce from Sarag and your plan to marry Onengan, right?"

Gunungsari nodded sheepishly and groaned. "You're right."

"I can't help you with your divorce," Sekartaji said gently. "You'll have to overcome Sarag's and her parents' fury on your own because you're at fault for what happened."

"Please don't blame me. Don't you pity me for having to live with a female whale?"

"Who forced you to marry Sarag? No one!"

"True, but the priest told me that my marriage would please the king."

"There were many other ways to please the king."

Both fell silent.

Finally, Gunungsari took a deep breath and said, "I'm here to ask you to help me propose to Onengan."

Sekartaji did not answer immediately. She looked at her younger brother's bowed head. "Of course, I will help you," she said, "but not now. You have to wait."

"Because of the threat from King Metaun?"

"Yes, that is one thing. The other thing is your unfinished business with Sarag. I am sure she still hopes for your return."

They fell silent again. After a while, Bayan came with snacks and warm drinks. The middle-aged handmaid, who had served in the palace since Sekartaji was a baby, had, as usual, eavesdropped on their conversation.

"Bayan, my brother Gunungsari wants to marry Onengan. What do you think?"

"After Raden Kelana has proposed to Your Highness, it will be Raden Gunungsari's turn to propose to Her Highness Onengan," Bayan said, hiding a smile.

"Yes, that's what I said." Sekartaji pursed her lips, making fun of her brother. "You have to wait."

"That means my marriage to Onengan will only take place if Raden Kelana wins the war and marries Sekartaji," Gunungsari concluded quietly. He looked at his sister. "Are you willing to marry Raden Kelana?"

Sekartaji did not answer her brother. Instead, she said to Bayan, "Emban, please bring me the gambang that Raden Panji gave me. It is in my room."

Sekartaji began to sing while accompanying herself with the gambang. But she stopped almost immediately. She turned to Bayan, "Emban, this gambang is out of tune. I know someone who can fix it."

Kebotendas was tuning the gambangs that the adipati of Blambangan had ordered when Bayan entered his shop with Sekartaji's instrument.

Kebotendas looked up from his workbench and glanced at the gambang Bayan had placed on the counter. "Can you leave your gambang?"

"When can you finish it?" Bayan asked. "The princess is eager to play it."

"You can pick it up in three days," Kebotendas promised, then offered, "Or would you rather I have it delivered to the keputren?"

"Yes, just send it there."

"It belongs to the crown princess of Kadiri?" Kebotendas asked.

Bayan nodded. "I also came to pick up the gambang she ordered." Bayan placed a few coins on the counter.

"Did she order a gambang?"

"Yes, the one on top of that shelf." Bayan pointed at the gambang Sekartaji had ordered when she visited the shop dressed as a peasant peddler. The princess had described the instrument to her.

The short conversation reminded Kebotendas of the people who had been haunting his dreams, the people associated with Angreni's murder.

After Bayan left, Kebotendas checked the gambang from the Kadiri keputren. He was familiar with the instrument; it had been made by Siwur, his father.

Kebotendas still remembered Siwur telling him about the first gambang that had made him proud. It was the one that was offered as a gift to the crown princess of Kadiri when King Amiluhur of Janggala, accompanied by the queen and his immediate family, visited the Kadiri Palace to propose to the crown princess for Amiluhur's son, Panji. The gambang Siwur had been so proud of, now lay in front of Kebotendas.

If he had not been ordered to kill Angreni, this gambang would not have been different from any other. Kebotendas's hands trembled when he picked up the instrument. His entire body shook as he began to strike the keys. He realized that he was unable to tune this gambang. It seemed to point at him as if he were a villain who had made the people associated with it suffer. Kebotendas sat with the instrument for a long time, doing nothing.

Onengan found him in that state when she entered the shop. She and two soldiers had followed Bayan as soon as Sekartaji's most trusted handmaid left the keputren to go to Kebotendas's shop. Bayan's trip to the gambang artisan's workshop had spurred her to go and see Angreni's killer.

"What's wrong, empu?" Onengan was struck by Kebotendas's appearance. "Are you sick?"

Onengan's question startled Kebotendas. He looked intently at the woman who was dressed like a princess. Then he lowered his gaze and muttered, "Maybe so, miss. My hands feel stiff, and I'm unable to play."

"You should take a rest then."

"I already promised to tune this gambang." Kebotendas bowed his head.

"Couldn't you tune it tomorrow? You're not feeling well now."

Kebotendas remained silent for a long time, then sighed. "I don't believe I will be able to tune this gambang tomorrow, or even the day after tomorrow." He looked down again and another silence fell between the princess and the artisan.

"This gambang belongs to my sister," Onengan said, breaking the silence.

Kebotendas shot her a quick glance, but kept his head down.

"If you don't believe me, you can ask those two soldiers." Onengan nodded at the two men standing outside the shop, a little distance away from them. "They are not in uniform, but you can check their bracelets, belts, and the kris they carry."

Kebotendas did not move.

The gambang which indeed had a unique appearance lay between them. After clearing her throat awkwardly a couple of times, Onengan said, "All right then. Let me take this gambang to my brother. He's quite good at tuning gambangs."

Kebotendas straightened in his seat and scrutinized Onengan. "What guarantee can you give me that I'll be able to return this gambang to its owner in good condition?"

"Have you ever seen this kris?" Onengan took out a kris that Brajanata had given her to show to Kebotendas if she ever found him.

Kebotendas swallowed nervously, as he looked at the kris in Onengan's hand. It was a duplicate of the kris King Amiluhur of Janggala had given him. He treasured it as if it were his own heart.

Onengan's possession of the kris was proof to Kebotendas that she was someone closely related to the king of Janggala, someone he could trust. Thus, he allowed her to take Sekartaji's gambang with her.

———•◆•———

Panji and his wives were chatting on the veranda at Tambakbaya when Prasanta interrupted them to announce Onengan's arrival.

"I will see her immediately." Panji followed Prasanta to meet his sister.

"You still remember my warning, right?" Panji whispered, taking a seat across from Onengan. "Don't forget, keep our relationship a secret. Call me Kelana Jayengsari."

Onengan nodded. "Yes, we won't let your wives or the people from the Kadiri palace find out. We already agreed on this, haven't we?"

Panji nodded. He was just worried that Onengan would forget and call him Panji.

"Can you tune this gambang?" Onengan asked and showed him the gambang she had brought with her from Kebotendas's shop. "It belongs to Sekartaji," she added.

"Tune this gambang?" Surprised, Panji asked, "Why don't you take it to the gambang artisan?"

"He is sick, and this gambang has to be returned to the Kadiri keputren tomorrow."

"Let me take a look." Panji swallowed hard when he recognized the gambang as the same one he had gifted to Kadiri's crown princess, Sekartaji. For a moment, Panji was catapulted back in time. He carefully stroked the instrument before he calmly said, "All right, I will fix it and return it to the princess tomorrow."

As part of his preparation to be the future king of Janggala, Panji had been taught to not only be good in strategy, swift in battle, and eloquent in speech, but also to be mature in religion and proficient in art. Panji excelled in singing and tuning the gambang.

After he tuned Sekartaji's gambang, Panji asked Prasanta to collect his wives. "I'd like the princesses to come here to sing," he said. "I'll accompany them."

"Where are Sariana and Sariani?" Panji asked when his wives had gathered and he noticed the twins were missing.

"Didn't you send them to observe the preparation of the Kadiri army to fight the enemy?" Prasanta reminded him.

Panji slapped his forehead and exclaimed, "Oh, that's right. I also sent Tunggulwulung to meet Kadiri's commander in chief."

Andayaprana, Citrasari, and Sundari took turns singing with the accompaniment of Panji playing the gambang. This way, Panji could be certain that the gambang bars were tuned properly.

"Let me deliver it to the princess tomorrow," Panji said to Onengan. She nodded in agreement.

After the singing and gambang playing was over, Panji and his three wives discussed the strength of King Metaun's troops. According to Sundari, King Metaun was a real person, even though her father had never met him. But Wiranata still believed that even if King Metaun were a real person, he was only being used as a foil by a group of people from King Garasakan's family. The discussion ended with the agreement to wait for further information from Tunggulwulung and the twins.

►——•••——◄

It was dusk when Panji and Citrasari arrived at the Kadiri keputren with the tuned gambang. Onengan had already told Bayan that the gambang artisan was sick and she had therefore asked Kelana to tune the instrument.

In addition to Sekartaji and her handmaids, many of the other princesses who lived at the keputren welcomed them. Everyone had a lovely time. But before the sun had set completely, Panji saw Sekartaji and excused himself.

After thanking Panji for tuning her gambang, Sekartaji said, "Go ahead, if you need to return to Tambakbaya so soon, Raden, but please allow Citrasari to spend the night here."

Panji granted his permission and left the keputren alone.

As soon as Panji left, Sekartaji asked Citrasari to play the gambang.

"Please forgive me," Citrasari shyly responded. "I'm not very good at it."

While Citrasari played the gambang, the handmaids served various refreshments. Citrasari played so well, that she amazed the other women.

When it was Onengan's turn to play, the women around her whispered, "Where did she learn to plan the gambang? She plays almost as well as our princess!" In Kadiri as well as in Janggala, a princess's beauty had to be complemented with being accomplished in playing the gambang and singing.

———◆———

In a corner of the Kadiri keputren near the palace kitchen, Sumbita and Banyakwulung stood talking. Banyakwulung, who lived in the Janggala's army barracks, had come on horseback to visit her. He had visited Sumbita three times since her stay at the keputren with Sekartaji.

Ever since he transported Sumbita to Usada Hall after she'd been seriously injured on the beach, Banyakwulung had felt that something was missing if a day passed without seeing Sumbita. Fate had united the two people from different castes. Now, alone with her at the keputren, Banyakwulung tried to unload a burden he had carried for several weeks.

"Sumbita, for some time I've been worried." Banyakwulung choked up. He had to swallow a few times before he was able to continue. "I'm worried that our relationship will come to an end."

"I'm sure that after I've accomplished my mission to kill Kebotendas, we will go our separate ways, Raden."

"Don't call me Raden," Banyakwulung snapped, then added softly, "Just call me by my name."

"It's hard to change a habit." Sumbita paused before continuing. "Besides, it is appropriate for me, a shudra, a member of the worker caste, to call you raden. After all, you *are* a kshatriya, a member of the military caste."

"Rules of the caste system are only written in religious books, Sumbita," Banyakwulung said firmly. "Before the arrival of these new religions of Buddha, Vishnu, and Shiva, the Javanese did not differentiate people based on their occupations or births. What separates one person from another is their way of life. The good deeds one does reveal a person's character."

"I've heard some kshatriyas speak like you." Sumbita felt a bit awkward speaking to Banyakwulung as if he were her equal, but she continued, "But as far as I know, to most kshatriyas, it is embarrassing to befriend a shudra."

"I don't want to be just friends with you," Banyakwulung said solemnly. "I want us to live together. I want you to be the mother of my children."

Sumbita held his eyes, then looked away. During the silence that followed, each of them seemed to be listening to their own conscience.

"I'm sorry if I made you uncomfortable." Banyakwulung felt that it might be better to leave Sumbita alone for a while, so he mounted his horse and headed for Janggala. On his way home, he looked at the rice fields and the farmers carrying their rice harvest and fruit to the market. He and Sumbita would be better off to live their lives as farmers and make a living by selling their harvest at the market. When he reached thirty years of age, Banyakwulung no longer wanted to be a soldier.

⊢——•◦•——⊣

Sekartaji really enjoyed the musical performance by Kelana's sister and his wife. After listening to Onengan, Sekartaji thought, *No wonder Gunungsari fell in love with her. She is not only beautiful, she's also talented.*

Sekartaji, Citrasari, and Onengan took turns playing the gambang, while Bayan, who couldn't play the instrument, was asked to sing. The song she sang was a humorous song and cheered the audience.

The song told the story of a priest who was asked to distribute the ceremonial meal to twenty people attending a prayer meeting on the seventh day of mourning the death of one of the villagers.

The prayer ceremony took place at night in the front yard by the light of torches. After prayers, the ceremony ended with the distribution of a whole chicken served on top of a bamboo tray that was placed in the middle of the twenty attendees.

As was customary, the priest had to break the savory and tender chicken into twenty pieces to be divided among the attendees as a complement to the rice and vegetables served on banana leaves.

While apportioning the chicken, the priest had to be accompanied by several village elders. Dressed in sarongs, the priest and elders crouched around the chicken. The priest was about to reach for the head — it was always the first part of the chicken to break off — when a sudden, strong wind came up and blew out all the torches. The priest, who could no longer see, now groped aimlessly for the chicken's head.

Suddenly, someone screamed in pain. When the torches were lit again, a village elder lay unconscious on the ground while the sacrificial chicken still had its head attached to its body. With its beak slightly opened, the chicken looked as if it was laughing at the priest.

Bayan's song was indeed funny, but people rarely dared to laugh openly. Giggling behind their hands, they put their heads together

235

and joked, "Just imagine, the way they crouched! It's obvious which chicken head the priest had plucked!"

No one noticed Gunungsari, standing hidden behind a tree, his eyes glued on Onengan. He imagined sitting so close to Onengan that she would feel his love while she played the gambang.

When the moon set, the women finally went to their rooms to sleep. Citrasari and Onengan slept in the same room with Sekartaji.

Gunungsari still didn't want to leave. Walking around restlessly, he stumbled upon Bayan, who had fallen asleep on a bench near the kitchen. Bending over her, Gunungsari whispered, "Bayan, wake up."

Startled, Bayan sat up and asked nervously, "What is happening?"

"Bayan, please help me," Gunungsari pleaded.

"What do you need, Raden?"

"Where is Onengan sleeping?"

"Why are you asking?"

"I want to surrender my life to her."

"Surrender your life? Please, reconsider it, Raden. What would people say when they hear of a divorced man sneaking into a virgin's bedroom? Besides, she's sleeping in the same room as Her Highness."

"Just tell her that I'm here to give my life to her," Gunungsari implored. "Here, give her this ring."

Bayan reluctantly accepted the ring and tiptoed to Sekartaji's room where Onengan was sleeping. Hoping that Onengan was not yet asleep, she peeked through the slightly parted window blinds.

"What are you doing here, Bayan?" Citrasari, returning from the bathroom, startled Bayan so much, she almost fell.

"Oh, it's nothing, Your Highness," Bayan stammered. "I wanted to get some tobacco to smoke."

"Tobacco? Smoke? What are you talking about?" Citrasari grilled, then added curtly, "You're strange, Bayan." Earlier, she had spotted Gunungsari hiding behind an orange jasmine tree. She now connected that fact to Bayan trying to sneak into Onengan's room.

Bayan softly interrupted her thoughts. "I have to do it for Raden Gunungsari."

"Go to bed. Let me take care of Gunungsari." Citrasari wanted to show Kelana that she, too, was skillful in handling situations.

Citrasari sneaked up to Gunungsari, who was still waiting for Bayan, and positioned herself behind a gardenia shrub next to him.

Citrasari picked three gardenia flowers, and threw them one by one at Gunungsari.

When the first one hit his cheek, Gunungsari looked around cautiously. He was still trying to figure out what was happening when the second flower hit him in the neck. When the third one hit his temple, he became annoyed and left.

⊢—•◦•—⊣

The next day, after accompanying Citrasari to the gate of the keputren, Sekartaji thought about the man who called himself Kelana Jayengsari. She became more and more convinced that Kelana was Panji in disguise. Apparently, Panji had not died in the ocean. Sekartaji was pleased with her own deduction.

On the other hand, she was bothered by Bayan's story about Gunungsari trying to meet Onengan alone at night in the keputren. The ring Gunungsari had given Bayan was proof of her story. *They must marry as soon as possible*, she thought.

That evening, Sekartaji visited a small shrine, located in a secluded corner of the garden. Bayan had prepared the flowers and incense, and sat on the floor ready to serve her mistress's needs as she prayed.

Sekartaji listened to the evening breeze carrying whispers that turned into song. It told her that Panji, her fiancé, was still alive. The sea had not taken him because he had not yet finished his tasks. But he no longer despaired about losing his wife as there was someone waiting to be his queen. The song ended with a question: Had Sekartaji received Angreni's jewelry? The singer provided the answer, *She had, of course.*

The song faded away as if its singer were walking away. The last words of the song said she and Angreni looked alike. The jewelry she had received from Raden Kelana was identical to the engagement gift she had received from Raden Panji, the crown prince of Janggala.

Panji, after studying the possible routes King Metaun's forces could take to attack the palace, had snuck into the keputren. When he saw Sekartaji enter the shrine, Panji, using the melody of an asmaradana, a love song, sung the lyrics he had composed.

Chapter 14

THE FLAME OF THE KADIRI PRINCESS

It seemed odd to Panji that he had not been introduced to Kadiri's general. But because it would be rude to ask for the introduction, Panji appointed Wiranata to make the connection.

Gunungsari was the first person Wiranata went to see.

"Raden Kelana is puzzled," Wiranata said when he met Gunungsari in the house he had moved to after divorcing Sarag. "To this day, in the face of impending war, he has not been introduced to Kadiri's commander-in-chief."

Gunungsari grimaced. "Don't be surprised; Kadiri does not have one."

"There's no commander?" Wiranata frowned in disbelief.

Gunungsari smiled wryly. "His Majesty the King of Kadiri is also Kadiri's commander-in-chief."

"Oh, I see." Wiranata paused. "The king must have reasons to hold on to the position."

"My father is worried about the relationship between the commander-in-chief, the court priest, and Bagong, the merchant. The priest's and merchant's influence in Kadiri is so strong, that the commander might only serve as an extension of their power, and that, of course, would be very dangerous."

"Are you saying that Kadiri once had a commander-in-chief?"

"Yes, but he was given a new assignment. He now supervises the priests and merchants in Kadiri. That task suits him better. He is more effective, as he is familiar with the religious figures and merchants."

"Do I need to meet him?"

"Why don't you instead meet the court priest and Bagong?" Gunungsari suggested. "They have more power in state affairs than the former commander-in-chief."

Considering that Gunungsari had recently divorced Bagong's daughter, Sarag, Wiranata decided to forgo meeting the richest merchant in Kadiri. Instead, he asked Gunungsari to take him to the court priest.

From his meeting with the court priest, Wiranata concluded that the king had downplayed King Metaun's threat, which was not only caused by Metaun's rejected proposal of marriage to Sekartaji. Wiranata also discovered that before proposing, King Metaun had been approached by many who had escaped the massacre by the previous king, King Jayabaya. It was this underground force that encouraged King Metaun to attack Kadiri. They had guaranteed to help him if Janggala sent troops to defend Kadiri.

Wiranata also obtained another, no less important piece of information from his meeting with the court priest. The priest gleefully told him that Janggala — having recently lost a good part of their army to a disaster at sea — was unlikely to defend Kadiri. Judging from the priest's demeanor, Wiranata felt that he had to be cautious of the priest.

Unlike Wiranata, who Panji had sent to obtain information from individuals unknown to them, Tunggulwulung was assigned to meet someone they already knew, Patih Gunabadra, the prime minister of Kadiri.

After briefly welcoming Tunggulwulung, Patih Gunabadra said, "It appears that your visit has something to do with preparations for war."

"Because you're one of the king's closest aides, it is more important that I get acquainted with you," Tunggulwulung said politely. "The preparation for war is just secondary."

"I am flattered, General," Patih Gunabadra said, pleased.

"As the king's closest aide, what do you know about the Kadiri army's preparation to face King Metaun's army?"

"The king was overly confident in thinking that his brother, King Amiluhur of Janggala, would help us," Patih Gunabadra explained. "We only asked for Raden Kelana Jayengsari's assistance after Janggala said they would not be able to help."

"Has the Kadiri army added more soldiers or weapons?"

"There has been a small increase in the number of weapons, but there has been no addition to the number of soldiers."

"Surely this big kingdom does not lack funding, or does it?"

"The kingdom's treasury has been depleted by religious matters," Patih Gunabadra said wearily. "Financially, the kingdom depends on the merchants led by Bagong."

His conversation with Patih Gunabadra left Tunggulwulung quite disturbed. He realized now that he could not rely on Kadiri's army.

———•◦•———

From Wiranata's and Tunggulwulung's reports, Panji deduced that King Metaun's threat to attack the palace was only meant to distract Kadiri's army. The real enemies were those who had escaped the massacre King Jayabaya had brought onto King Garasakan's descendants.

Tunggulwulung had reported that Patih Gunabadra suggested Panji's troops join forces with Kadiri's army to defeat King Metaun. Wiranata had reported that the Kadiri court priest had suggested that Panji deploy his entire army to attack King Metaun. Neither the prime minister nor the court priest suggested that Panji's troops guard the border. This aroused Panji's suspicions of a conspiracy within the palace. Panji asked Gunungsari to facilitate a meeting with the king and prime minister to present his concerns.

Panji was certain that King Metaun's attack at the front of the palace would only be a decoy. The most dangerous attacks would be those coming from behind and from the wings of the palace.

At Gunungsari's suggestion, the king invited Panji to the palace. Reports from the border patrol confirmed the sighting of enemy troops.

Inside the palace, Patih Gunabadra said, "I have observed King Metaun's troops' movements for more than a month, Your Majesty."

"What is the result of your observations, Patih?" King Amerdadu asked.

"They will use all their strength to break into the palace from the front. They are like a python ready to strike a lamb. They could easily take the palace. I suggest we concentrate on defending the palace's entrance."

"General Tunggulwulung, what do you think about the patih's suggestion?" Amerdadu asked.

"I don't agree with deploying Kadiri's entire army to hold King Metaun's attack at the front," Tunggulwulung said. "Some troops must remain to guard the border."

"Before deciding, I will ask Raden Kelana's opinion," Amerdadu said.

"After listening to Patih Gunabadra's opinion and General Tunggulwulung's objection, I will take the middle ground," Panji said.

"What do you mean by the middle ground?" Amerdadu frowned.

"My men and I will hold King Metaun's troops back from the front of the palace, but I will also position some of my men so they can help the border guards in the event they are attacked."

"Yes, I can understand your strategy." Amerdadu turned to Patih Gunabadra. "Patih, what do you think about Raden Kelana's plan?"

"Forgive me, Your Majesty, I disagree. Deploying a separate force from the main Kadiri army merely to await a possible attack at the border only benefits one party."

"Only benefits one party?" Amerdadu frowned again. "What do you mean by that?"

"By not holding the front line at the palace gates, Raden Kelana and his men will be in the safest position. So what does the Kadiri army benefit from their presence? Nothing!"

"What is your rebuttal, Raden Kelana?" Amerdadu shifted anxiously in his seat. "Do you still want to divide your men and have them waiting for an uncertain attack?"

"We will abide by Your Majesty's decision," Panji replied indifferently. His purpose of coming to Kadiri was to solve problems, not create them.

For a moment, Amerdadu sat quietly, thinking with his head bowed. After suddenly looking up as if asking for guidance from the gods above, the king said firmly, "Raden Kelana's army will join our troops that are blocking the enemy from entering the front gate, but he will be positioned in the rear. The border guards will remain at their posts and report any sighting of approaching enemy movements."

Everyone bowed their heads. No one said a word. Amerdadu broke the tense silence by ordering everyone to leave and prepare for the coming invasion of the enemy.

Before returning to Tambakbaya, Panji approached Patih Gunabadra and said, "I want to see the commander of the border guards." Panji intended to order the border guard commander to immediately dispatch a horseman wearing a headdress of young coconut leaves if they sighted the enemy.

⊢—·•·—⊣

Prasanta rushed to Panji to report that enemy forces had crossed the border and were now slowly, but surely, approaching the town square of Kadiri's capital. Not only had soldiers been killed at the border, but residents who lived nearby the route had also fallen victim to King Metaun's army.

Panji, who had been on standby for two days, said goodbye to his wives to go to war. Andayaprana wanted to participate and, riding the elephant she brought from Bali, joined Panji.

Panji's men immediately positioned themselves on the town square and waited for the Kadiri troops to meet the advancing enemy.

At the Kadiri keputren, Sekartaji also readied herself to participate in defending the palace. Dressed as a soldier, she rode along with several guards, ready to protect the keputren against the enemy's attack.

A handmaid who had passed through the war zone whispered to her friend, "It seems that there will be competition between Her Highness Sekartaji and Her Highness Andayaprana."

"What competition?" the other handmaid asked.

"A competition for Raden Kelana's love."

"Hush!"

The king of Kadiri, as the commander-in-chief, was in the midst of his army that moved to meet the advancing enemy. More than ten thousand soldiers crowded the streets.

Panji turned toward the soldier on his left and ordered, "You, ride south immediately. Do as I told you earlier." Then, turning to the soldier on his right, he ordered, "You, ride north. Carry out the orders I gave you."

Without a word, the two soldiers turned and galloped their horses in the direction Panji had sent them. Panji turned and rode his horse east, toward the palace.

Meanwhile, fighting had erupted at the southern boundary. As hundreds of enemy troops moved towards the border, their spears, sailing through the sky like metal waves, could be seen from afar.

As Panji had ordered, a horseman at the border immediately covered his head with a headdress of young coconut leaves and rushed his horse towards Panji's men stationed as the rearguard of Kadiri's army at the palace gate.

When the scout that Panji had sent south ran into the horseman with the headdress, they exchanged information before each continued toward their destination.

Panji's scout who was told to go to the northern border found a riderless horse, grazing on the roadside. A soldier lay on the ground next to it, covered in blood. Before exhaling his last breath, the soldier gasped, "Enemy…enemy…" Panji's scout immediately returned to his main force for help.

Panji arrived at the eastern border just as the border patrol frantically announced the enemy's arrival. He immediately ordered a soldier to ask for reinforcement from his main force. Panji, himself, was getting ready to meet the enemy marching towards the border. From afar, the enemy's spear tips gleamed menacingly.

Tunggulwulung ordered thirty soldiers to ride their horses to the eastern border where Panji was now. Then he told Wiranata to lead another thirty soldiers towards the northern border. He, himself, took thirty soldiers to the south. The remaining eight soldiers were ordered to help Andayaprana fight at the front.

"Archers, ready! Release on my command!" Panji shouted after his thirty soldiers arrived.

The enemy had not expected to be attacked by archers and had not prepared their shields. Panji's arrows killed dozens of enemy soldiers.

The shower of arrows shook the enemy's confidence. Their soldiers no longer marched in orderly formation towards the battle. Many of them ran frantically to escape.

Panji charged into the battlefield, throwing his kepel. The explosions confused the enemy even more.

These tactics had been discussed by Panji, Tunggulwulung, and Wiranata a week ago. The three different platoons, in three different places, used the same strategy. They reduced the number of enemies with arrows, confused them with kepels, and finished them off with swords. Indeed, it turned out that the enemy's strength was concentrated in these three locations, and not in the group directly led by King Metaun.

The thousands of Kadiri soldiers did not meet any significant resistance in the front line. King Metaun's force, much smaller than the Kadiri army, tried to avoid direct confrontation. They split up into two forces. Acting like a crocodile opening its mouth to catch its prey, they surrounded thousands of Kadiri's soldiers and showered them with arrows.

The Kadiri soldiers could not do anything except take cover behind their shields.

Riding high up on her elephant, Andayaprana could clearly see the enemy's movement. She soon realized that riding at such height did not give her much benefit; instead, it might even endanger her. She quickly slipped off her elephant and joined Panji's soldiers in front of the palace. They asked her to tell the king to advance his troops instead of waiting and hiding behind shields.

After breaking through the enemy line, Amerdadu, the king of Kadiri, riding his elephant, finally spotted King Metaun, also riding an elephant. The two kings approached each other.

Both armies automatically formed a circle around the two kings who were ready to do battle. Both kings carried long spears hanging from their elephant's back.

"Do you have anything to say before I kill you?" King Metaun shouted, seated on his elephant.

"Give me your head as a souvenir!" King Amerdadu roared and threw the short spear he held in his left hand.

King Metaun, who was focused on the long spear in his opponent's right hand, did not expect such a sudden attack. The short spear tore through Metaun's shoulder and blood gushed.

Amerdadu immediately thrust his long spear directly into King Metaun's chest. The Kadiri army cheered as King Metaun crumpled and fell off his elephant's back.

Kadiri's army paid for their victory with the lives of dozens of soldiers. Panji did not lose any of his men, although a few were lightly wounded. When Panji and his men regrouped in the town square, they were hailed not only by the residents, but also by Kadiri's soldiers.

"Did you look at King Metaun's corpse, Raden?" Tunggulwulung asked as they walked away from the town square.

"He turned out to be the former Kadiri commander-in-chief, whose position was eliminated by the Kadiri king," Wiranata, who was walking beside him, answered.

"I find it strange that His Majesty did not recognize his own general," Tunggulwulung grumbled.

"No one could have recognized him," Wiranata said. "He had painted his face and disguised his voice."

"Was he the one who proposed to Her Highness Sekartaji?"

"Of course not," Wiranata snorted. "The one who claimed to be King Metaun's messenger said that Metaun was not from Kadiri or Janggala. I think that he was Adipati Burik from Kaburikan. Gunungsari said there were pockmarks on his face."

"Does this mean that King Metaun and his kingdom don't exist?"

"I'm sure a group of aggrieved people exist. Most of them are probably descendants of King Garasakan; the rest would be followers of Janggala's prime minister's older brother."

As the two warriors talked, it became increasingly clear who had orchestrated the insurgence.

While the Kadiri authorities busily cared for wounded soldiers and carried home the fallen ones, Panji and his men returned to Tambakbaya. The exhausted men had fought an army ten times their number. No one noticed that the Kadiri king, escorted by a dozen soldiers, followed them.

As Panji rode through the gate at Tambakbaya, he collapsed on his horse.

Those riding next to him, jumped off their horses and carried him into the house.

The king followed everyone into the room where Panji was laid on the bed.

Meanwhile, the king's corpsmen treated the injured soldiers.

Banyakwulung and Sumbita, now newlyweds, sat on the porch of the house Sekartaji had provided for them. Sumbita talked about her plan to end Kebotendas's life.

"I know you've been practicing martial arts in preparation to face Kebotendas," Banyakwulung said gently.

"Yes, because I don't want to borrow your hand to kill him." Sumbita had rejected her husband's suggestion that he capture Kebotendas, so she could just kill him.

"Then please allow me to watch from a distance. Are you going to confront him tomorrow?"

"No, the day after tomorrow."

Both of them fell silent. They had only been married for one week — a wedding without a reception party.

The following day, Sumbita told Banyakwulung that she was going to the market for groceries. Banyakwulung, now a farmer, was busy in the back yard. He did not expect Sumbita to head for a house with a thatched roof, where Kebotendas lived.

Sumbita had observed Kebotendas for a month. She knew where he lived and had tracked his daily activities. She knew exactly when he would go to the market to buy equipment for his workshop and when he would return home. Sumbita had decided to ambush Kebotendas on the road near the river when he returned from the market.

"Do you still remember me?" Sumbita, dressed in Banyakwulung's soldier uniform, stepped onto the road in front of Kebotendas.

Stunned, Kebotendas stared at her for a moment before he murmured, "Yes. It's been almost a year."

"One year, two years, three years, or forever; time could never erase my hope of seeing you again," Sumbita snorted and reached for the kris on her belt.

Kebotendas blinked his eyes. He still had to convince himself that he was not dreaming. He had dreamed of fighting Sumbita more than once. "You still want to prolong our feud?"

"Our feud will last until the day you die."

"Your grudge against me is very deep."

"It is not a grudge, but an obligation, an obligation that I owe to my mistress. Once I fulfill my obligation, my debt is paid."

"I see; we will repeat our fight soon enough and, in the end, one of us will die. Please listen to my explanation before that happens."

"Go ahead; I'll listen."

"His Majesty, the king of Janggala, assigned Raden Brajanata to kill Lady Angreni because the patih's daughter was the reason Panji cancelled his engagement with Kadiri's crown princess, Sekartaji. The cancellation of the engagement could lead to a war between the two kingdoms, which would cost thousands of lives. To avoid that, King Amiluhur of Janggala ordered the death of Angreni.

"But His Majesty worried that Raden Brajanata would not have the heart to perform his assignment, and ordered me to do it for him.

"His Majesty was right to be worried. Raden Brajanata could not kill Angreni. Therefore, I had to follow the king's orders and carry out the task." Kebotendas paused before crying out in anguish, "Am I wrong? Didn't I simply do my duty?"

Kebotendas felt immense relief that he was able to finally say these words to Sumbita. In his dreams, his tongue was always tied when he tried to explain what happened and reveal his feelings.

Why did you want to carry out that task? Sumbita wanted to respond. *I suspect that you had a personal reason why you were willing to do it.* Instead, she could only snort.

"Am I wrong for being loyal to the kingdom?" Kebotendas almost pleaded. "The kingdom protects people like you and me. The kingdom also makes us prosperous. Because of the kingdom, we can live a civilized life, unlike the animals in the forest. Am I wrong for having the desire to be a part of the kingdom?"

"Protectors do not kill innocent people," Sumbita snapped. "Otherwise, they're like thugs asking for protection money. And as far as making us prosperous, in addition to paying taxes, we still have to work hard to earn a living." Sumbita wiped the blade of her kris against her thigh and snarled, "I think that's enough. Get ready!"

"I'm glad you chose the kris as the weapon for my death. Death by the kris is a civilized death, unlike animals that are slaughtered with machetes or stabbed with spears. I'm ready now," Kebotendas said calmly, as he drew his own kris.

The fighting was fierce. Kebotendas wanted to end the fight as soon as possible. Relying on his agility, he thrust and slashed his kris while dodging and jumping away from Sumbita's attacks. He could tell that Sumbita had been training hard for weeks to prepare for this fight. He had never expected Sumbita to hunt him down.

As Kebotendas grew more tired, Sumbita thrust her kris into Kebotendas's stomach. He uttered a muffled scream and collapsed.

Sumbita stood over Kebotendas, who lay holding the wound in his stomach. "I deliberately thrust my kris into your stomach, not your chest, Kebotendas. Your words softened my intention to kill you because I realize now that you're just a fool, not evil. I let you live, to beg for help from the kingdom you defended so fiercely."

Leaning over him, Sumbita thrust her kris into Kebotendas's calf and then into his thigh. When Kebotendas screamed and rolled over, Sumbita thrust her kris into his other thigh and calf.

No longer able to scream, Kebotendas gasped with saliva and tears wetting his pale face. When another thrust drove Sumbita's kris into his right arm, he didn't feel any pain. His body, now covered in blood, was numb.

"Ask your kingdom to support you," Sumbita said contemptuously. Before walking away, she added, "I didn't harm your left hand so you can still wipe yourself after defecating."

On her way home, Sumbita saw a carriage with an emblem of the Janggala kingdom. She mustered her courage and stood in the middle of the road, with spread arms, to stop the carriage.

"Sir," Sumbita said after the carriage stopped. "A Janggala soldier is dying on the roadside, over there."

The two people in the carriage were Kusni and Tandang. They immediately jumped out of the carriage and ran down the road. As soon as Tandang reached the bloody, crumpled body lying on the roadside, he shouted in surprise, "Tendas? Is that you?"

Tandang stared at Kebotendas in disbelief. As a trained soldier, he could immediately judge how badly injured his brother was. Noticing that Kebotendas was trying to speak, Tandang brought his ear closer to his brother's face.

Kebotendas whispered, "Mirah is yours. You're lucky..."

Sumbita turned and ran away from the two people who were busy helping Kebotendas. A stone's throw away from where she had stopped the carriage, she saw Banyakwulung running towards her.

———•———

On their way to take Kebotendas to the royal physician — the same one who had also taken care of Sumbita a year ago — Kusni, who was sitting next to Tandang as the coachman, said, "There's a story about two brothers fighting over a girl written in the holy book."

"Are you referring to the Kudasrenggara?" Tandang asked.

"No. I dare not say that the Kudasrenggara is a holy book. However, I admit there are many valuable lessons that I learned from it."

"I didn't fight with Tendas over a girl." Tandang turned to look at Kebotendas, lying on the carriage's back seat.

"Oh?" Based on the conversations Kusni had overheard when he was at Kebotendas's house, and the words spoken just now when Tendas lay in the middle of the road, he knew that Tandang was Kebotendas's real brother, and the siblings had been fighting over a girl.

"Can I tell you a little bit about Tendas, my younger brother?" Tandang did not want Kusni to draw the wrong conclusions.

Kusni nodded and glanced at Kebotendas, who now lay quietly, but could hear their conversation.

Tandang started his story. "Our family lives next door to a wayang puppeteer who has a daughter, Mirah. We both like her. As an older brother, I let Tendas have Mirah. I moved out, hoping that my absence would bring them closer. At the time I left home, Janggala's army was recruiting soldiers.

"My job as a soldier is to guard royal officials who are traveling outside the kingdom. But I also have another, secret, duty. I draw maps of the places I visit, to document information which might be useful in case we go to war in that region. I'm telling you about my secret assignment because it involves Raden Brajanata, and I know how close you are to him.

"When I was not on duty, I went home. Mirah always visited me. When I knew for sure that the relationship between Tendas and Mirah had not worked out and that she, in fact, was waiting for me, I couldn't help but welcome her in my heart. This clearly broke Tendas's heart. His attitude towards me changed greatly.

"I didn't know what to do. Fortunately, my assignments eased my stress. But one time, when I was on leave, Mirah asked me to take her away. With her parents' permission, I took her with me.

"I knew from my fellow soldiers that Tendas had also joined the army. But strangely, I never saw him at the barracks or at the palace. We never saw each other again — not until today, when we found him lying on the roadside." Tandang turned to check on Kebotendas.

———•◦•———

The news that Raden Kelana Jayengsari had fallen unconscious after winning the battle quickly reached the Kadiri palace.

Sekartaji immediately went to Tambakbaya, where she met the king, who had come earlier. Sekartaji took a seat beside Panji's bed. Looking at him closely, Sekartaji thought, *Raden Kelana is pretending. People who pass out are usually pale. He's quite smart. By pretending to be unconscious, he will not be hailed as a hero. I know he doesn't like being treated that way.*

"Does Raden Kelana usually faint after fighting?" Amerdadu asked Prasanta, who stood next to him.

"It has become a habit of Raden Kelana Jayengsari, Your Majesty," Prasanta said. He knew that Panji was not unconscious but rather needed to quickly regain his strength. By pretending to be unconscious, he could recuperate faster.

"After he has completely recovered," the king paused, glancing at Sekartaji, "I will keep my promise and immediately marry him to Sekartaji."

It was true that Panji was only pretending. He indeed did not want to be hailed as a hero, and he wanted to rebound quickly without being disturbed. But also, he could not bear to see the corpses of the Kadiri fighters he knew.

As Panji lay with his eyes closed, he thought, *Wiranata was right.* King Metaun — or whoever claimed to be King Metaun — was not important. A group of people, the descendants of King Garasakan who had escaped King Jayabaya's persecution, were the main instigators of the war. Panji had unknowingly met some of them in Pucangan when his aunt Rara Suci, introduced them as distant relatives.

Panji knew from the beginning that King Metaun's proposal to Sekartaji was only an excuse to attack Kadiri and kill King Jayabaya's descendants. Internal conflict and royal rivalries did not die easily.

King Amerdadu and Panji's other visitors left. After the king's carriage began to move towards the palace, Tambakbaya turned quiet again.

Sekartaji was the only person at Panji's bedside. She felt compelled to see Kelana wake up before leaving. Sekartaji began to sing.

Panji slowly opened his eyes, then sat up.

"Everyone is worried about you, Raden Kelana." Sekartaji, still sitting on the chair beside Panji's bed, gave him a scrutinizing look.

"Yes, I know." Panji now sat cross-legged on his bed.

"I'm sure that you *do* know, since you did not faint and definitely were not unconscious." Sekartaji looked away to hide her smile.

"I…" Panji smiled sheepishly, realizing that Sekartaji knew he'd been pretending.

"Never mind," Sekartaji teased. "There, you can pass out again." She gave Panji's shoulder a gentle push, and he fell back on the bed. Long after Sekartaji, escorted by several soldiers, returned to the Kadiri keputren, Panji could still feel her soft touch on his shoulder.

The king's announcement of the marriage of Sekartaji to Kelana Jayengsari spread quickly throughout the country. Everyone looked forward to this royal wedding.

Prasanta was the happiest of all. He had known now for almost a month that soon after Panji had fought his wars, Angreni would be reincarnated. And he was sure that Sekartaji would be the vessel of Angreni's reincarnation.

The only four people in Kadiri unhappy with the news were the court priest, Patih Gunabadra, the prime minister, Bagong the merchant, and his daughter Sarag. They disappeared from the public eye after Kadiri defeated King Metaun.

The next evening, Panji came unannounced to the keputren to visit Sekartaji. All the soldiers and handmaids in the palace now knew Panji and allowed him to enter.

A full moon hung high in the Kadiri sky. When Panji entered the keputren, Sekartaji stood waiting for him, as if expecting his arrival. The moon above her lit her pretty face.

"My dear Sekartaji," Panji said, as he stepped closer.

"Kelana," Sekartaji replied.

The two beloveds, long separated by an uncertain fate, faced each other in a tranquil silence.

"You are Panji, aren't you."

A turtledove cooed several times.

"Yes, my dear," Panji said.

"I express my deepest condolence for Angreni's passing," Sekartaji whispered.

"She is not gone," Panji said. "She now lives within you."

In the keputren's garden, the full moon above Sekartaji was exactly the same as the one that had shone above Angreni on the evening Panji proposed to her in the patih's garden.

"You are my queen," Panji said.

"May I tell His Majesty that Raden Kelana Jayengsari is actually Raden Panji?" Sekartaji asked.

"Not now. Let the people enjoy their happiness for a while in peace. The truth might startle them."

The full moon witnessed the two lovers embracing each other. The moonlight on Sekartaji stunned Panji momentarily. He felt as if the woman in his arms were Angreni but also was Sekartaji, *loro-loroning atunggal*, the two had become one.

Panji's marriage to Sekartaji was a grand celebration. For several days, guests were treated to lavish banquets. Perhaps it would have been even more festive if the war had not killed dozens of Kadiri soldiers. To honor the families who had lost loved ones, there were no gamelan, song, and dance performances, nor martial arts competition and cockfighting.

—•—

Panji and Sekartaji were at the keputren, discussing the proper time to marry Gunungsari and Onengan, when a soldier on horseback galloped into the compound and dismounted.

"Raden," he reported breathlessly, "the border patrol reports a large army from Janggala that appears to be ready for war approaching the border. There are about a thousand of them, mostly veterans who are only deployed when the kingdom faces great danger. The Janggala soldiers set up camp at Sumampir Village, and all the inhabitants have fled to the city. They're afraid of the Janggala soldiers."

"All right," Panji said. "Go tell General Tunggulwulung about this also." The soldier made a quick bow then ran to his horse.

"Do you think that the Janggala army will attack Kadiri?" Sekartaji couldn't hide her anxiety. She called to her beloved handmaid, "Bayan! Have you heard the news of the Janggala army at the border?"

"The rumor is still vague, Your Highness. But according to a servant whose family lives in Sumampir Village, the Janggala army is here only to kill Raden Kelana Jayengsari, Your Highness's husband." Bayan was no less anxious than her mistress.

Sekartaji was astonished. "What has my husband done wrong, Bayan?"

"Raden Kelana has insulted Janggala because he dared to marry Your Highness, who is still betrothed to Janggala's crown prince, Raden Panji."

Later that day, the Kadiri king met with court officials and those closest to him, including Panji. His Majesty opened the meeting with the news he'd heard from the spies and border patrols. "There are almost a thousand soldiers," he said. "A messenger delivered a letter demanding that we hand over Raden Kelana Jayengsari by tomorrow afternoon before sunset. They want to kill Raden Kelana Jayengsari because he dared to marry Sekartaji, who is still engaged to Raden Panji, their crown prince."

Only anxious breathing broke the tense silence in the audience hall.

"Raden Kelana," the king said, turning to Panji, "don't worry. We will defend you against them,"

For a long time Panji remained deep in thought. Finally he said, "Your Majesty, I would like to thank you for your willingness to defend and protect me. However, please forgive me, I do not want to add to the number of war casualties. Let me surrender myself to the Janggala army tomorrow morning."

Everyone was shocked. The king stared at him with wide eyes. A startled Gunungsari almost fell out of his chair.

Silence fell over the hall again.

Finally, the king said softly, "You can surrender and accept a death sentence, but what about your loyal soldiers? I'm sure that your soldiers will not allow you to be killed like that."

"I will instruct my soldiers not to fight back," Panji said.

"Well, if that's what you want," the king said sadly, then added, "But your wife, Sekartaji, must also be willing to hand you over to the Janggala army."

"Of course, Your Majesty. It is of utmost importance that Sekartaji is willing to let me go."

The meeting ended with sighs and moans from the distraught attendees. Many covered their faces. Some of the officials shed tears. It had not yet been a week since Kadiri celebrated the victory of Kelana Jayengsari, who had helped them to defeat King Metaun, and now everything had to end in this terrible way.

———•◦•———

The news that the Janggala army was set to deliver a death sentence to Raden Kelana Jayengsari and that he planned to accept it willingly had reached Panji's wives. Andayaprana was the first to question Panji, "Do you really want to surrender to Janggala?"

"Why not? I'm afraid to fight against Janggala."

"Afraid?" Andayaprana said in disbelief. "How strange. You've never been afraid to go to war. But if you are afraid to fight them, I will go to Bali this afternoon and return tomorrow with Balinese soldiers to fight against them!"

Sekartaji embraced Andayaprana and said, "Please don't go. Just believe what Raden Kelana has told me: The Janggala army will not harm him."

After hearing Sekartaji's words, everyone calmed down. They knew that Sekartaji was a crown princess with great insight. All of Panji's wives believed that Sekartaji must know something they didn't.

⊢⎯•❖•⎯⊣

Prasanta decided to go alone to Janggala's camp at Sumampir Village. As soon as he arrived, even before he could reveal his identity, Prasanta was arrested and tied to a coconut tree.

Prasanta scowled at the soldier who had captured him and growled, "Is this how a soldier behaves? You just beat someone you don't know?"

"Do not talk too much," the soldier scolded. "We're on the brink of war. Anyone suspicious must be arrested."

"Oh, I see. I'm now even more convinced that you really are stupid."

"No one calls me stupid!" The soldier rushed at Prasanta and was about to punch him when others in the camp who had overheard the squabble stopped him.

"Aren't you Raden Panji's aide?" a soldier asked, recognizing Prasanta.

"Yes, I am." Prasanta was secretly relieved but snapped, "Call your commander if you don't want to be punished!"

The soldier quickly called Brajanata, who hurriedly untied Prasanta and apologized for his soldier's carelessness.

"Where have you been?" Brajanata asked, astonished. "Are you here to serve the king of Janggala now that Raden Panji is gone?"

"I serve Raden Kelana Jayengsari," Prasanta answered straightforwardly.

"You're serving the wrong man," Brajanata said grimly. "We came here to kill him."

"What has he done wrong?"

"He dared to marry Sekartaji, the crown princess of Kadiri," Brajanata said. "Don't forget, Sekartaji is still Panji's fiancée."

"What if the King of Kadiri protects Raden Kelana?"

"It means that the King of Kadiri humiliates us. And in that case, we're ready for war." Brajanata looked around. The people who surrounded them became increasingly agitated as they listened to the conversation.

Prasanta and Brajanata stood looking at each other for a moment. Finally, Prasanta said loudly, "Raden Brajanata, I am here to tell you that Raden Kelana Jayengsari is Raden Panji in disguise."

"What?" Brajanata shook his head in disbelief. "Is what you say true?"

"You can cut my head off if I'm lying."

"I don't need your head, Prasanta. I have only one wish. Go home and come back with Panji as soon as you can."

———•◦•———

Back at Tambakbaya, Prasanta reported to Panji about the situation in Sumampir Village, leaving out the part that he had been captured. The worried princesses secretly eavesdropped on the conversation. As Prasanta's report unfolded, the princesses whispered to one another, "This means that Raden Kelana Jayengsari is the crown prince of Janggala." Andayaprana impatiently exclaimed, "Now we don't have to worry anymore!"

Panji heard her and turned. "Please be quiet," he said sternly. Turning back to Prasanta, he said, "Continue your report."

"Raden Brajanata wants to see Your Highness as soon as possible."

"If that's what he wants, tell him that Panji invites him to come to the Kadiri palace tonight." Panji pulled a small kris out of his cummerbund and handed it to Prasanta. "Give this kris to him. He'll definitely recognize it."

Prasanta bowed hurriedly, then spurred his horse towards Sumampir Village.

"Onengan," Panji said to his sister, standing behind him, "Tell Gunungsari that my companions and I would like to see the king. Ask him to arrange everything."

Panji shaved and dressed so that he looked as he did when he was crown prince of Janggala. He deliberately arrived early at the palace and waited in front of the gate. When he heard footsteps, he walked towards the sound.

"Panji?" Brajanata immediately recognized the figure in front of him.

"That's right, Brajanata," Panji said coldly.

Brajanata held back on his intention to approach and hug his brother.

"Please answer my question. Are you the one who killed my wife Angreni?" Panji asked sharply with a threat in his voice.

Brajanata did not answer.

The two of them stood facing each other in silence. The flames from the castor oil lamps, illuminating the palace surroundings, flickered. A night heron flew squawking above them. Brajanata's guards calmed their restless horses.

"I gave my kris to you," Panji said. "Now kill me. I will defend myself as best I can." Panji stared at Brajanata who wouldn't meet his eyes. They could hear each other's heavy breathing.

Brajanata didn't move.

Panji stood frozen.

Their natural human instinct under threat kicked in, and their muscles tightened. In the distance, an owl hooted. The sound was sad and eerie.

As Panji slowly walked towards Brajanata, hurried footsteps came closer.

Prasanta, followed by Sumbita, suddenly appeared. "Sumbita," Prasanta pulled Sumbita forward, "tell Raden Panji and Raden Brajanata what you told me."

After prostrating, Sumbita told the story Kebotendas had told her about Angreni's death. With tears rolling down her cheeks, she ended her story with her fight against Kebotendas.

Panji and Brajanata walked slowly closer to each other. It was not clear who took the first step. The two half-brothers embraced, speechless. Brajanata sighed. Stammering he apologized for causing Angreni's death by adhering to their father's — the king's — orders.

Panji calmed Brajanata. He told him that no one was to blame in this matter — it was fate. Then the two princes walked side by side toward the Kadiri palace.

Kusni, Kertala, and Banyakwulung were standing under the blooming champaca tree outside the palace. A little behind them, Tandang and Mirah were sitting side by side. When Sumbita and Prasanta walked toward them, they all ran to meet the two. Then, everyone, except Prasanta, stepped into a carriage that belonged to the Janggala kingdom. Prasanta waved as the carriage rolled away and then walked into the Kadiri palace.

In the balairung, Amerdadu, King of Kadiri, was surrounded by nobilities and his closest aides.

The king asked Brajanata, as the commander of the Janggala army, why he had brought his troops to Sumampir Village.

Brajanata said that Janggala's mission was fulfilled because Raden Kelana Jayengsari was none other than Raden Panji Inu Kertapati, the crown prince of Janggala.

Listening to Brajanata's explanation, the king rose speechless from his throne. Tears glistening in his eyes, he sat down again and looked heavenward for a long time. When he smiled, everyone present rejoiced.

In the year of 1185 CE, Panji Inu Kertapati became the king of Kadiri, with the royal title Kameswara, while Sekartaji, his queen, was also known as Seri Kiranaratu.

⊢—•◦•—⊣

GLOSSARY

Adipati: rank in Javanese nobility, to distinguish /address the lord of a region the size of a district

Asmaradana: love song

Asmaragama, anala, ajuwita, and atantra: a series of handbooks on making love

Balairung: royal audience hall where the king receives guests

Bandayuda: a special soldiers' training camp for close combat

Brahmins: the highest Hindu caste consisting of religious leaders and priests

Dinda: endearing address for younger female

Emban: handmaid

Empu: master artist or craftsman

Gambang: a wooden xylophone

Gamelan: Javanese musical ensemble

Kang / kakang / kanda: endearing address for older male

Kenyakadiri: a love song for a girl from Kadiri

Kepel: a hand grenade named after a Javanese fruit

Keputren: a compound where all the women of the court live

Ki: address for an older or respected male

Kris: a short double-edged dagger functioning as both a man's weapon and jewelry

Kshatriyas: the second-highest Hindu caste, consisting of kings and nobilities

Kudi: a small machete

Lontar: a type of palm tree. Lontar leaves were used as writing materials as far back as the fifth century BCE, and perhaps earlier.

Loro-loroning atunggal: the two had become one

Nira: liquid extracted from the male flower of the palm tree

Nyai Patih: address for the prime minister's wife – could be viewed as "Mrs."

Pandanus: a kind of palm-like tree whose long leaves are used for weaving mats

Paseban: a large, open audience hall where the king's guests wait

Patih: prime minister

Pendapa: a large open pavilion in front of dignitaries' residences where guests are received

Raden: address for male nobility

Semar: one of the gods in Javanese mythology, who was incarnated as a servant for righteous royalties, and who had a duty to guide and protect them

Shudras: the lowest Hindu caste, consisting of peasants and laborers

Vaishyas: the third-highest Hindu caste, consisting of traders and craftsmen

Wayang: puppet

Junaedi Setiyono was born in Kebumen, a regency in the southern part of the Indonesian province of Central Java, on 16 December 1965. Setiyono acquired his university degree at the Muhammadiyah University in Purworejo, a small city near Yogyakarta. In 2013, Setiyono was awarded a scholarship by The Ohio State University in Columbus, Ohio, to conduct research as a part of his doctorate degree in language education, which he received in 2016 from the State University of Semarang.

Setiyono worked in a non-governmental organization (NGO) and as a high school English teacher. Since 1997, he has taught at his alma mater in Purworejo, usually on the subjects of writing and translation.

Setiyono started his literary career writing short stories for newspapers and magazines published in Purworejo, Yogyakarta, and Jakarta. He won several awards in short story writing competitions. His first novel, *Glonggong* (Penerbit Serambi, 2008), won the Jakarta Art Council Novel Writing Award in 2006. In 2008, the same novel was on the five-title shortlist for the Kusala Sastra Khatulistiwa Literary Award, which recognizes Indonesia's best prose and poetry. His second novel, *Arumdalu* (Penerbit Serambi, 2010), was on the ten-title shortlist for the Khatulistiwa Literary Award in 2010. In 2012, the manuscript for what would become his third novel, *Dasamuka* (Penerbit Ombak, 2017), won the Jakarta Art Council Novel Manuscript Award. The novel was translated into English in 2017 and published under the same title by Dalang Publishing. The novel won the 2020 literary award of the Indonesian Ministry of Culture and Education.

About the Translator

Oni Suryaman was trained as an engineer, but mostly works in education and as a translator, with English and Indonesian as target languages. Suryaman started his teaching career in Jakarta at the Monash College — an affiliation of the Monash University in Melbourne, Australia. He currently teaches test preparations for SAT, GRE, and GMAT.

Suryaman began to translate technical documents and textbooks during his college years. He has translated English-language fiction and non-fiction works into Indonesian for several publishers in Indonesia, including the following:

• *Trisurya* (Kepustakaan Populer Gramedia, 2019) from *The Three Body Problem* by Liu Cixin (Chongqing Press, 2008), translated into English by Ken Liu, winner of the 2015 Hugo Award (Tor Books, 2014);

• *Madiun Dalam Kemelut Sejarah* (Kepustakaan Populer Gramedia, 2018) from *The Residency of Madiun, Priyayi and Peasant in the Nineteenth Century* by Onghokham (Yale University Press, 1975);

• *Asih Asah Asuh* (Kanisius, 2016) from *Teaching & Supporting Children with Special Education Needs & Disabilities in Primary School* by Jonathan Glazzard, et al. (Learning Matters, 2015);

• *Yesus* (Gloria Graffa, 2008) from *Jesus, An Intimate Portrait of The Man, His Land, and His People* by Leith Anderson (Bethany House, 2005).

Suryaman also published two papers in Indonesian addressing science fiction topics: *Seksualitas, Gender, dan Institusi Perkawinan dalam Karya-karya Fiksi Ilmiah — Sexuality, Gender, and Marriage Institution in Science Fiction Works* (University Sanata Dharma HISKI Seminar Proceeding, 2017); and *Snow Crash Sebuah Studi Kasus Literatur Fiksi Ilmiah Pascahumanisme — Posthumanism in Science Fiction*, a case study of *Snow Crash* by Neal Stephenson (Bantam Books, 1992, University Sanata Dharma HISKI Seminar Proceeding, 2019).

Suryaman published one picture book in Indonesian, "I Belog," an adaptation of a Balinese folktale (Kanisius, 2017). This book was performed in a dramatic adaptation at the Asian Festival of Children's Content (AFCC) Singapore in 2017.

Later on, his love for literature made Suryaman pursue a career as a literary translator. *Ciuman Sang Buronan — The Kiss of An Outlaw* (Gading, 2019) is a collaborative Indonesian language translation by Yogyakarta translators of a short story collection in English by international women authors.

He has also translated short stories for the Your Story page of Dalang Publishing's website, dalangpublishing.com.

Panji's Quest is Suryaman's first literary translation of a full-length work into English.

Among all genres of literature, Suryaman loves science fiction the most. The American sci-fi authors who influenced him are Ursula K. Le Guin, Ray Bradbury, and Arthur C. Clarke.

Oni Suryaman lives with his wife, Caecilia Krismariana Widyaningsih, a published children's book author, on the outskirts of Yogyakarta, away from the busy city life, where he can do what he loves most: educate children and write fiction.

Suryaman loves to watch movies, particularly the *Star Trek* series, and enjoys tinkering with paper, textiles, and yarn. He is involved in his local home school communities and the city's Credit Union. Suryaman can be reached via email at oni.suryaman@gmail.com.

My Name is Mata Hari
Remy Sylado
Translated from the Indonesian by Dewi Anggraeni

My Name is Mata Hari tells the story of Margaretha Geertruida Zelle, a young Dutch woman married to an older military officer assigned to the Dutch East Indies. Claiming her mother's Javanese ancestry, she changed her name to Mata Hari, Malay for "eye of the day."

As Mata Hari, she danced on stages across Europe and the Middle East, and took many high-ranking military and government officials as her lovers. Convicted of espionage during World War I, she said at the end of her tumultuous life, "I am a genuine courtesan. And I am a dancer in the true sense."

Price: $17.95
Paperback: 342 pages
ISBN: 978-0-9836273-0-2

Potions and Paper Cranes
Lan Fang
Translated from the Indonesian by Elisabet Titik Murtisari

In Lan Fang's award-winning novel, Sulis is a young woman selling potions in Surabaya's harbor district. She meets Sujono, a day laborer with dreams of becoming a freedom fighter, and whose passion for Matsumi, a geisha called to Java by a Japanese general, is destined to ruin all of them. Each tells the story of their lives during the Japanese occupation of Java and Indonesia's transition from a Dutch colony to an independent republic.

Price: $17.95
Paperback: 252 pages
ISBN: 978-0-9836273-3-3

Kei
Erni Aladjai
Translated from the Indonesian by Nurhayat Indriyatno Mohamed

At the end of Suharto's New Order, the Kei people hold on to their traditions as they flee the violence that divides Muslim from Christian and destroys the villages. Namira, a Muslim girl, works as a volunteer in a refugee camp when she meets Sala, a young Protestant man. Grounded in the islander's belief of "We drink from the same spring and eat from the same land, the land of Kei," the two fall in love amid the chaos that will soon separate them.

Price: $17.95
Paperback: 228 pages
ISBN: 978-0-9836273-6-4

Daughters of Papua
Anindita Siswanto Thayf
Translated from the Indonesian by Stefanny Irawan

Seven-year-old Leksi lives in modern-day Papua with her grandmother Mabel and her mother, Mace. Her companions are Pum, an old dog of unknown ancestry, and Kwee, a pig. Together they look back at the past, as they face an uncertain future. In *Daughters of Papua*, the present is marked by a contentious election, with the gold company that wants to rob Papuans of their heritage the only winner.

Price: $17.95
Paperback: 204 pages
ISBN: 978-0-9836273-9-5

The Red Bekisar
Ahmad Tohari
Translated from the Indonesian by Nurhayat Indriyatno Mohamed

The *bekisar* is a fine crossbreed between jungle fowl and domestic chicken that adorns the houses of the wealthy. Lasi, whose father was a Japanese soldier, fair-skinned and beautiful, is such an acquisition for a rich man in Jakarta. She is born in a village where the main source of income is tapping coconut palms for their rich sap, or nira. Her life takes an unexpected turn when she is betrayed by her husband and flees to Jakarta. She meets Mrs. Lanting, procuress of companions for men in high government and social circles, who sells her to the rich Handarbeni. Lasi enjoys her new splendor as a much-desired ornament, but is alarmed when she discovers the marriage is a sham. When she reconnects with Kanjat, a childhood friend now grown into a man, Lasi and Kanjat rediscover their affection for each other. Their bond is the village, its people and traditions. Together they struggle to free Lasi from a net of power, corruption, and deceit.

Price: $17.95
Paperback: 294 pages
ISBN: 978-0-9836273-2-6

Love, Death and Revolution
Mochtar Lubis
Translated from the Indonesian by Stefanny Irawan

During the early days of their nation's revolution, Indonesians were driven by passion and built a future on dreams. In a world still reeling from World War II, Major Sadeli of the Indonesian Army Intelligence travels to Singapore tasked with establishing naval and air routes to Sumatra and Java, as well as securing weapons and radio equipment vital to the revolution. His desire for Indonesia to be prosperously independent, and independently prosperous, forces him to choose between personal happiness and commitment to a higher cause.

Price: $17.95
Paperback: 324 pages
ISBN: 978-0-9836273-5-7

Cloves for Kolosia
Hanna Rambe
Translated from the Indonesian by Miagina Amal

Elderly widower Gamati swears to save his family line from extinction
when he and his family fall victim to the infamous plunder expeditions
of the VOC, the Dutch East India Company. To escape the colonialists'
cruelties, he leads his orphaned grandchildren and a small group of
fellow villagers to the safety of another, more remote, island north of
their current location. The birth of his great-grandson Kolosia during
the voyage assures Gamati of his family's ability to sail the Moluccan
seas freely for generations to come.

Price: $17.95
Paperback: 350 pages
ISBN: 978-0-9836273-8-8

Blood Moon Over Aceh
Arafat Nur
Translated from the Indonesian by Maya Denisa Saputra

The story is set between 1989 and 2002 in Alue Rambe, an isolated
agricultural village south of Lhokseumawe City, in Aceh, Indonesia.
Born in 1976, into a farmer's family, Nazir's life becomes a part of
Aceh's dark, rebellious history that recounts the injustice the Soeharto
government imposed on the Acehnese.

Price: $17.95
Paperback: 354 pages
ISBN: 978-0-9836273-4-0

Dasamuka
Junaedi Setiyono
Translated from the Indonesian by Maya Denisa Saputra

A Scottish academic, journeying to the island of Java in 1811, is quickly drawn into the struggle of the Javanese people as they fight back against colonial powers and their own corrupt aristocracy. Willem Kappers, a Scottish scientist, learns about intrigue in nineteenth century royal Javanese court and witnesses colonialism change powerful kings into puppets of the Dutch and English authorities. Kappers's involvement with an ambitious Javanese nobleman, Dasamuka, gives the reader an intimate glimpse into the struggle of the Javanese commoner against the oppression of the reigning sultan, as well as the colonial powers.

Price: $17.95
Paperback: 266 pages
ISBN: 978-0-9836273-1-9